M   CARRI
Carrington, Tori.
Dirty laundry : a ?
Metropolis novel /
       R00233108.

SEP   2009

DIRTY LAUNDRY

OTHER FORGE NOVELS BY TORI CARRINGTON

Sofie Metropolis

Dirty Laundry

A Sofie Metropolis Novel

TORI CARRINGTON

A TOM DOHERTY ASSOCIATES BOOK

NEW YORK

This is a work of fiction. All the characters and events portrayed
in this novel are either fictitious or are used fictitiously.

DIRTY LAUNDRY

Copyright © 2006 by Lori and Tony Karayianni

All rights reserved, including the right to reproduce this book,
or portions thereof, in any form.

A Forge Book
Published by Tom Doherty Associates, LLC
175 Fifth Avenue
New York, NY 10010

Forge® is a registered trademark of Tom Doherty Associates, LLC.

ISBN 978-0-7653-1241-9

Printed in the United States of America

We dedicate this book to
Melissa Ann and Jacqueline,
who never cease to amaze us with their
warmth, wit, intelligence, and generosity.
And, as always,
to our sons Tony and Tim,
με αγαπη.

R0023310830

Rec0233105830

ACKNOWLEDGMENTS

After having penned over thirty novels, the only knowledge that we can lay claim to with any certainty is that each book is a collaborative effort that reaches outside our own obvious teamwork. In ways both big and small. In no specific order, here are the people to credit for this novel's existence:

Our sons, Tony and Tim, who are a fathomless source of inspiration and information merely by existing. By looking at life through your beautiful eyes, we're able to be your age all over again . . . with, of course, the wisdom of the years that have gone between. You both are the hearts and the souls and the reflectors of our own existence.

Our agents at Trident Media Group: the extraordinary Robert Gottlieb, Hilary Rubin, Jenny Bent, Alex Glass, Kimberly Whalen, and everyone else who works behind the scenes to cover the business angle of our lives so we may focus on the creative end without worry.

Melissa Ann Singer, Linda Quinton, Tom Doherty, Elena Stokes, Melissa Broder, Natasha Panza, Anna Genoese, Dot Lin, and everyone at Tom Doherty Associates for their unwavering belief in us and our Sofie . . . and for keeping us in frappés!

Author publicist Patricia Rouse, who blew us away with her efficiency and munificence while organizing and overseeing our first two-month, cross-country Baklava Express Tour. That we can still humbly call you friend after all this, well, speaks volumes. Are you up for another round?

Cooking with Georgia host Georgia Sarianides and her daughter, Despina, and son, Pete, for demonstrating how wonderfully small the world really is.

Our friends up north at H. B. Fenn: Heidi Winter, Leo MacDonald, Cheryl Westcott, and Janis.

The many booksellers and fellow readers at Borders, Barnes and Noble, and the countless indies we have encountered and continue to encounter in our travels. Please check out our Travel Blog at www.sofiemetro.com for a complete list and photos.

An acquaintance known only as Tony-the-Italian, whom we met in Astoria Park, who humorously and colorfully explained the secrets of maneuvering in overdrive while towing an RV over mountain roads. Elvis thanks you.

The many Greek and Cypriot Americans we met during our 2005 tour for proving that no matter where you are, "home" can be found in the hearts of those with whom you cross paths. This includes, but is certainly not limited to: Elena and Carolina Maroulleti of New York's bilingual Aktina 91.5 FM; Sotirios Agelatos of Tampa's WPSO; George Sarris and his daughter Dorothy of the fantastic Greek restaurant the Fish Market in Birmingham, Alabama; Christina Tomazini of Books & Company in Dayton; the marvelous Maria Contos of Chicago; Pam, Donna, Ida, and Kathy of Sharon, Massachusetts; Peter Gaveras and his son Lee of Plymouth; Christine Alexiou of Purple8 Pictures; and Houston B. Dalton manager Kay Miriam Vamvakias, her gregarious father-in-law, and the rest of the family. Meeting all of you was one of the many highlights of our trip! Here's to our paths crossing again . . . hopefully very soon.

And to the Saturday Club: Andreas, George, Chris, Frixos, Makis, and Costas.

And, finally, the neighborhood of Astoria. Whenever we feel homesick, a few days spent walking your aromatic streets, drinking coffee in your corner cafés, and enjoying the company of your many denizens reminds us that Greece is not as far away as we think. *Zeto E Ellas!*

DIRTY LAUNDRY

One

ONE OF THE GREAT THINGS about being a private dick—aside from saying those words and presuming to lay ownership to something possessed only by men—is that it gets you out of going to Sunday Mass. Well, okay. It's not so much the Mass I have a problem with. Rather, it's the prospect of having to attend with my mother, Thalia Metropolis, that makes me cringe. Aside from her smooshing my face into various Greek Orthodox religious icons propped up just inside the door of St. Constantine's, I'd have to sit next to her. And thus would endure much fussing and pulling and poking to make sure my rarely worn blouse was unwrinkled and that my hot pink thong wasn't showing through my miniskirt. And forget all the gossip I'd have to catch up on. Frankly, I didn't care whether Mrs. Stefanou was suing her hairdresser because he turned her hair orange or that Mr. Zervas had "personal" problems and had gotten a free trial of Viagra. (Trust me, if you knew Mr. Zervas

---

you wouldn't want to think of him in that regard either. Especially not in church.)

I have more important things to do with my time. Like serve papers.

My name is Sofie Metropolis, PI. Okay, so I wasn't born with the title, but I liked tacking it on if only because it detracts from the obvious Greekness of my name. Are you Greek American? Then that means you or one of your family members owns a café, a restaurant, a diner, or a club, sometimes all of the above (in my case my family members fell into the former two categories). Especially in Astoria, a one-time predominantly Greek neighborhood in Queens, one of the five boroughs of New York City.

I became a PI five months ago (really a PI-in-training because I can't become a certified private investigator in New York for another two and a half years). That's when I caught my would-be groom Thomas-the-Toad with his tux pants around his ankles on the day of our wedding . . . and it hadn't been my thighs he'd been wedged between. The moment was life changing in many ways, the biggest change being my new vocation. And while my current assignment proved that even the job of private investigator wasn't all it was cracked up to be, it was better than dividing up the contents of the tip jar any day.

And besides, it got me out of learning that Mr. Zervas was taking Viagra and chasing his seventy-year-old wife around the dining room table with his pants down around his ankles.

My professional philosophy was pretty simple: Screw with me, get a bullet in the knee. That's what happened to one of my recent clients when it turned out he had set me up as an alibi to his murderous intents on his wife, then switched his aim to me when I figured it all out. Word had it Bud Suleski would have a limp for life, which meant he couldn't run away and was quite the popular guy at Rikers as a result.

My personal philosophy . . . well, I was still working on that. And that wasn't an easy position to be in when you're Greek. Greeks seemed to know exactly where they are, how they feel, what opinions they hold every moment of every day, no matter if they're later proved wrong. Look up "Greek" in the dictionary and you'll find that "conviction" is part of their heritage, along with much spitting and shouting and interesting hand gestures.

"Live and let live." Maybe I'd go with that for now until I figured out something better. Then again, no. Because I wouldn't mind if my ex turned up dead. "Live and let one person die"? Doesn't have the same ring to it somehow.

Anyway, on this sweltering Sunday morning in August, at just after ten, I sat in my classic Mustang convertible (read: Bondo Special) outside an apartment complex in Jackson Heights, wishing for air-conditioning and hoping to spot one very wily Mr. Eugene Waters.

Serving court papers made up a nice percentage of my Uncle Spyros' agency's profits. And while I normally didn't serve, the success rate of our top two servers dropped when it came to Mr. Waters. Over the past week, neither of them had been able to get the guy to accept landlord dispute papers, and the deadline was fast approaching. Yes, after two failed attempts, the agency could go the nail and mail route, meaning I could nail the papers to his door (or slip them under it), then mail two additional copies, one regular and one certified, to Mr. Waters. But the reason why Uncle Spyros and his agency were popular in the serving business was because he didn't like to do that. The client wanted the papers served in hand? Then in hand was how they would be served.

So I'd rolled my eyes and told everyone I'd do it myself. I mean, how difficult could it be?

Rule number 565: Never underestimate the potential of any case to turn dangerous or complicated, or both.

My uncle Spyros—the certified PI, my mentor, and owner of the agency where I work—was fond of rules. And while I was exaggerating the number of this one, the rule itself stuck in my mind. Which would make my uncle happy. Me, I made a face and determined I should come up with my own list of rules. The first of which would be to ignore Uncle Spyros' rules.

Muffy barked from the backseat as if putting an exclamation point on my ruminations.

I stared at the scruffy Jack Russell terrier. It had been two months since my mother's neighbor and best friend Mrs. K had gone on to the Big Hindu Heaven in the sky, and Muffy the Mutt had been promoted from rescued pet to my pet. And I had the bite marks to prove it.

I wouldn't go so far as to say that Muffy and I had become friends. But we had reached a truce of sorts. An "I won't mess with you if you don't mess with me" attitude that was working out so far. Except when I was leaving the apartment. Somehow he—yes, Muffy is a he—sensed when what I was about to do might be marginally exciting, and he found a way to follow me out and jump in the back of my car.

He rarely followed me when I went to my parents' house up the block from my place, however. Then again, I didn't much like how my paternal grandmother eyed him while she diced vegetables either. I mean, dog meat couldn't be that far from goat meat, could it? And seeing as Yiayia had lived through some difficult times back in the homeland, like World War II, communist guerillas, and two military juntas . . . well, I decided I didn't want to pursue that particular line of thought.

"Bingo."

I switched my attention from the dog to first-floor apartment number sixty-nine. A short, thin black man had stepped outside—was that a pink satin bathrobe with feather cuffs he was wearing?—looked around, then bent over to get the Sunday *Times* I'd put out there. (I knew few people who could resist a paper put right outside their door, especially on a Sunday, although I suspected Mr. Waters was the type who would probably steal his neighbor's paper.)

My brand-spanking-new pair of K-Swiss hit the pavement as I got out of the car, capturing my attention where they contrasted against my jeans so that I nearly closed the door on Muffy when he followed after me. I growled at the dog then hurried the fifty or so feet to apartment number sixty-nine.

"Excuse me," I said. "I was hoping you could help me . . ."

Mr. Waters eyed me warily, then Muffy.

"I'm lost and need some directions."

He went inside the apartment with the newspaper then slammed the door.

Humph. Maybe Pamela had tried the "plant the newspaper then pretend to need directions" angle already.

I left the map around the sealed documents and sighed, Muffy panting at my feet as if waiting to see what I would do next.

I knocked on the door.

"Please . . . I've been driving around in circles for an hour. If you could at least let me use your phone to call my aunt . . ."

A muffled, high-pitched male voice came from the other side of the door. "We ain't got no phone. Go away."

"Maybe you could take a look at my map . . . tell me where I'm going wrong?"

"I ain't from around here."

"Me neither," I said in my best defeated-tourist voice, hoping my Queens accent wasn't too strong. "I just drove all night from Ohio, and I'm tired and I'm lost and I could really use some help right now."

"Ohio?"

A spark of hope. "Yes."

"Where at?"

I searched my mind for a city name. "Toledo," I said, remembering M*A*S*H reruns. Klinger's favorite oath had something to do with a Holy Toledo, and he was always talking about the city as home. (Okay, I'm a TV-rerun fanatic. So sue me.)

I heard the lock give and the door opened on the chain. "I got people in Cleveland."

I smiled. "Nice city, Cleveland."

He slammed the door again.

Okay, maybe Cleveland wasn't nice. But I'd bet the people were a hell of a lot more hospitable.

"Please," I said again, employing a politeness that might not be natural for most native New Yorkers, but would be for an Ohioan. "My aunt was expecting me four hours ago and is probably worried sick. She's got this heart condition . . ."

"Call her on a pay phone."

"I'll pay you for your trouble."

Silence, then, "How much?"

"How much you want?"

The agency got seventy-five dollars for each set of papers we delivered in hand, so I figured it wasn't worth my time to offer him more than say twenty.

"Twenty dollars."

Figured. "I can give you five. I don't have much money. You see, I lost my job in Ohio and used the last of my savings to come here to live with my aunt until I get back on my feet."

Where did I get this stuff? It might worry me that I was so adept at lying except that I was enjoying the rush too much. Especially since I didn't lie well when it came to items of a personal nature.

Although I kind of wished I made up a Vegas showgirl story instead. It would have been much more interesting.

I looked down at my tennis shoes, jeans, and fitted black tank. Then again, it also probably would have been less believable.

"Ten," he said.

"Deal."

The door opened again on the chain. I thrust the map at him.

"You see, I'm supposed to get here . . ." I said, pointing to a spot near Forest Hills.

He wasn't taking the map.

"And the best I can figure is, I'm here."

I pointed at a spot near Astoria.

"Naw, you're not there. You're here," he said, poking at the map with his index finger but otherwise not touching it or the papers it was wrapped around. "Where's the ten?"

I resisted an eye roll and dug in my pocket for the promised money. It was the principle of the thing.

He took the ten and stuffed it into the front of his pink robe. A robe that was gaping a little too widely for my liking. And he smelled suspiciously like marijuana. Which might explain the pink robe.

"So that must be my first mistake," I said, referring to the map again. "The directions my aunt gave me take me this way." I indicated an area around Flushing Meadows in Corona.

"No, no. Don't go that way. You'll only circle back. Here, let me show you . . ."

He took the map and the papers within.

I resisted the urge to squeal in delight—at least I think I did—as I jumped away from the door.

"You've been served," I said.

He dropped the map and the papers and slammed the door. Shit.

Officially I had served the papers. All I needed to do was place them in his hands and say the words. But with the papers lying at my feet and the door closed on my face, I didn't feel like I'd accomplished the job somehow.

I could go back to the car and sit and wait to see if he picked them up. But I got the distinct impression that even if Waters opened the door, the last thing on his agenda would be picking up those papers.

So I picked them up instead.

Waters shouted from inside the apartment. "You know, you ain't supposed to be serving no papers on a Sunday anyhow. If I had half a mind, I'd take those stinkin' papers and get the whole thing thrown out of court on account of your serving on a Sunday."

Was he right? Was I not supposed to be serving on a Sunday? Well, that didn't make much sense. Sunday seemed like the perfect time to serve papers. Then again, Eugene Waters probably knew a whole hell of a lot more when it came to this stuff than I did.

Probably I should have gone to Mass . . .

HOME. ALTHOUGH I'D BEEN LIVING on my own for the past five months, I still referred to my parents' place as home. And had basically accepted that I probably always would.

One of the nice things about "home" was that I could always tell what my mother was cooking the instant I walked into the house. Today it was fricassee. Or at least the Greek version of it. When I was ten I went to Jenny Tanner's house for dinner once and her mother had served a completely different fricassee, something involving chicken in a brown sauce and rice. The Greek version included a large cut of lamb, greens, and dill with an egg and lemon sauce all over the top that made your mouth water when you smelled it.

Today was no exception.

One of the downsides of "home" was facing my feuding father and grandfather.

I walked through the living room where my father and my maternal grandfather both sat—I stopped to kiss each on the cheek—reading different sections of the *Times* in different recliners while simultaneously ignoring each other. On the tension scale, silence was good.

I moved into the kitchen and greeted my mother and my paternal, eternally black-clad grandmother, then I put Muffy in the backyard (it was the size of a postage stamp and enclosed by other houses), where he seemed to let out a sigh of relief that he'd passed Yiayia without incident, no matter how hot it was outside.

"You missed church," my mother said, shoving a platter full of fresh, cut bread and feta cheese into my hands.

"I told you I had to work."

She made a disapproving sound and pushed me through the door into the dining room, her own hands full of food. "What you do is not work. What you do is dangerous."

I didn't think my mother would ever get over the fact that I had shot someone. Up until that point she hadn't known I owned a gun, or that I was licensed to carry (which means carry concealed). Now every time I see her or talk to her on the phone, she brings it up as if I'll offer to get rid of it if she asks just one more time. And since the incident was something I didn't particularly like to remember either—I hated guns—I hadn't liked talking to my mother much lately.

"Did I miss anything?" I asked, following her back into the kitchen where Yiayia was putting her contraband bottle of rye back into her deep dress pocket after having knocked back a hefty swallow.

"You missed taking in a bit of God," my mother snapped.

What was it with mothers and guilt?

"And you missed seeing the Protopsaltis' new daughter-in-law."

"Ah." Actually, *that* I would have liked to see. If only because Yanni Protopsaltis had had the guts to actually marry outside Greek bloodlines. Not only that, but he'd been married in a civil ceremony without his parents' knowledge and his new wife was of Vietnamese extraction.

I could imagine the entire congregation turning when the family entered, openly staring at the young couple, some of them probably crossing themselves three times to ward off the evil that had befallen the Protopsaltises.

Only a Greek could understand the power of a Greek family when it came to matters of marriage. Take me, for example. One of the reasons I'd become engaged to marry Thomas-the-Toad Chalikis was that my family had made my life an unbearable hell until I agreed to marry somebody. And Thomas-the-Toad emerged as as likely a candidate as any.

Too bad he'd forgotten that getting married usually would mean he'd have to withdraw his candidacy as lover material for other women, more specifically, my maid of honor and best friend at the time.

At any rate, I would have liked to have gone to church if only to invite the newlyweds over to my place for dinner or a drink or something. Or at least give them a huge thumbs-up sign right there in front of God and everyone.

"Oh, and Apostolis Pappas is missing."

Thalia said this just as she disappeared through the kitchen door with the last of the platters and called everyone for dinner.

She couldn't have surprised me more if she'd told me Muffy was on the menu.

Apostolis Pappas owned the neighborhood dry cleaners. Only I called him Uncle Tolly, along with pretty much the rest of the neighborhood, mostly because of the pieces of ouzo candy he always gave out to the kids, along with a lot of hair ruffling.

I looked over Yiayia's shoulder where she stirred something on the stove. "What does she mean by missing?"

My paternal grandmother was as old as Methuselah and looked it. She merely slid a glance at me then reached for the bottle in her pocket again. She shook it, indicating she needed to be replenished.

"I'll bring something by tomorrow," I told her, following my mother out into the dining room.

My father and grandfather were now seated at the table, as

were my sister, Efi, and her many piercings and tattoos, and my brother, Kosmos, both younger than me by a few years—Efi a few more than Kosmos—and as different from me as a spoon and a fork.

"What do you mean by missing?" I asked my mother.

Yiayia wandered in and took her seat and the family began loading their plates with food.

My grandfather crossed himself, offering up a silent prayer, and everyone else followed suit. I sank into my chair and did the same.

"Just what I said."

Trust my mother to bring up the Protopsaltis' Vietnamese daughter-in-law over a missing Uncle Tolly.

Efi, who sat next to me, leaned closer. "They think it's the mob."

My eyebrows shot up. The mob and Uncle Tolly?

"The mob had nothing to do with it. If you ask me, he finally wised up and left that old battle-ax he's married to," my grandfather said, getting the plate of fricassee before my father and nearly emptying it. My father looked at my mother and my mother automatically began forking half the food from my grandfather's plate back onto the platter, then onto my father's plate.

War averted.

"For all we know, he's laying in a ditch somewhere waiting to be discovered," my brother said.

We all stared at him.

"What? He's not exactly a spring chicken anymore."

My grandfather narrowed his eyes at him. "He's two years younger than me."

We all cleared our throats and concentrated on our plates.

"It's probably the heat," my father said. "The heat makes people do strange things."

The heat. I could relate to that.

This August had to be one of the hottest on record, and no matter how high the air-conditioning was set, I couldn't seem to cool off. My skin seemed forever covered with a thin sheen of sweat, and I showered and changed clothes no fewer than three times a day: I just wanted to be sure I didn't smell like a good many of the Greeks in the neighborhood, mostly older, who'd been raised during a period in the old country when clean water was at a premium and you were lucky to get one shower a week.

Of course, the futile activity did absolutely nothing to alleviate the itchiness I felt right there, just below my skin. It made me fidget when I sat, and I caught myself scratching more times than I cared to count. I was pretty sure I knew what was responsible for the itch. Something aggravated by the high temperatures and not treatable by imbibing massive quantities of water, applying lotion, or a trip to the doctor.

I caught myself scratching my arm and stopped.

"Anyway," Thalia said, pouring red *boutari* wine into small juice glasses and nudging me to pass them down until everyone had one. "I told Aglaia that you'd stop by after dinner and see if there's anything you can do."

I grimaced. And it wasn't because of the lemony sauce I'd just filled my mouth with.

Just call me Sofie Metropolis, personal private investigator to my mother.

Two

THE GREAT THING ABOUT DREAMS is that you have absolute power over the actions of the players. This control is especially useful when it comes to *wet* dreams. And I was liking everything about being the commander of this one. In it, I was having yummy bounty hunter Jake Porter do all kinds of naughty things to my sex-starved body that went well beyond the spicy kisses he'd given me a couple months back, which were more than enough for my imagination to build on.

"You're beautiful, luv," he murmured in his rumbling Australian accent, his mouth in an area that caused my back to arch and my thighs to tighten against the pillow I'd woken up to find wedged between my legs more than a few times lately.

"Yeah?" I breathed, licking my lips.

"Yeah. Let me show you how beautiful . . ."

The only problem was the sound effects weren't exactly in sync with my dream. Was Porter growling? Yes, Porter was definitely growling. Not exactly something you wanted your partner to be doing while concentrating on such a delicate area of your anatomy.

I shifted in the dream to try to stop the sound. It increased.

It was pretty bad when you sweated even in your dreams. And not exactly the type of sweat you welcomed either.

I snapped awake to discover with relief and disappointment that it wasn't Porter who'd been growling but rather my new roommate. And while he was of the male persuasion, he was completely the wrong species. Muffy the Mutt had the far corner of my top sheet between his sharp little teeth and was madly working it back and forth, off my person.

"Go away, hellhound." I flopped back onto the bed.

Story of my life, really. Just when things started getting interesting—*bam!*—something happened and I was not only back at square one, I was stomping my feet at the injustice of it all.

Muffy's nonstop, machinelike growling spiked every time he tugged on the sheet.

Then I remembered it had been so hot last night that I'd closed all the windows and switched the air-conditioning to high, meaning the Muffster didn't have access to the fire escape and the roof beyond, where he did most of his business.

We played tug-of-war with the sheet as I looked at the clock. Just after six. Way too early for civilized folk to even think about getting up. Especially on a Monday morning.

The smell of something unpleasant filled my nose. I stared at the dog. Over the past two months, I'd learned the finer points of canine farts. But somehow I didn't think I'd ever get used to them.

"All right, all right," I muttered, finally giving in and crawling out of bed. "Can't a person have some privacy already?"

Muffy leapt to the floor, ran toward the door, then circled back again indicating he really had to go.

I crossed my apartment in my old Mets T-shirt and bare feet and threw open the sash over the fire escape. Muffy leapt out and scampered toward the roof.

I shook my head and took a deep breath. The thick, humid air that hit me full in the face made me want to slam the window shut again. Instead, I adjusted it so it was open wide enough for the Jack Russell terrier to get through then went into the kitchen to make my morning frappé. Iced coffee and a pickle in hand, I collected my *Daily News* from outside the door, probably brought up by Mrs. Nebitz, my neighbor across the hall, who always seemed to be after the worm. Which is probably why I never got it, early or otherwise. I snapped the newspaper open to read the Daily Dish. After taking in my fill of gossip I already knew about, I turned to the Boroughs section.

"Astoria Man Missing: Foul Play Suspected."

Uncle Tolly.

I hadn't gone over to the dry cleaners after dinner yesterday like my mother asked. I'd been too stuffed and too hot to do anything but come back to my place and take a nap, then veg out in front of the television for the rest of the night with the remote fused to my hand.

I looked toward the open window. Muffy had yet to come back in. I sighed and put the paper on the kitchen table and followed the Uncle Tolly story to another page. It didn't tell me anything I didn't already know from my mother and the rest of my family. Aglaia Pappas had called the police at around ten P.M. Saturday night to report her husband missing. He'd gone out for an after-supper walk at seven and had never come back.

Since Uncle Tolly didn't suffer from Alzheimer's and had

been in good health when he'd gone for his walk, the police had instituted a twenty-four-hour waiting period as they did in most missing persons cases. Which meant they should have started looking for him last night. The piece outlined how he and his wife had operated the dry cleaners for the past forty years and were pillars of the community.

I knew the couple didn't have kids. I also knew that they seemed to have aged together in such a way that it was almost impossible to tell the two apart. They put on the same weight, got almost the same haircut, and aside from Aglaia's ample bust size and their difference in temperament, it was easy for those who didn't know them to get them confused altogether.

I made a face and took a hefty sip of my frappé. Put it this way: I usually planned my visit to the cleaners to coincide with when Uncle Tolly was most likely to be working. Like first thing when they opened in the morning.

"What, you don' like job? To other cleaner go," Aglaia had told me in broken English when I'd taken my flea market area rug in to be cleaned two months ago and the dyes had run.

Funny, she never spoke to me in Greek even though her English was atrocious. Probably she was trying to improve her vocabulary.

Probably she did it just to be ornery.

Muffy came dragging his butt into the kitchen, looking like he hadn't accomplished the business he'd intended.

"I told you that you shouldn't have had the *kalia* last night."

He barked at me.

Since his previous owner, the late Mrs. Kapoor, had been from Bangladesh, the dog seemed to prefer a curry-laden diet over everything else I tried to feed him. I knew it couldn't be good for him but, hey, he'd lived this long—I think he's about four—and who was I to judge anyone else's eating habits? I liked to dip pickles into my morning coffee. (No, I'm not pregnant. You had to have sex to get pregnant. And I don't think dreams count, no matter how wet.)

I shrugged and while reading the next item in the paper put fresh water in the dog dish and filled the other bowl with dry food. He sniffed it, drank some water, then walked back out of the kitchen to sit in the open window. Probably I should have closed the window. I didn't want the air-conditioned air to waft down the street to my mother's house so she could call me and ask why the window was open. But Muffy looked so miserable I didn't have the heart.

Did they sell laxatives for dogs?

I looked at the clock on the wall. It was too early to go to the office where I had five open cases to work on, one comp case (a worker's compensation case where I hoped to catch a guy who supposedly had a debilitating back injury doing something like hauling a refrigerator over one shoulder), three cheating spouse cases (so not my favorite), and one background check on a Con Ed employee that included a spot tail.

The cleaners, however, opened at seven, in time for the morning, before-work rush. A good time to pay my promised visit seeing as Aglaia would be busy. Stuffing the rest of the pickle into my mouth, I headed for the bathroom and the shower.

THE CLEANERS WAS CLOSED.

I stared at the sign in the front window as I shut off my car engine and listened as it coughed and sputtered into silence. Whoa. In none of my twenty-six years had I ever seen the cleaners closed on a Monday morning. In fact, after Friday, the day was probably one of their busiest of the week. You know, packed full of those who had gotten up in the morning only to forget they had nothing to wear to work so they make a mad dash to pick up their things from the cleaners. I slowly got out of the car, remembered Muffy had stayed back at the apartment waiting to do his business, and closed the door. A light was on in the upstairs apartment as the days had already begun to shorten and dawn was farther away than it used to be.

I stood on the sidewalk for a long moment ignoring that I was already sweating. Literally, that is. Although figuratively I wasn't much looking forward to talking to the overbearing woman who hadn't asked for my help. But the thought of facing my mother again without having visited compelled me to step to the door and ring the bell. A moment later, a voice barked, "Who's the hell is it?"

I grimaced. "Mrs. Pappas? It's Sofie. Sofie Metropolis? Perhaps my mother—"

I was buzzed in. I'd half-expected her to make me stand on the sidewalk to explain everything, perhaps even conduct my questioning from there. But there I was climbing a dimly lit stairwell up to an apartment I doubted many had visited since the couple had spent so much of their time downstairs.

The first thing I smelled was the scent of fried fish. *Bakaliaro*—cod—to be exact. And not of the fresh variety, but the salted. Whenever my grandmother fixed it, the house stank for days. My mom said it's an old country thing. While you can buy the fish fresh in abundance nowadays, back then you couldn't, so the older generation had gotten used to eating the salted.

I don't even want to say what I thought it smelled like. Unwashed old woman provides a hint.

"Come, come," Mrs. Pappas said, opening the apartment door and ushering me inside.

I gave my cramped surroundings a quick once-over. It looked like the place hadn't been painted or redecorated in the forty years the couple had lived there. The paint was at best a fading beige that once may have been white, every spot taken up by a framed photo of some sort, which was odd considering the couple didn't have children and had no other family in the States. I stepped to take a closer look and found they were all black-and-white and sepia prints they'd probably brought with them from Greece, with a few color shots sprinkled in that were likely sent in Christmas cards. Handmade doilies covered everything from the dining room table to the sofa arms and the backs of the chairs.

The place wasn't all that dissimilar to other Greek-American households in that it seemed the occupants had never really adopted their new country but rather lived in a kind of Greek limbo.

I watched Mrs. Pappas' short, solid frame as she went into the small kitchen to put her Greek coffee cup and saucer into the sink then brush Melba toast crumbs from the table. I couldn't help thinking she looked like E.T. in a flowered house-dress.

"I so glad you come," she said as she rushed into the other room. "You help open. Come."

Uh-oh . . .

"Mrs. Pappas, I didn't come here to—"

"Never mind. Come, come."

She picked up a key ring and led the way downstairs and back outside. Parked in front of the cleaners was a brand spanking new Mercedes I'd glimpsed earlier but hadn't paid much attention to because I'd been staring at the CLOSED sign. I considered it now even as I thought about what I was going to say to get out of toiling away in a dry cleaners all day.

"Tolly's."

I looked at Mrs. Pappas. "What? The car?"

"Yes. I told him not to buy. You know what he say to me? Shut up. Shut up. Can you believe?"

Actually, I had yet to move beyond the fact that Uncle Tolly had bought a Mercedes when his apartment hadn't been painted in forty years.

"Come, come."

She finished putting up the metal security gate and opened the door.

Moments later, she was handing me plastic-wrapped clothing from the back of the shop to hang in the front.

"Mrs. Pappas, I didn't come here to work."

She appeared not to hear me as she shoved another armful of clothes at me.

"My mother thought I might be able to help you find Uncle Tolly."

She stopped and stared at me suspiciously. "Find? Why would you be able to find?"

Hmm . . . I found her question curious. Why would she be asking me why I thought I'd be able to find him? Could it be that Mrs. Tolly had done away with the old man herself and stashed him somewhere nobody would find him?

I'd heard a rumor somewhere that undiluted dry cleaning solution ran a close second to acid when it came to dissolving the hardest to dissolve.

Then I realized that like my mother she probably gave me zero credit when it came to my new job. "I'm a PI, Mrs. Pappas. You know, a private investigator."

"I thought you work at your grandfather's *cafeneio*."

"I did . . ."

"I have no money for an investigator private."

I hung up the clothes in my arms only to have another batch shoved at me. "No, no. I wouldn't charge you, of course."

This got the older woman's attention. She stopped in the doorway. "Why you no charge me? You think I too poor?"

"You just told me you didn't have money to hire an investigator."

"I told you I don't want an investigator."

Okay . . .

This was one argument I really wasn't up to having so early on a Monday morning. The agency assistant, Rosie Rodriguez, would be coming into the office at eight. Maybe I'd beat her there if I could shuffle a little closer to the door and make my escape.

"If you want to pay me that's fine," I said.

"Pay you for what?" she asked. "The mafia killed my husband."

That was a serious charge to make, even for a half-baked woman who smelled like salted fish.

I shuffled uncomfortably. I didn't like that this was the second time someone had linked Uncle Tolly and the New York City mob in the same sentence. "How do you know he's dead?"

"How do I know he's dead, she asks. I know he's dead because he didn't come home, that's how I know he's dead."

She snorted indelicately, her gaze going through the window and settling on the car outside.

"Actually, maybe you can help me," she said finally. "I need for you to find my husband's body."

I resisted the urge to stick my thumbs into my eye sockets until I heard a satisfying pop and took out a policeman's type pad from my back jeans pocket.

"So you can bury him." A lot of Greek Americans took their loved ones back home to be buried with other relatives and the like. Maybe Mrs. Pappas wasn't as bad as I thought.

"Bury him? Do you know how much it costs to bury somebody? No, I want you to find his body so I can sell his car."

"YOU'RE NOT THINKING OF TAKING on this case, are you, luv?"

When I came out of the cleaners, I was so preoccupied with thoughts of Uncle Tolly's body lying among the other un-marked graves in Potter's Field on Hart Island and of Aglaia counting crisp one hundred dollar bills after she sold the Mer-cedes that I was wholly unprepared for the sentence and the man who uttered it.

I turned to find none other than the growling object of my subconscious desires leaning against the brick of the building, his arms crossed over his enormous chest.

Jake Porter.

Okay, let me get this out of the way up front: I have not slept with Porter. Oh, not from lack of trying—mostly on my part. But from lack of interest—mostly on his part. He'd worked on making my car a happy Sheila—even though I'd named her Lu-cille, but I don't think he means "Sheila" as a name anyway—and has a habit of showing up when I least expect it. I met him during one of my first cheating spouse cases five months ago, then he'd turned up while I was working the Suleski case. He'd taken apart my garbage disposal to retrieve my engagement ring (an accident—I swear), only so I could find out the rock was CZ, not the diamond that had been in it when my grandfather Kosmos had given it to my slime of an ex to propose to me.

Is all that clear?

No?

Well, that's okay, because the mess of my mind pretty much covered how I felt every time I saw major hottie Aussie Jake Porter, who I thought was a bounty hunter, but I suspected might have some kind of murky government ties. A sort of chaos swept over me and I became all too aware of that itch I couldn't seem to scratch and how long it had been since I'd felt the touch of a man where I would most like to be touched.

But, aside from a kiss or two, and the heart-pounding, suggestive grins he sometimes gave me, I haven't been successful in getting him to take care of my little problem.

Yet.

I smiled.

"Well, look who blew back into town," I said, really meaning "life," as in mine, instead of "town."

"Who said I ever left?"

"I did."

I walked toward my car, overly aware that I was wearing my usual uniform of jeans and stretchy top and sneakers and wishing I had on something different, like a snug red summer dress and strappy heels, no matter that it was Monday morning and I normally wouldn't be caught dead in such an outfit. He followed.

"She needs a nice long bath."

"Mmm," I said in response to his comment, probably because I was incapable of much more.

"Mrs. Pappas has some interesting theories about her better half."

I eyed Porter. He was six foot five or so and had sandy brown hair and one of the naughtiest grins I'd ever seen.

And the last time I saw him, he'd cast himself in the role of my protector.

The role I wanted him to play was something altogether different.

So you could say he and I had a conflict of interest.

"Heard about that, have you?" I unlocked the passenger door of my Mustang and swung my purse inside.

"Hard not to. Word's all over."

I squinted at him. "And your interest in Uncle Tolly is?"

He leaned against the car. "Gave me an excuse to come over and say hello."

"So my possibly working the case must also be making the rumor rounds."

He didn't say anything, which I took to mean yes.

Didn't surprise me really. Although I'd only officially taken on the case five minutes ago, it's likely my mother had been talking to everyone as if I was already working it at some point yesterday. Which meant the whole of Astoria, if not Queens, knew what I was up to. Well, at least those who were interested, anyway. And since I'd shot Bud Suleski in the knee, there seemed to be more of those lately.

"Is there some specific reason you wanted an excuse to see me?" I asked, although I wasn't entirely sure why. Probably because I wanted him to tell me he'd missed me as much as I'd missed him. Mostly because I didn't want him to be around because of the case I'd just taken on.

He merely grinned at me in that way that left me wondering if he was amused or attracted. Or possibly a little of both.

He pushed from the car. "You might want to advise your client to lower her voice when it comes to her thoughts on her husband's whereabouts."

"That's why you came over here?"

"Mmm."

Ugh. I thought I'd made the grunt but couldn't be sure.

Just when I thought Porter was going to walk away and leave me wondering about his words and his motivation for saying them, he leaned down and kissed me full on the mouth.

And I was so unprepared that I could do little but stare at him.

He chuckled and walked away, leaving me a puddle of quivering female flesh right there in the middle of the sidewalk.

Double ugh.

Three

That was what the gold-and-black lettering on the window read even though my Uncle Spyros hasn't physically been in the office for the past three months. He was in Greece. And it was beginning to look like he might never come back. Which didn't bother me in the least because it gave me free reign of the place.

"You didn't deliver the summons," Rosie stated rather than asked when I entered, five minutes after scraping myself off the sidewalk after Porter's kiss.

Okay, maybe I didn't have total free reign. There was the sometimes irritating Puerto Rican office manager who was probably twice the man my uncle was despite her dish-sized dimples and huge breasts, displayed today "to their utmost flattering degree," as she liked to put it, in a tight, low-neck red shirt. Aside from a slight aversion she had to neighborhood vampires, she was pretty cool.

"No, he found me out," I said, checking through the messages on my desk. "Is it true you're not supposed to serve papers on Sunday?"

She stopped chewing her ever-present gum. "You tried serving him on a Sunday?"

That was all the answer I needed. I figured it would be a good idea if I looked into this stuff.

"Are there any other rules designed to give the innocent a head start?"

"Yeah. Like you can't serve from eight in the morning till nine, and from five to six. Oh, and after ten o'clock at night."

I gaped at her. "That's like the only chance you stand of finding anyone home if they work."

Rosie shook her head. "Tell me about it. I keep telling Spyros we should start nailing and mailing."

Sounded like a plan to me. But I wondered what impact it would have on that portion of the agency's business if Spyros did change the policy.

"I got us a new case," I told Rosie, deciding I didn't like serving anymore and that after this one my serving days were over.

She sorted through paperwork on her desk. "Oh? Did someone lose a pet?"

I stared at her, not appreciating her sarcasm because I had those five open cases I was working on, and a growing roster of successes, no matter how small. Still, I wondered how long it was going to take me to live down the two missing pet cases I'd taken on already.

At any rate, Mrs. Pappas had hired me—at a quarter of the going rate, but Rosie didn't have to know that yet—to find her husband's dead body.

At least it wasn't another missing pet case. Or cheating spouse.

And didn't involve following around people for background checks and waiting for comp cases to do something noteworthy, which was surprisingly often.

"And if he's alive?" I'd asked Aglaia.

"Then you don't get paid."

I explained while Rosie actively nodded.

When I finished, she tsked-tsked several times and said, "Poor Uncle Tolly."

"You know Uncle Tolly?"

She waved at me, causing the hundred silver bangle bracelets she wore on her right wrist to jangle. "Of course I knew . . . know Uncle Tolly. Everybody knows Uncle Tolly. He used to give out those little black licorice thingies when I was a kid." She stared at me. "You don't think he's dead, do you?"

I frowned as I absently folded one of the message slips from my mother into a paper airplane. "Unfortunately, it's a possibility."

Rosie gave a visible shudder that jiggled her breasts.

What I wouldn't give for breasts like that.

Of course, I'd made the mistake of saying something similar to Efi, my younger sister, and she'd suggested that I have my breasts augmented. But since I nearly fainted at the mention of the word "needle," I didn't think I could handle the stress of an entire operation.

Besides, whatever happened to what God gave you being good?

I stared at my own modest bust then Rosie's and sighed. That belief had gone the way of bra burning and completely died with the advent of reality television.

Rosie looked around as if expecting someone to be lurking in the shadows, her mouth working a million miles a minute on her chewing gum. "You don't really think the mob had any-thing to do with it, do you?"

"There is no mafia," I told her. Hey, that's what the crime families claimed, anyway. Despite news to the contrary in the papers and on local television almost all day, every day.

She stared at me as if I'd lost a few worry beads on the way to the agency that morning.

"Oh, all right, I had the same thought," I said, although Mrs. Pappas had been the one to bring up the possibility. And my sister Efi before that. "What, the dry cleaner laundering more than clothes?"

Rosie looked around again.

"Hey, your brother is the manicurist to the mob, isn't he?" I asked her.

She stared at me again, all big eyes and frozen mouth. "Uh-uh. Don't even say it."

"What?"

She pointed a fingernail at me that bore a decal of the American flag. "You keep me and my baby brother out of this."

"Out of what? I was just going to suggest that maybe you give me his number, you know, so I can see if he's heard any-thing on the mob grapevine."

"Uh-uh. One moment you're filing somebody's nails, the next you're wearing cement boots at the bottom of the East River. No way."

"Come on, Rosie, I'm not sending him undercover or any-thing."

"You don't have to. All it would take is one phone call from you and my brother would be mob history." She was shaking her head so that her large silver hoop earrings bobbed. "Nobody, but nobody messes with the DiPiazzas."

The name rang a bell. "DiPiazza. As in Tony DiPiazza?"

"Oh, boy." She put a hand to her chest as if the mere mention was enough to send her into cardiac arrest. "He's the absolute worst out of the bunch."

"I used to go to school with a Tony DiPiazza. I wonder if he's the same guy."

Rosie continued shaking her head, her short, dark curls waving at me as she went back to her desk. "I don't even want to know."

"But—"

She put her fingers to her ears. "Not a word. I don't want to hear nothing about no DiPiazzas."

"Fine," I said. "Anyway, I'm not going to go down that road unless I'm convinced the possibility of mafia involvement exists. First I'm going to check area hospitals and the like, see if maybe he didn't fall down and hit his head or something."

Rosie was nodding. "Yeah, yeah. Maybe he's got that . . ." She snapped her fingers. "Amnesia. One of the characters on my soap she got amnesia last year? Couldn't remember a thing. Not even the father of the baby she was pregnant with." She shook her head. "So sad. At least my sister knows who the father of her baby is. He might be a no good son-of-a-bitch bastard, but she knows who he is. Oh, did I tell you she reached the seventh-month mark yesterday? She's—"

I tuned Rosie out. This time, I was the one who fought putting my fingers in my ears . . .

I DROPPED BY THE 114TH Precinct to put out a few feelers on Uncle Tolly and was told they were looking into it, which essentially meant they hadn't done anything yet. So I drove by

Eugene Waters' place only to find him not home, then on to Flushing. I chose a spot under a tree to park across the street and up the block from the house of Charles McCutcheon, the subject of my comp case. The thing about being a PI is that more often than not you find yourself working out of your car, not your office. Which usually was okay with me, if only because it got me away from Rosie on her chattier days. If only it wasn't so hot and if my target was more active than a sloth who'd just been fed and didn't need to eat for another week at least.

I looked at the open front door to the house in question. The top part of the screen wilted out, empty beer cans littered the front porch, and I knew my subject himself would make an appearance soon to claim the sagging lawn chair that would probably topple over if it hadn't been propped against the wall of the one-story structure, which was in dire need of renovation.

Charlie was twenty-six (it surprised me that he was my age, if only because I didn't know any guys my age that looked the way he did), had worked as a baggage handler at LaGuardia for five months before apparently lifting the too heavy luggage of someone like Paris Hilton, injuring a sensitive disc in his upper vertebrae that supposedly resulted in a significant loss of mobility of his left arm.

All well and good, you say. An unfortunate accident that left the victim unable to work and therefore entitled to worker's compensation.

Only this was the third time this particular victim had petitioned the state agency for permanent disability status in the past three years. And his "family physician" was suspected of making false diagnoses and coaching his patients to feign injury for a percentage of the compensation award.

If you asked me, I thought they should go after the doctor.

Flick him off the radar screen and his patients would fall like dominoes in neat succession after him. Then again, who was I to judge? Apparently, two other larger agencies had tried but failed to get the dirt on McCutcheon, which was the reason I was working on it. And when I proved this guy was capable of doing more than sitting in his battered lawn chair all day knocking back cheap beer and expanding his belly by noticeable degrees, the agency would make a tidy little profit and possibly get more comp cases thrown its way.

I sighed, took a deep sip from my frappé before it got too warm, then reached for my cell phone. At least I didn't have to actually sit all day waiting for Charlie to lift more than his beer hand. It was during boring stints like this that I actually got more accomplished than I did at the office. I didn't know how investigators coped before the advent of cell phones.

Consulting a list Rosie had made up for me before I left the office, I started my search for the missing Uncle Tolly. I contacted area hospitals, including those in and around Manhattan. I reasoned that since the Ditmars stop on the W and N trains was within walking distance, he could be just about anywhere. Not only in New York. But around the country via Grand Central Station. Or the world for that matter, considering both LaGuardia and Kennedy airports were in Queens.

Nobody in any of the area hospitals had an Apostolis Pappas or a John Doe fitting Uncle Tolly's description.

The information both relieved and concerned me. So he wasn't lying comatose somewhere. But if he wasn't, where was he?

My cell phone rang where I still clutched it and I jumped.

"You're ignoring my calls again," my mother said.

"No, I'm not." Liar. "I'm on a case." At least that much was true. If you could call what I was doing working a case. I stared at where Charlie's door was still open, the chair still empty.

Truth was, I *was* ignoring my mother's calls. I'd prefer to talk to her when I had some solid news to report. Checking in with her and telling her what was going on every five minutes would only slow me up. Not to mention drive me batty.

"What's up?" I asked.

"What's up? What's up? Is this the way you talk to your mother? Like she's one of your friends?" She spoke in Greek to someone on her end. Probably my grandmother. I could see Yiayia nodding then calling me a name that would be cause for a fight in other cultures, but was par for the course within the Greek community.

Geez. "Sorry, Ma. I'm just a little busy, that's all."

"What did Tolly's wife have to say? Is there any news on him yet?"

I didn't have to ask how she knew I'd gone to Aglaia's. Probably even before I left the cleaners, the news had traveled the length of the phone tree a committee of women had started at the church years ago. It had been created for things like helping get the word out on deaths so the community could help the grieving family. Probably it was used more to talk about Mr. Zervas taking Viagra.

"Unfortunately, no. I've got a call into the police and just checked all the area hospitals. Nothing."

"I could have told you that. Aglaia already called."

"Yes, but someone matching his description could have been brought in between then and now."

"Oh. Sure. I hadn't thought of that."

"That's why I'm the PI and you're my mom."

"You're not a PI."

Right. The only time I rated the title was when she needed me to help out her or one of her friends.

"Speaking of which, can you stop by here later?" Thalia asked. "I have . . . something to ask you."

She'd dropped her voice as if trying to stop my grandmother from overhearing her. I could have saved her the effort. Yiayia heard everything. This despite the fact that she appeared deaf to the world.

Still, that my mother was trying to keep my grandmother out of something intrigued me.

Unless it had something to do with my ex . . .

"If this is about Thomas—"

"No, no," my mother answered quickly. "Nothing to do with Thomas."

"At least not now, anyway," went unsaid, because both of us knew that ugly chapter of my life hadn't completely closed yet. Partly because I still had unopened wedding presents in the corner of my bedroom. Mostly because my parents still wanted me to marry him.

Then there was the fact that my grandfather Kosmos still faced charges for breaking Thomas' nose two months ago. And forget the disastrous results of my parents' attempt to reconcile Thomas and me like he'd done nothing more than wear different-colored socks on the day of our wedding.

At any rate, thankfully, not much had happened on the reconciliation front lately. But I didn't kid myself into thinking my family was giving up.

Still, I said, "Fine. I'll stop by when I have a chance."

"Good. Good. I'll make your favorite."

Thalia broke the connection, leaving me to wonder not only what she was going to fix for me—everything was my favorite—but also why she was fixing it.

I groaned, praying that it had nothing to do with any more favors for her friends.

Movement at the house up the street. Only instead of seeing Charlie in a pair of baggy Bermudas, a dingy wife-beater tank top and dollar-store flip-flops, I watched as he straightened the lapels on a beige linen jacket that shouldn't have clashed against his navy slacks but did. Maybe it was the black T-shirt he wore underneath and the thick white neck brace he had on. I dunno.

At any rate, I surmised that it must be hearing day.

I exchanged my cell phone for my camera—which is really my brother Kosmos' camera, even though I'd bought it (long story)—and took a few shots of Charlie trying to look like an invalid as he awkwardly maneuvered himself behind the wheel of his old Pontiac. He drove away.

Some days it just didn't pay to be a PI.

I shook my head, put the camera down, then pointed my own car in the direction of the office.

Fifteen minutes later, after fighting an elderly woman—who thankfully was not Greek—for a parking spot (I'd never challenge a Greek woman for fear that the evil eye would be focused on me), I stepped back into the office, glad for the air-conditioning that instantly enveloped me.

"Got another one on the line," Rosie said across the office.

I looked at her. At this rate "another one" could mean anything from another missing person, another missing pet, to another set of fingernail decals.

I put my camera and cell phone down on my desk along with the Charles McCutcheon file and Eugene Waters' summons.

"Another what?" I dared go where I shouldn't.

"Another cheating spouse case. That's two more of them this morning. Must be that time of year."

That time of year? Like that time of the month? Interesting comparison. Like a never ending menstrual-like cycle of the seven-year itch.

Speaking of itches, I caught myself scratching my arm and stopped.

"Every time is that time of year," I complained.

Truth is, cheating spouse cases are my least favorite cases. Seemed everyone wanted to get dirt on his or her spouse. Considering my own recent experiences, I just didn't like the many glimpses the cases gave me into the darker side of relationships.

A month or so ago, one of my targets, Lisa Laturno, caught me snapping pictures of her and her partner coming out of a seedy motel room. Instead of screaming and making a fuss or trying to hide, she'd casually approached me where I'd sat in my Mustang. She hadn't made a grab for the camera and the damning undeveloped film inside like I'd expected her to; she'd invited me for coffee.

"What is it that makes you meet someone for five minutes of nookie in a crappy motel room?" I'd asked her after an awkward exchange on how hot it had been that summer and how we were both looking forward to fall.

The pretty brunette had shrugged and said, "I don't know. The newness of it, I guess. The excitement. The risk alone gives the encounter a kind of danger, a rush, that's . . . well, mindblowing. The best orgasms I have are with ugly guys I never see again."

I was pretty sure I sat there gaping at her as if she'd just told me the key to eternal life was giving great blow jobs.

"But you have a husband, two kids, and a vacation house in the burbs," I'd said. "What would make you jeopardize all that for a quick roll?"

"Ah, therein lies the key to the thrill. The fact that I am jeopardizing so much." She'd re-crossed her legs as if the idea alone gave her a thrill. "Hey, don't get me wrong. I love my husband and our family and our life together. This, my hobby, just reminds me how much I do love them all." Then she'd smiled at me. "Aren't you wondering why I'm not surprised to find you following me?"

"Because you're being bad and bad always gets caught?"

"Because you aren't the first PI my husband's hired. And you won't be the last." She'd looked pleased, but with what I hadn't been sure. The fact that she'd shocked me? "He always forgives me."

I realized she'd been pleased she was getting away with obnoxiously bad behavior.

And I'd been sick to my stomach.

It was the first time I'd heard the word "hobby" being linked to "infidelity." But I had the feeling it wouldn't be the last.

All things considered, I'd rather wait for guys like Charles McCutcheon to forget about their neck braces and lift cars so pretty girls could change their flat tires.

Rosie put the two new case files on top of my desk and I stared at them as if afraid they might bite.

"Rosie, tell me something," I asked after she'd returned to her desk to sort through the fresh batch of court documents that needed to be served.

"What?"

"Why aren't you a full-fledged PI?"

She stared at me. "What, do I look stupid to you or somethin'?"

"Are you calling me stupid?"

"No. I'm just saying I'm not stupid."

That didn't make any sense to me but I wasn't going to argue the point.

And Rosie apparently wasn't going to offer up anything additional either.

The cowbell above the doorbell rang and Pamela Coe, one of the agency's best servers—she'd had a one hundred percent success rate until Eugene Waters—sauntered in looking like the thousand bucks she could sometimes pick up in a week.

I squinted at her, an idea playing on the fringes of my mind as I watched her and Rosie discuss what was what and Pamela took a handful of summonses and put them in her designer bag that I was pretty sure she hadn't bought on Canal Street.

"Pamela, you got a minute?" I asked when she turned to leave.

The too pretty blonde blinked at me. Probably because I hadn't spoken two words to her since I started working at the office, much less indicated I'd known her name.

"Sure," she said. "What you got?"

You can take the girl out of Brooklyn, but you can't take Brooklyn out of the girl.

I smiled and emptied my guest chair of ongoing and new case files, hoping Pamela's response to my idea of promoting her to part-time investigator wasn't going to be, "What, do I look stupid to you or somethin'?"

Four

TURNED OUT MY MOTHER DIDN'T want to talk to me about Thomas after all . . . only I had the icky feeling I was going to wish that's what was on her mind by the time she finished with me.

I stopped by my parents' house for dinner—which was served at around one—you know, considering my mother was making whatever my favorite is. And as I was knocking back some major forkfuls of chicken and homemade *hilopites*—Greek egg pasta cut into small squares—in red sauce seasoned with cloves, I was growing overly aware that no one else was around and that my mother was silently watching me.

It wasn't the watching me part that made my neck hair stand on end. It was that she was silent while I ate. And that my grandmother didn't seem to be around anywhere. And my grandmother was always around everywhere.

"Where's Yiayia?" I asked warily, looking as if she'd materialize from somewhere out of the shadows merely by my mentioning her.

"Upstairs lying down."

Since the contraband I'd promised was in my purse, and she had been running low last night, that meant someone else had supplied the bottle of rye that had sent her up for a nap. Had grandma enlisted Efi's help? No, my sister was only nineteen and couldn't buy liquor. Not that she couldn't get a hold of it if she wanted to, but I could see Efi giving my grandmother a stare and walking away without saying a word if asked to make the liquor run.

Then again, I always suspected my mother knew I was supplying Yiayia with a bit of hooch on the side. Did she have her own supply for when she wanted to get rid of her nosey mother-in-law for a while?

The more I thought about it, the more my appetite vanished. But not before I did some major damage to the plate.

"Okay, spill," I said to my mother after clearing the table and putting my plate in the dishwasher.

"Here, here, have a *tiropita* first."

Tiropitas were small feta cheese pies that were best straight out of the oven. As these were. But it was my mother's stalling when moments before she'd been a blink away from hurrying me up that halted my hand.

"Come on, Mom. You might as well say whatever it is you want to say and get it over with."

She sighed and wiped at the table with her ever-present apron. "You're right, of course. It's just that this isn't something I ever thought I'd say, and the words seem stuck in my throat."

I snuck one of the *tiropitas*. It might not help her talk, but it would help me listen.

"It's about your father . . ."

I nodded, getting a can of Diet Coke out of the refrigerator with which to wash down the cheese pie.

"I believe your father is . . . what I mean to say is . . . God I can barely even think the words . . ."

A warning gong went off inside my body, vibrating every part of me. I could count the times my mother had been speechless on one finger: now.

"I think your father is being . . . unfaithful to me," she finally said.

I sat back in my chair as if physically slapped, a half-eaten *tiropita* in my hand.

Truth was, my mother had been acting a little strange lately. Ever since her neighbor and best friend and Muffy's previous owner, Mrs. Kapoor, died two months ago. They'd been tighter than canned stuffed grape leaves, and Mrs. K's death had come as a surprise because no one had known she was sick.

Right after, Thalia had seemed to call me every hour on the hour, sometimes just to breathe over the phone. Especially after she'd found out I'd shot Suleski in the knee. It was as if she was afraid something might happen to me.

Or, more likely, afraid something age-related might happen to her.

I put the *tiropita* down. There were few things that could keep me from enjoying a good *tiropita*. This was one of them.

I brushed buttery phyllo dough crumbs from my hands. "Don't be ridiculous. Dad never even looks at other women."

Mostly because when he wasn't working, he had his nose

stuck in the *Times* or one Greek-American newspaper or another. But I didn't think it prudent to point that out.

"Nonetheless . . ." My mother shrugged, not giving an inch. "Impossible."

She shook her finger at me. "There is no such thing as impossible. If it's one thing I've taught you kids, it's that."

"My going to Mars next year isn't even a remote possibility."

She didn't waver. "I want you to look into it."

I knew she was talking about my father and not Mars and I nearly choked on my own saliva as I looked at the door and gauged my chances of getting through it without committing to do something I absolutely did not want to do.

"No way."

I noticed then that Thalia was tightly holding a paper napkin and that her dark eyes were rimmed with red.

Oh, boy.

Say what you would, but I was afraid my mother really thought my father was playing hide-the-salami with another woman.

I reached out and took her hands in mine. Something I wasn't used to doing. Usually it was her holding my hands.

"Ma, there's no way Dad would be unfaithful to you," I told her softly.

She sniffled and I wondered if the handholding bit was a good idea.

"How do you know that?"

I raised a brow. "How do you know that he is?"

She stared at me. "Because women know these things."

I determined I'd rather have been physically slapped. I hadn't known about Thomas. So what kind of woman did that make me?

I took my hands back.

"Have you asked him?"

I'd rarely seen my mother do an eye roll but now she gave me one that could rival the best. "Of course I didn't ask him. We've been married thirty years. Besides, when it comes to matters of this nature, you don't ask. You find out."

I decided I needed to get out of there. Trying to serve those pesky papers was better than sitting across from my mother torturing herself with the thought that my father was being unfaithful to her.

"I've got to go," I said.

She grasped my arm in that way only mothers knew how to do. "You'll look into it for me? Find out who she is?"

"I will not. I already know he's not doing anything. He loves you too much."

Then I remembered that cheating wife I'd had coffee with a month or so ago. Hadn't she also loved her husband and kids? Was it true that clandestine sex had nothing to do with love?

The only problem in this case was that if my father was messing around, my mother would never forgive him. Oh, she'd never divorce him. But she probably would serve his privates up for Sunday dinner.

MY NEXT STOP WAS THE butcher shop next door to the dry cleaners. I didn't bother taking my car from the agency because of parking trouble this time of day, what with everyone jockeying for a spot so they could catch the train into the city. Which was a good thing because it made it easy for me to avoid Aglaia's seeing me. Like with my mother, I'd prefer not to speak to her until I had something solid to offer up. At least that was my story. And I was sticking to it.

The butcher, Plato Kourkoulis, and Uncle Tolly went way back. Back to when they first opened their businesses within a few months of each other. Often was the time when you'd find one of them in the other's shop shooting the crap, as they say.

Frankly, I'm convinced Greek men are bigger gossips than the women, despite the prevailing belief that the opposite was true. The difference lay in that the women are much more open about their nefarious activities while the men are in a state of constant denial.

A large copper cowbell rang above the door as I entered the butcher shop. Plato always kept his place clean and neat, the cuts of meat fresh and arranged in a well-refrigerated display case against the left wall. His wife had died about a decade or so ago so he was on his own now, no mention of the possibility of his remarrying because, well, Greeks didn't remarry. In fact, if Plato were to be seen with another woman, it would probably send the other Greeks into major, frenetic crossing mode.

I wasn't sure why that was. Maybe they believe God only gave them one shot at the marriage deal. So when that one shot was over with, they didn't bother to look for another shot.

Or maybe there just weren't that many options available to them unless they went outside the Greek community. And to marry outside the Greek community brought down a penalty worse than death. Just ask my uncle Spyros. He'd done it two times.

I wondered where that left me in the marriage deal. I'd had my one shot and look what happened. And since there weren't exactly any Greek men knocking down my door, I wondered if I'd end up like Plato.

Or worse, like my uncle Spyros.

"Sofie!"

That's what I liked about the male Greeks. No matter what they were doing, or how hard a day they were having, more of-ten than not they would throw open their arms and greet you like a long lost relative back for an unexpected visit.

"*Yiasou, Kirie Platona*," I greeted back, taking his large, cal-loused hands. "How are you doing today?"

"Good, good. Business is good. Day is nice."

The day was hot, but I wasn't going to contradict him.

An uncharacteristic frown pulled down the side of his face. "But I can enjoy none of it, what with my best friend and neighbor missing and all."

I nodded, having known Uncle Tolly's whereabouts would be of huge concern to this big bear of a man. "That's what I was hoping to talk to you about. You wouldn't happen to have any ideas where Uncle Tolly might be, would you?"

He scooted back behind the display counter and tugged out a tray of thickly cut pork chops. "I wish I could tell you, Sofie. I wish I could tell you." He put on disposable plastic gloves and sorted through the meat. "I haven't been feeling very well since he disappeared. 'Aglaia,' I told his wife, 'I think he's gone off and taken up with another woman.'" He chuckled without hu-mor at this. "But both of us know he would never do that."

Sounded like my earlier defense of my father to my mother. "Are you sure?" I asked.

"What, and leave his pride and joy behind?" He gestured to-ward the front window where the back of the Mercedes was plainly visible.

I squinted at the car. I hadn't noticed before that it bore a van-ity plate. It read: *Adi yia*. Which roughly meant "Go in health."

"When did he buy the car?" I asked.

"Just last month. I don't think he's even made the first payment on it yet."

I made a mental note of that.

Could Uncle Tolly be having financial trouble?

Plato was shaking his head. "No, no. I'm afraid I'm going to have to agree with Aglaia on this one. It's a case of foul play."

"How so?"

"He started getting these . . . visits from one of those DiPiazza boys about five months or so ago."

Not good.

"Do you know what the connection was?"

He wrapped two chops in plain white paper then taped the package closed. "No, no. And Tolly wouldn't tell me either. He'd wave his hand at me and tell me to forget about it."

Which guaranteed that Plato wouldn't.

"Here," he said, handing me the package of chops. "These are for you."

When I was younger, sometimes Plato would give me packages to take home to my grandmother. Gifts, he would say. Back then Yiayia had done a lot of the shopping, you know, when she wasn't two sheets to the wind and more mobile than she is now.

"Please. It's a gift from me. Just think of your Uncle Plato when you enjoy them."

I smiled at him. "Thanks. I will."

I started for the door, opening it in time to let the Widow Vardis in.

"Sofie! How nice to see you," she said, somehow managing to look cool in all black.

"*Yiasou*, Mrs. Vardis. Are you doing well?"

"Fine, fine."

She leaned her metal cart against the wall, obviously out for an afternoon of shopping.

"Glad to hear it."

I rounded her and opened the door.

"You'll let me know if you find out anything?" Plato called out.

"You'll be the second to know." Or the third or forth, considering I had my mother waiting in the wings.

I STOOD NEXT TO UNCLE Tolly's new Mercedes and tried to get a peek inside. I wasn't taking any chances that the alarm would go off, so I cupped my hand over my eyes and made sure I didn't come near to touching the shiny surface of the car or the window. Aside from a black set of *koboloi*—Greek worry beads—hanging from the rearview mirror, there was nothing to indicate anyone had been in it at all, much less driven it recently.

I'm not sure what alerted me to the fact that I was no longer alone, but I looked up to find Pimply Pino climbing the curb, yanking his pants up as he tried to look official in his NYPD blues. It wasn't working.

"I hear you're working the Apostolis Pappas case," he said, considering me, then the car.

Pino and I went way back. All the way back to his pimply childhood when he had gotten his head caught in the cemetery fence during a prank; it had taken a firefighter's lock cutter to free him. I knew him even before that, when he was just plain irritating and the most picked on kid in class at St. D's. His mother was Italian, his father was Greek, so he'd always been the half-breed, the outsider whose mother didn't go to the church but whose father made sure he did.

I'd felt sorry for him once for about five seconds. About the time it took me to figure out it was more fun to tease him than pity him.

Oh, and he was no less irritating now than he'd been back then. But life was not without a sense of irony: as a New York City police officer, he was now the one picking on me. Constantly.

"Yeah," I said in answer to his question about working Uncle Tolly's case. "Any news at the precinct?"

"Not anything I can share."

That more than likely meant nothing. Especially since a detective was probably working the case and Pino wouldn't have access to any information to share.

I turned to look into the backseat of the Mercedes.

Pino sniffed and hiked up his pants again in a way that made even me wince. "I wouldn't be doing that if I were you."

"Oh? Why not?"

"Because it's private property. And likely evidence in the case."

I shrugged. "All the more reason for me to look."

"I received a complaint about you snooping around here."

I snapped upright. "What?"

It was obvious he was trying hard to suppress a grin. "That's right."

I looked around, searching for moving curtains or silhouettes in windows. All I saw was Plato the butcher still talking to the Widow Vardis, and Aglaia completing a customer order. I didn't think either one of them would call me in.

I crossed my arms over my chest, not sure if I bought into what Pino was saying. Then again, I hadn't known him to lie. Except in the third grade when he'd claimed he hadn't touched my desk and I'd found a garter snake inside it. Even then he'd been bad at lying and I'd been expecting something. What *he* hadn't expected was for me to put the snake down the front of his pants, and he ran, screaming, from the room.

"Who called in the complaint?" I asked.

"Can't tell you that. It's confidential."

"Don't I have the right to learn the name of my accuser?"

"You haven't been arrested."

What was left hanging was an aggravating "yet."

But then again, what would he arrest me for? Working a case I clearly had a right to be working?

I looked back at the Mercedes. Unless, of course, the car did turn out to be a crucial piece of evidence in Uncle Tolly's disappearance.

I thought of the Stephen King book *Christine* and shuddered.

I shrugged again. "Fine. I'll leave then."

Pino followed me for a couple of steps and I turned, catching him up short.

"You know, Pino, you really should look into taking some time off. Hassling me full-time has got to make a hell of a dent in your love life."

What both of us knew was that Pino, pimply or otherwise, didn't have a love life.

Then again, neither did I.

And that upset me more than Pino's pestering me.

"You be sure to keep us informed if you come across anything important inre to the case."

"Inre." Now there was a word. And one I was certain Pino used every chance he got.

I gave him a thumbs-up although it was another hand gesture altogether that I wanted to give him as I walked up the street, well away from him.

Five

OKAY, SO NOW I HAD two people linking Uncle Tolly to the mob: his wife Aglaia and Plato the butcher. I walked up Steinway and stopped in the agency, which was sandwiched between a fish store and a Thai restaurant, to ask Rosie if anything had popped up. Since nothing had, and any footwork on my other cases needed to be done at night, I continued on to Broadway and my father's restaurant. I figured now was as good a time as any to find out why my mother thought he was being unfaithful to her.

Of course, going to my father's dictated that I would also be across the street from my grandfather's café. And no matter how hot the day, it was pretty much guaranteed that Grandpa Kosmos would be sitting outside playing *tavli*—backgammon—with one of his friends.

And there he was.

Both my father's and grandfather's places were on corners and had awnings and tables and chairs set up on the wide sidewalks of the side streets. At night, both were packed with people looking to get out a bit and, since New York's citywide smoking ban went into effect, those wanting a place to smoke. During the day, the outside areas were pretty much deserted. At least during this blasted heat wave.

Except for my grandpa Kosmos. According to him, the heat here in the U.S. was nothing compared to the heat back home. Truthfully, I couldn't imagine anything being worse than this.

"Sofie!" he called from across the street.

Experience told me that if I did anything more than wave, I would end up in an apron, waiting tables for the rest of the afternoon. And not only would that not get me what I was looking for—namely evidence that my father was not being unfaithful to my mother—it would get me into trouble with my father.

I'm a little unclear on all the details of the longtime dispute between the two most important men in my life, but from what I understand my grandfather is still upset that my father stole his best waitress—my mother—then turned the Greek café he'd given them as a wedding gift into an American restaurant. (Actually, half the items on the menu were Greek, even if the place was called the Metropolitan Restaurant and was known for its steaks.) So to get back at my father, Kosmos opened the Cosmopolitan Café directly across the street.

I really didn't get the whole feud thing. The only thing I knew is that I'd spent a great deal of my life—along with the rest of my family—trying to keep from getting involved in it.

"Sofie, *ela etho, koritsi mou,*" said my grandfather, calling me to come over.

"I can't right now. Business. Maybe I'll stop in later," I called, then with a wave ducked inside my father's restaurant.

I made a note to myself to sneak out the back and circle around the block so I wouldn't have to see my grandfather. Had I been thinking, I would have done that on the way in. But the heat had swollen my brain, and I wasn't capable of more thought than putting one foot in front of the other.

Don't get me wrong. Out of all the members of my family, my grandfather and I got along best. He and I were kindred spirits, I liked to think. But ever since he'd asked me to find a stolen war medal for him—a medal I couldn't talk to anyone about and no one in my family ever discussed—I'd been avoiding him somewhat. It wasn't that I didn't want to find the medal. It was just that paying gigs kept getting in the way of the free favor. And my mother's favor currently took precedence over Grandpa Kosmos'.

My father's restaurant was nice. Big, roomy burgundy leather booths and chairs. Huge tables draped with white linen tablecloths with fresh flowers set in the middle. Gleaming wood paneling and a long mahogany bar that also boasted leather-covered stools. It was between the lunch and dinner hour, so the only customer in the place was Costas Gounaris, who really wasn't a customer but a friend who sometimes liked to escape his office for the relaxed environment of the restaurant. He always sat in the far corner booth and even now typed on his laptop computer without looking up to see who had entered.

"Hey, Sof," the tender called as he dried glasses behind the bar. "How they hangin'?"

Nick Boutsas was younger than me and a little cockier than his average looks should let him get away with. But he was a good worker. Always on time. Always willing to go the extra mile. Which earned major points with my father.

"They're, um, hanging," I said, suppressing the urge to glance down at my chest because, hey, I'm not a masochist. "My father around anywhere?"

"Yeah, he's in back checking some orders. Why don't I get you a drink and I'll let him know you're here. The usual?"

I nodded and took one of the stools near the door.

Moments later, I had a tall frappé in front of me that I sipped as if I'd just survived a ten-mile hike through the Mojave rather than a ten-block walk.

Nick disappeared through the door leading to the kitchen and I sat back. My sister Efi usually worked dinner, her argument being the tips were better at that hour. My sister was far savvier than I ever was. I'd never worked the dinner crowd when I was her age, preferring to have nights to myself so I could go clubbing and generally get into all sorts of trouble.

I heard a distinctly female laugh come from the back. Nick flirting with one of the waitresses? Probably. The guy lived to flirt. And to ask questions about hanging body parts.

I swirled the froth in my frappé with my straw and did a double take as I spotted my father's grinning face through the round window in the swinging kitchen door. Another laugh and my father changed positions with a pretty waitress I wasn't familiar with.

The door opened and my father came out.

"Sofie!" he called.

I was busy trying to get a gander at the waitress he'd been obviously flirting with.

My father . . . flirting. The possibility remained so far-fetched that I resisted the urge to pinch myself to make sure I wasn't in the middle of a bad dream brought on by my mother's ridiculous suspicions.

I'd grown up with my father always a big part of my life.

Worked in his restaurants for too many years to count. I knew how he operated. Never was there a time I caught him flirting with the help. In fact, I've rarely ever seen him crack a smile at work. He was always too busy seeing to details, making sure enough steaks were marinating in his special sauce, that employees were on time, and that the tablecloths were clean. While he didn't bark at his workers like my grandfather was often known to do, he wasn't overly friendly with them either.

Which made what I'd just witnessed stand out like a bruise on otherwise perfect skin.

"To what do I owe this pleasure," my father said, taking my hands in his across the bar.

I leaned over to kiss him on both cheeks and then sat back staring at him, words somehow not coming to me right then.

Was my mother right? Was my father taking some liberties with his staff?

I caught my own double entendre and suddenly felt sick.

"New waitress?" I choked out.

"Who?" He looked around the deserted restaurant then back at the door. There was that grin again. "Oh, you must mean Magda. Yes, she's new."

Magda.

"I hired her last month. Quite a girl."

Not a good worker. Or punctual. Or an asset to the restaurant, which were all ways my father usually described his personnel.

Quite . . . a . . . girl . . .

I looked at my watch, not sure I could deal with this right now. "Look at the time. I completely forgot I have an appointment in ten minutes." I took a deep gulp of my iced coffee—not a good idea because I got iced coffee headache—then leaned across the bar again and gave my father a quick kiss. "Thanks for the frappé."

Then I dashed for the door in a way I was sure was anything but discreet, much less elegant.

MUCH LATER THAT NIGHT, I paced the length of my apartment, back and forth, forth and back. I'd made the rounds on my five currently open cases—six counting Uncle Tolly, seven my mother's personal favor, but I wasn't counting that—only to find that the three spouses under suspicion of extracurricular activities were tucked in for the night with their rightful partners, the worker's compensation recipient suspected of fraud was slumped in his front porch chair with a cooler full of beer cans, and the Con Ed employee was working late.

Muffy's nails clicked against the polished patches of wood floor between area rugs as he mimicked my movements, probably thinking this was some sort of exercise program. I absently reasoned that I probably should take him out for a walk every now and again. While he got pretty good exercise running up and down the fire escape to the roof, I didn't think that was enough.

But Muffy and his lack of exercise weren't currently what I was worried about. Instead, I kept running the memory clip of my father and Magda through my mind, with the echo of my mother's words playing like background music.

Pericles Metropolis had always been Papa or Dad to me. I had never really stopped to take a good look at him as a man. And given that closer look I was now taking, I saw a tall, good-looking man who was aging well. His hair wasn't so much gray as it was silver. And it wasn't silver all over but rather at the temples, enhancing the blackness shot through with silver of the rest of his hair. Time had etched lines around his mouth and dark eyes, but rather than detracting from his looks, they seem to add to them; when he smiled at you it was really something.

My mother hadn't weathered the years quite as well. Her graying hair was simply gray. And she wore it in the same style she'd had for decades, long and pulled back from her face in a bun. If she'd once had a nice figure, now it was blurred by a few extra pounds and made worse by the shapeless dresses she wore.

And I couldn't remember the last time I'd really seen her smile.

Muffy barked at me and I realized I'd stopped pacing. I stared at the mutt and the way he panted at my feet. I suppose I should be thankful he wasn't biting me, but a sinister part of me wanted to lock him in his room.

Essentially, Muffy's room was the second bedroom. For the first few nights of our relationship, I'd locked him in the bathroom to make sure he wasn't offered any prime ops to sink his sharp little teeth into my flesh . . . again. But I'd quickly figured out that locking him *in* the bathroom meant locking myself *out*. And since I didn't think it a good idea to go to Mrs. Nebitz's every time I had my own business to see to . . . well, Muffy and I had settled on the second bedroom as his personal domain. It held my old area rug—formerly flea-infested, it had begun to unravel and its dyes ran with the addition of a few drops of water—a couple of chew toys, and a large dog bed I'd picked up on special from the pet shop down the street. I was thinking about putting my ex-groom's leather Barcalounger in there, too, since Muffy was the only one who used it, but hadn't decided on that yet.

"Books . . ."

Muffy cocked his head and made an inquisitive sound. I wasn't all that sure where the thought had come from myself. Divine intervention? Or was it connected to decorating ideas, because I'd thought about turning Muffy's room into a library before he'd become my hairy roommate? Or was I so desperate to think about something other than the possibility that my father was helping himself to the help that my mind was simultaneously reviewing the Uncle Tolly case?

Whatever it was, I thought I was onto something.

I glanced at the television where a rerun of *Seinfeld* was on (the one where Kramer decides to get into the rickshaw business), then at my watch. After eleven. Surely too late to pay Mrs. Pappas a visit.

Then again, what else did she have to do?

I grabbed my purse and headed for the door, Muffy following on my heels.

"No," I said, poking my finger in his general direction yet far enough away so he couldn't decide to relieve me of the needed digit. "You stay here and watch television."

He barked and stood his ground. I crossed my arms and stood mine.

Finally, he made a sound of exasperation somewhere between a growl and a sneeze and stalked over to the Barcalounger. He climbed up on top, did his round and round bit, then lay down, his head on his paws, glaring at me.

"Be good," I told him.

I opened the door, dashed out, then quickly closed it. But as I was locking it, I became aware of a familiar panting sound at my feet.

How had he gotten out without my seeing him?

I sighed.

"Fine. But you're staying in the car."

I PARKED BEHIND UNCLE TOLLY'S Mercedes and cut the engine, much as I had done a good eighteen hours earlier. The dry cleaners was dark, as was the apartment above it. Well, what had I expected? While Mrs. Pappas might be worried in her own way, it wasn't in a way with which I was familiar.

I got out of the car and quickly shut Muffy inside. He scratched at the mostly closed window—I left all the windows open a crack for circulation—and barked. I smiled and waggled my fingers at him.

"Gotcha."

Feeling pleased with myself, I turned toward the cleaners. On Monday, the street was eerily quiet at this time of night. I knew on Broadway a few blocks up, and farther down the street nearer thirty-first, there would be traffic and people out, but here not a soul braved the streets and nary a light shone from apartment windows. New York was strange that way. So many people, yet the city could be so quiet.

I shivered despite the heat and stepped toward the window of the dry cleaners, cupping my hand to block out the street-light as I looked inside.

Movement.

I jumped back slightly, unprepared to see anyone inside.

Was Mrs. Pappas putting in overtime?

I looked through the glass again. If she was, why did she have all the lights off?

I knocked on the door. "Mrs. Pappas? Are you in there? It's Sofie. Sofie Metropolis."

Nothing.

I tried the handle.

It turned and the door opened.

I wasn't sure if that was a good thing or a bad thing.

"Mrs. Pappas?" I called out again. Or at least I think I did. I'm pretty sure the words came out as a whisper.

It didn't take long to figure out she wasn't in there. I wrinkled my nose at the scent of cleaning solution and . . . was that cigarette smoke?

Had Aglaia taken up smoking?

I pushed aside the plastic-covered clothes hung on the outside pole, ready for customers to pick up in the morning, business apparently going on as usual. A small voice told me I really shouldn't be doing this. That maybe I should go out to the car and use the cell phone I'd left in there to call 911 and report the movement I saw. Or maybe ring the upstairs apartment to wake Mrs. Pappas. At the very least, let Muffy out so I wouldn't be alone.

Instead, like the stupid person Rosie accused me of being that morning, I pushed forward.

My right foot settled on something slippery. I immediately pulled my foot back. What was that? Something wet? Something slimy? Say something like blood?

I leaned down and with a shaking hand I reached out.

A dry cleaners bag.

Right. Blood.

I picked up the wrapped blouse that must have fallen from the bar and hung it up again. Probably that's the movement I'd seen. Probably Mrs. Pappas hadn't hung it well and it had fallen, causing me to think someone was inside.

I stepped into the back toward the office I knew was off to the left.

And the unlocked door? That irritating voice in my head asked?

My heartbeat accelerated.

Probably Mrs. Pappas was a little preoccupied and had forgotten to lock it.

Righ—

A plastic-covered suit grabbed me from behind.

I screamed and battled against the slick plastic being held by a very real someone on the other side of it. An arm snaked around my neck and snapped my head back while another arm tightened like an iron vise around my waist.

Rosie was right: I was stupid.

Six

"ARE YOU SURE YOU DIDN'T pick the lock yourself? Isn't that on page two of the PI's handbook? Knowing how to pick locks?"

I stared at Pino, resisting the urge to give him an eye roll. "I haven't turned page one yet."

A half an hour had passed since the attack of the molesting suit. Surprisingly, the Suit had released me almost as quickly as it had grabbed me. Probably because of the pitiful sounds I'd made. One of my worst fears as a kid had been suffocating in a plastic bag. If that fear had anything to do with my brother Kosmos putting a Ziploc bag over my head and trying to seal it, I wasn't copping to it. Mostly because I'd done worse to my younger brother.

Unsurprisingly, Pimply Pino was the first officer on the scene after I scrambled to my car for my cell and called 911. Didn't the guy have a life? I swear it seemed he was on duty 24/7.

I guess for him being a NYC police officer wasn't just a job; it was an adventure.

I looked at Mrs. Pappas, who was examining the suit in question as if to make sure she could still give it to the customer.

"Step away from the suit, ma'am," Pino said.

Was it my imagination or had his hand budged closer to his firearm?

His attitude looked like something out of a bad B movie, and I was having trouble digesting it, along with the moment of terror I'd just lived through.

Mrs. Pappas looked at Pino like neither him nor the gun concerned her. "What, what? The owner is one of my customers best. He wants suit tomorrow. He's going to get suit."

"I'm afraid that's not going to happen, ma'am," Pino said. "That suit is evidence."

My shoulders dropped a couple inches from where I sat on a chair against the wall. "Oh, for the love of God, collect the plastic and be done with it already. The suit didn't attack me; the guy behind the suit did. And if there are any prints, they'll be on the plastic."

It appeared the idea hadn't occurred to Pino as he stepped between Aglaia and the suit. He put on latex gloves he'd pulled from a bag in his back pocket and went about putting the protective plastic into a large Ziploc bag.

I shuddered.

Truth was, the incident had shaken me more than I cared to admit. Although I was a PI and registered to carry concealed, I'd been physically threatened only twice. And Bud Suleski had earned a bullet in the knee for his efforts.

"Why did you break into the cleaners?" Pino asked, his job

collecting the plastic done, his job trying to get me to 'fess up to something I didn't do continuing.

"I told you, the door was unlocked."

"Impossible," Aglaia said, helping me not at all. "I lock door before I go upstairs."

"The door was unlocked," I reiterated. "Correct me if I'm wrong, but doesn't it stand to reason that the man who attacked me would have been the one to unlock it?"

My two companions had an *ah* moment that made me want to hang my head and cry.

Maybe it was the late hour.

"I was at home going over my notes on the case," liar, "when it occurred to me that the accounting books could maybe help me, so I drove here, saw movement, thought it was Mrs. Pappas inside, and found the door unlocked."

"And that's when you were attacked."

I nodded and bit my lip to keep from saying something sarcastic. Sarcasm would get me nowhere.

"You want see Tolly's books?" Aglaia asked.

I nodded.

She went into the back room and returned a minute later, depositing three large leather-bound ledgers into my lap.

Apparently, Uncle Tolly hadn't heard of the invention of the computer.

"Good?" Aglaia asked.

"Great," I said, wondering exactly what I had let myself in for.

"Can I sell car now?"

THE FOLLOWING MORNING, I WAS well into my second frappé as I went over the mammoth ledgers at the agency.

Rosie sat on at her desk the other side of the open-air part of the office pretending she didn't know what I was doing; she seemed to think her merely being in the same room with me while I was going over the books was some sort of prosecutable offense with the mob. Kind of like the Medusa syndrome. Look at Medusa, turn to stone. Look at the books, get popped by the mob.

It was only ten A.M. and my mother had called twice already. I'd told her I was busy with a client and that I would call back, but I didn't want to call her. Truth was, I still wasn't sure what to make of what I'd seen between my father and Magda yesterday. And if there was one thing Thalia was very good at, it was pulling things from me I wasn't ready to give. She seemed to home in on any kind of information she was looking for and extract it with the precision of a surgeon. Only I didn't want to give her this information because this information was damning and could have a major impact on life as I knew it.

So I decided that I would have to confront my father head on.

Exactly what that meant, I wasn't sure, but I had to know before I could figure out what action to take next.

I wondered if threatening to shoot him in the knee would fix the situation.

What was the penalty for shooting your father?

I realized that I'd already pretty much made up my mind on the issue of my father's fidelity: namely that he was guilty. And that bothered me more than I wanted to explore just now.

I heard Rosie make a tsking sound. "If you knew what was good for you, you'd stick with finding people's pets."

This and she didn't even know about last night and the incident with the Suit. Namely because I hadn't told her.

I moved the ledger I wasn't reading and opened another one on top of it. "Everybody's a critic."

Truthfully, what she'd said stung. I'd only handled two missing pet cases—one of them now *my* pet—and a few dozen other cases. Surely by now I should've shaken the pet detective stigma. Apparently not.

She popped her gum for several moments, then said, "I know about what went down at Uncle Tolly's last night."

I finally looked at her.

"What? You don't think I have my ways?"

"Nothing happened."

She gaped at me. "Nothing happened? Nothing happened?" She crossed her arms under her breasts. "Oh, my God! One minute you're just walking down the street, the next you're laying face down in a pile of wet cement that has your name written all over it."

"The guy could have broken in looking for money."

"At a dry cleaners?"

"Sure, why not? There's cash on hand."

"Everybody knows that old woman sleeps with all her cash in her mattress."

I had noticed a difference in the entries in the two books I had open. More specifically that they listed different amounts on the same dates. They were also entered in different colored pencils.

It had taken me a little while to familiarize myself with Tolly's method of bookkeeping, and to dust off my own rusty skills when it came to financial matters. I'd taken a course at Queensborough Community College after high school and talked my grandfather into letting me do his books, hoping it would get me away from waiting tables. It had. For a while. Until I completely computerized Grandpa Kosmos' system, nearly sending him into cardiac arrest (he was convinced that anything on a computer was at risk of being looted, even though the ancient processor wasn't hooked up to the Internet). But that had been some time ago and Tolly used a different accounting system.

I said to Rosie, "Okay, so going by your logic, my attacker was waiting in the dry cleaners, you know, on the off chance that I might stop by at eleven-thirty at night so he could attack me with a suit then let me go."

She stopped chewing her gum. "You just don't get it, do you? The guy was probably after the same thing you were."

We both stared at the books.

"And you know what that means, don't you?"

I swallowed hard. Yes, I did know what that meant. It meant that the guy last night hadn't been some random burglar but had, indeed, been a member of the mafia looking to collect any damning evidence from the premises. And if the guy had been from the mob, then last night could have turned out very differently for me.

"Look at this," I said, following one line in one book to the same numbered line in the other. "Uncle Tolly was keeping two sets of books."

Rosie leaned over me to look at the entry, then caught herself and snapped upright, nearly putting one of my eyes out with a breast. "Uh-uh. I ain't looking. In fact, I'm going to ask that you get those things out of here. I don't want them anywhere near my person."

"They aren't anywhere near your person. They're across the room from your desk."

"They're in the same building. And you know what *they* do to buildings."

They set fire to them, I thought.

I gave a heavy sigh. "I think we're both watching way too much television."

"Uh-uh. It happens all the time. All you got to do is turn on the news. It's just nobody talks about it because nobody wants to get torched."

The bell above the door clanged and Rosie jumped. I was pretty sure I did, too.

"Jesus, Joseph, and Mary," Rosie muttered under her breath. "Give a body a heart attack, why don't you?"

The young woman who had walked in blinked at her as if she'd spoken a foreign language. "Excuse me?"

Figuring Rosie didn't need the extra stress of feigning civility just then, I asked, "Can I help you?"

She was probably about my age, I guessed, with short brown hair, and she wore the latest in urban chic. "Yes, I'd like to see Mr. Metropolis, please."

"He's not available," I said, getting up and extending my hand. "I'm Ms. Metropolis. What can I do for you?"

"Actually, it's not for me. It's for my aunt."

That helped a lot.

I only prayed it wasn't another cheating spouse case. I had my quota of those.

"What's the matter regarding?"

"My crippled cousin's ferret."

Crippled . . . cousin's . . . ferret.

It was more than her choice of words that was cause for pause, it was the meaning behind them.

In my book, a ferret was little more than a glorified rat.

I squinted at her. "Isn't it illegal to keep ferrets as pets?"

She raised her penciled-in brows. "Is it?"

"Yes, I think it is."

"Then how did my aunt buy it for my cousin?"

Good question. Out of state, maybe? Or maybe they had an underground pet supplier in the city, you know, just to spite the law.

"Anyway," she said, "my cousin's been in a wheelchair for the past year—she's got that disease that *Back to the Future* guy's got. At least I think that's what it is."

"Michael J. Fox?"

"Yeah, that's him. Anyway, the day before yesterday, she couldn't find him—the ferret—anywhere, you know? My aunt's afraid he got caught behind the refrigerator or something and his dead corpse is going to stink up the place."

"So tell her to move the refrigerator."

She stared at me. "She did move the refrigerator. And everything else she could. She's pretty sure Fred's not in the house."

Fred the Ferret.

I swallowed a sigh. Maybe Rosie was right. Maybe I should have gotten Uncle Tolly's books out of the office. More accurately, maybe I should have gotten myself out of there before I could agree to look for this woman's poor crippled cousin's ferret Fred.

"Oh, come on, Sof," Rosie said. "It's a sign. Not two minutes ago I was telling you to forget about those books and look for people's pets, then just like that this lady—"

"Jennifer Lopez."

Rosie stared harder at her, apparently deciding that the girl wasn't the J.Lo the name instantly brought to mind, then continued, "Miss Lopez here walks through the door." She crossed herself. "Divine intervention, that's what this is."

A load of crap, that's what this was.

And I didn't want to add a ferret to my list of roommates;

I had enough on my hands with Muffy. And if the ferret case turned out anything like the Missing Muffy case, I'd end up sharing my pillow with Fred.

"Forget about it." I stepped toward my desk to retrieve the ledgers and leave.

Rosie tsked loudly. "Oh my God, I never knew you were so . . ."

She looked so disappointed that I did what I shouldn't have. I stopped and waited for her to finish. "What?"

"Cruel."

Somehow she made the word sound like it had three syllables and was the worst word in the English language.

Go . . . to . . . the . . . door, I ordered my feet.

"Look," Lopez said. "I've been to three agencies so far and they practically laughed me out the door." She reached into her purse and came out with a wallet. "I'll pay whatever it takes. Just find Fred."

Probably I'd have ended up taking the case anyway, I told myself. I watched her count out twenties until she reached a hundred. The money had nothing to do with it.

Who was I kidding? At this point in my investigative career, every dollar I racked up made me feel more deserving of my title.

I looked at Rosie even as I picked up the books from my desk. "Write down her name and address for me. I'll see if I can't squeeze in a few minutes today or tomorrow to take a look."

Rosie's dimples popped at me. "You know what you are? You're a saint. That's what you are."

My chest puffed out; "saint" was much better than "cruel" any day.

I SAT AT MY KITCHEN table back at my place, Uncle Tolly's accounting ledgers spread out in front of me. There was no doubt about it. The dry cleaner had been keeping two sets of books. One that showed a large income, another that showed a more modest and likely more accurate income.

Which meant that probably he had been laundering more than clothes.

Oh, boy.

I leaned back from the books much as Rosie had done earlier.

Okay, so I had no real personal experience with the Cosa Nostra, you know, aside from that which I'd seen on the news or in the newspapers or movies. *The Sopranos* was one of my favorite shows, but since the family lived in Jersey . . . well, they weren't real to me beyond the fact that they were fictional. Oh, sure, I knew lots of people who outwardly looked like they were from the cast of *The Sopranos*. The guy up the street was a dead ringer for Tony Soprano, or rather the actor James Gandolfini. And there were even a few guys that looked like Marlon Brando's Don Corleone (hey, Italians were everywhere in New York, and the Greeks were kissing cousins), but suspected involvement in any "family" was generally joke material rather than the source of any real fear for me.

You better watch out. You don't want to mess with Jenny Pastrami or else her older brother will breaka your kneecaps. Ha ha!

You know, that sort of stuff.

But while I'd never been a victim of a violent crime—Bud Suleski aside—I knew those who had. And was well aware of the possibilities.

There was a knock at my door.

I stared at the locked barrier like the boogeyman might plow through it at any moment. Why? Well, because as far as anyone knew, I was at work. And since no one had buzzed from downstairs for access to the hall, that meant whoever was on the other side of that door had probably been following me.

Truth be told, I wasn't looking forward to another struggle with the Suit anytime soon.

And I didn't have anything in the apartment with which to protect myself. My Glock was locked in the glove box of my car. And given my experience with knives two months ago, well, I wasn't about to reach into any of my kitchen drawers either.

I looked around. Where was Muffy when you needed him? Souvlaki? He was at your feet. Boogeyman at the door? Nowhere in sight.

Probably he was on the roof trying to see to a bit of business of his own.

Great.

So I grabbed a crystal vase from a nearby table—a wedding gift from a cousin in California—and stalked toward the door. I looked through the peephole. No one.

Another knock.

I nearly jumped out of my K-Swiss.

Okay. I had one of two choices: I could ignore the unwanted visitor and pretend I wasn't there, or I could open the door and confront them.

I chose the former option.

Another knock and the doorknob moved.

Not good.

"Sofie? Sofie, are you in there?"

Every muscle in my body relaxed at the sound of my across-the-hall neighbor, Mrs. Nebitz.

I put the vase down on the hall table and undid the chains and locks on the door.

"Hi, Mrs. Nebitz."

The reason why I hadn't seen her through the peephole was because Mrs. Nebitz was probably all of four feet eight inches tall and looked like the type of grandmother every kid conjures up when they imagine grandmothers. (You know, ones that didn't dress in all black, eye the family dog to measure it for pot size, and hide a bottle of rye in their robe pocket.)

"I'm sorry if I startled you," she said. "It's just I saw you come home and wondered if you wanted some *rugelach*."

I eyed with longing the plate of great smelling and probably warm cookies she held out. Mrs. Nebitz made some of the best stuff I'd ever tasted, and some of the worst. This offering was most definitely one of her best.

"Thank you."

I took the plate. Several sister plates of which were still in my dishwasher and probably should be returned before Mrs. Nebitz ran out of dishes and stopped bringing me stuff.

"I also wanted to ask if you knew who was in the car out front."

"Car?" I barely managed to squeeze the word out of my throat.

Could it be Jake Porter? Then again Mrs. Nebitz knew Jake—she called him "that nice Mr. Porter"—and aside from being disappointed that he wasn't Jewish, appeared to like him.

"Yes," she said. "I noticed the car pull up right after you and, well, it's been there ever since."

Despite the hair standing on end up and down my arms, I smiled. "I'm sure it's no one, Mrs. Nebitz, but I'll check it out."

As soon as I closed the door, I put the *rugelach* on the hall table next to the vase and moved slowly to the window. Standing out of eyeshot, I looked to the east side of the street. I didn't see anything out of the ordinary. Being careful not to be spotted, I moved to the other side of the window and considered the west side of the street. There! A dark sedan was sitting parked under a tree, the two occupants' attention apparently on my third-floor apartment.

Oh, boy. Just what kind of trouble had I let myself in for this time? I mean I wanted to find Uncle Tolly, but not if it meant taking a swim with the fishes in order to do so.

I grabbed my purse and my car keys and left, suddenly feeling unsafe in my own apartment.

Seven

MY VISIT TO JENNIFER LOPEZ'S cousin's house in Woodhaven had started out as a way to see whether the suspicious car parked outside my apartment would follow me. When it didn't, I decided I might as well get the details on the ferret out of the way. If luck was on my side, Fred would have shown up under a pillow or something between the time Lopez asked me to look for the rat and now.

I knocked on the door to the simple, contemporary two-story brick house. Some of the properties in this area had enough room to stretch your arms out on either side before touching the neighboring houses. This was one of those. Which meant lots of places for the little bugger to hide. Great.

Maybe it wasn't too late to get out of doing this.

The girl in the wheelchair who opened the door told me the ferret had yet to turn up. She looked like she'd been crying and that someone had taken away . . . well, her ferret.

The fact that she was in a wheelchair pretty much told me

86 TORI CARRINGTON

she didn't have the Michael J. Fox disease (Parkinson's) as Lopez had said, but something else. A friend's sister had MS. I wondered if that's what this girl had.

"Michaela! Haven't I asked you a million times not to answer the door without asking who it is first?" A woman who looked an awful like my new client but twenty years older stopped behind the girl. "Who are you?"

"Sofie. Sofie Metropolis? Jennifer might have told you I was coming by?"

The woman poked her head out, looked up and down the street, then yanked me inside and closed the door.

"I can't believe she sent you over here. We don't want any trouble."

"I'm sorry, but your name is?"

"Mud, if you have anything to do with it."

Hookay.

"I take it this has something to do with it being illegal to keep ferrets in the city?"

"No, it has to do with you wearing jeans illegally. Of course, it has something to do with that."

"This is a private matter. There's no reason for the authorities to be involved."

"Famous last words. I wouldn't have bought the damn thing if I'd known it was illegal."

What did she think? That she could be arrested for keeping a ferret? From what I understood, the law was pretty lax. If they received a complaint, they confiscated the ferret but they didn't charge the owner.

Of course, if the reason behind the law was true—that the wanna-be rats attacked babies in the park—maybe it should be enforced more diligently.

"Mom, stop, please," the girl said, tugging on the woman's shirttail. "Sofie's going to find Fred for me."

Whoa. Now I understood why Jennifer had refused to leave the agency until I agreed to take the case. There were probably few people who could resist the heartbreaking sound of the girl's voice, wheelchair aside.

She was eight, maybe, ten at best. It was hard to tell because of her condition. And if it weren't for the wheelchair you most likely couldn't tell she was sick. She looked like a honey-skinned little angel with huge dark eyes and curly brown hair.

The other woman looked at me again, probably thinking the same thing I was.

"I'm sorry I was so rude." She wiped her hand on her jeans and held it out. "I'm Delores and this is my daughter Michaela."

"Nice to meet you," I said, shaking her hand, then when the girl offered hers, I shook that as well.

A little while later, I was armed with a blurry photo of the ferret, had a history of his habits (he liked to sun himself on the porch when it wasn't too hot and he was always limited to Michaela's lap), and knew his favorite snack, bananas.

By the time I left, I also felt a growing need to find this little girl's pet for her, unsuspecting babies sunning themselves in their carriages in the park be damned.

I stood on the porch looking around the cozy area, then went down the stairs and poked around in the bushes. I wasn't kidding myself that it would be that easy but I didn't want to rule anything out either. Five minutes later, I had completely rounded the house, looking inside garbage cans, peering around shrubs, and toeing anything Fred could possibly hide behind. I sighed when I found myself back in the front, empty-handed.

Could pet-napping be to blame as had been the case with

Muffy? I had to consider all possibilities. Even if I didn't think a ferret was capable of pissing anyone off by taking the neighbor's newspaper or biting passersby.

Or was it?

I looked up and spotted something that gave me a whole lot more to worry about. The dark sedan that had been parked outside my apartment building? Well, it was now parked across the street here.

Seemed I'd been mistaken: I had been followed.

I DIDN'T FEEL COMFORTABLE GOING back home or to the office so long as my new friends were on my tail. I guess because home was my sanctuary and I didn't want them tainting that. And the office . . . I could already see Rosie hiding under her desk and insisting I leave and take the guys with me.

My parents' house and my father and grandfather's places were also out of the question. Thalia would probably get her broom out and chase the car down the street, and my father and grandfather . . . well, I wasn't sure what they would do, but I suspected whatever it was it would include their clientele. (You haven't lived until you've seen someone chased by a dozen old Greek men shaking their fists and spitting Greek profanities that had far too much to do with a goat's anatomy.)

So I drove around Queens for a while, not trying to lose my tail, but trying to get a better look at the driver and his sidekick, which wasn't easy to do with the tinted glass. There were two of them. And I was reasonably sure they were Italian, though this was mostly because of the nature of Uncle Tolly's case rather than any visual confirmation. Truth was, without asking, I couldn't really tell the difference between a Greek and an Italian.

And I wasn't about to speak to either one of the guys in the car. Better I should look like I didn't know they were following me.

Curiously, I found myself a couple blocks away from Eugene Waters' place. I picked up the papers. I had four days left to deliver them or the point would be moot. It wasn't so much that the agency couldn't spare the delivery amount we'd lose. But start falling through and the client—in this case a big law firm in Long Island City—went looking for other deliverers, of which there were plenty in New York, meaning the loss of a big chunk of income that would surely gain my uncle Spyros' notice.

Ah, yes, Uncle Spyros. He was to blame for my being a PI at all. Or to credit, depending on what kind of mood I was in. I looked at the car still lurking in my rearview mirror and decided to blame him. Right now, I could be serving Greek coffees and getting updated on gossip at my grandfather's café, or making good tips at my father's restaurant, rather than being chased by the mob.

The spot directly outside Waters' apartment building was free but I made a point of parking around the other side lest he remember my car. I tried not to be obvious as I watched the sedan cruise by. It parked in the space I'd left free.

Yeek.

Palming the legal papers, I climbed from the car. Within moments, I was knocking on the same door I had a couple of days earlier, checking my watch to make sure I was following the rules set by the Big Process Server God in the sky.

"Who the hell is it?" the same whiny male voice yelled through the steel barrier.

"Sofie. Sofie Metropolis," I called back.

I don't think I gave him my name on the first go around.

Maybe the no-nonsense approach would get me what being sneaky hadn't.

He opened the door, no chain, no skulking, just stood there staring at me like he half wondered if he knew me.

Then he placed me and slammed the door in my face.

Great.

There it was. The opportunity to slap the papers in his hand, inside his apartment, and I'd been so stunned my ploy had worked I'd merely gaped at him.

I knocked on the door again. "Mr. Waters, this isn't going to get you anywhere. You know and I know that what I'm holding is a petition to sue. If you don't face it now, you'll have to face it later."

He told me to do something that was physically impossible with the papers.

Then again, maybe not.

At any rate, it was something I wasn't interesting in doing with the papers.

"Mr. Waters, I'm going to stand out here all day if I have to."

Oh, but that was lame. What happened when I had to go to the bathroom? I made a face. Of course, the power of suggestion would have to kick in then and I felt the sudden urge to go.

I knocked harder and nearly fell back flat on my butt when the door swung open. But rather than Mr. Waters facing me, a woman about four times his size and girth stood filling the doorway to overflowing. She was wearing the same pink satin robe with feathers at the cuffs Waters had been wearing the other day . . . and was showing me far more flesh than I wanted to see.

"What in the hell do you want!" she not so much said as blasted.

"Hi," I said with a shaky smile, feeling almost as frightened facing her as I did the Suit last night. "I'm Sofie Metropolis."

"I didn't ask what your name was, I asked what the hell you wanted!"

I was pretty sure she'd blown my hair back with that one, with a little spittle included.

I held up the papers. "I'm here to deliver these to Mr. Waters." I swallowed hard as she opened her mouth to blast me again. "Are you Mrs. Waters?"

Mrs. Waters would be just as good as Eugene himself. Just so long as I delivered it to someone who had close contact with him.

"What if I am?" She showered me again.

I'd braced myself that time, holding my breath and squinting my eyes to minimize any damage she might do.

I took her hand with my left then slapped the papers into her palm with my right.

"You've been—"

"Uh-uh. Oh no you didn't!"

Before I could get the words out, she was slapping the papers so forcibly against my chest she knocked the air clean out of me and knocked me back on my butt.

"Now go on! Get your narrow white behind out of my sight before I decide to do more than that!"

The door slammed again.

Great.

And in case I wasn't humiliated enough, a light wind caught the papers on the sidewalk, threatening to blow them away. I moved my foot and trapped them against the cement with a K-Swiss.

A couple of tenants walked around me, the woman giggling. I suppose I should be grateful they didn't just walk over me.

I stared at the door as I lifted one hand, then the other, both of them covered with mud. My visit must have fallen just after watering time, although the dead grass around me said they could have turned on the sprinklers just for my benefit. I slowly got up. Of course, it only stood to reason that my butt and my hands had firmly hit the mud. And there was nowhere for me to wipe it.

Aw, hell.

Figuring my jeans were beyond redemption anyway, I rubbed my hands on the front, then wiped as much of the mud as I could from my posterior.

I walked toward my car. I was angry enough to want to scream. Instead, when I would have turned the corner into the back lot, I did an about face and stalked toward the sedan instead.

I knocked on the darkly tinted window with the back of my muddy fingers.

The window automatically lowered a couple of inches, although I couldn't see but a sliver of dark eyes.

"Whaddya want?"

Italian. Definitely Italian.

"Why in the hell are you following me!" I shouted, taking some lessons from Mrs. Waters.

The window went back up, the equivalent of the door slamming in my face. I stalked back to my car, supposing it was long past time for me to see if Tony DiPiazza was indeed the same Tony DiPiazza I'd gone to school with. And find out if these two goons were connected to him in any way.

Eight

OF COURSE, LUCK—NAMELY MY current lack of any good luck—would dictate that the one person I would run into when I looked like I'd just lost a mud-wrestling contest would be my ex-maid of honor, Kati Dimos.

Two minutes and nobody will see me, had been my thought when I'd stopped off at See Foods to pick up some dog food for Muffy and some heavy-duty soap for myself.

Ten seconds and I'd run headlong into Kati.

Kati was short for Ekaterina. And we'd been friends forever. Well, before she'd decided that five seconds of showing my groom what color underpants she had on was worth more than a box of pictures of us doing all that silly stuff best friends did. There was the one shot where we were both dressed like Smurfs for *Apokries,* which is the Greek answer to Mardi Gras and Halloween rolled up into one. (We'd been seven, and my mother thought the blue and the white symbolized something related to Greece.) At ten, we'd taken the same gymnastics class, and there were countless blurry shots of us on a balance beam or during a floor exercise in which you couldn't tell who was who. At twelve, we'd bought the same white bikinis and posed for my mother in the backyard like we were Madonna instead of the board-flat preteens that we were.

But never, ever, had we competed for the same guys, stolen each other boyfriends, or slept with the other one's groom.

Never, ever until five months ago, that is.

"Sofie!"

It made no nevermind to me that I also appeared to be the last person on Kati's "want to see" list. Probably because she looked like a million bucks to my half a cent.

"What, um, happened to you?" she asked, openly eyeing my mud-covered jeans.

"Hazard of the job."

She nodded as if completely understanding. Which would be something because I'm not sure my response made much sense to even me. "You're working with your uncle Spyros now, right?"

"Right."

I realized that I hadn't kept up on her activities at all while mine were probably listed in the weekly *Astoria Times,* you know, just so everyone could see what a mess I was making out of my life since the day of my almost wedding, since I'd fed my engagement ring to the garbage disposal.

Was she still a paralegal with that attorney's office?

Did her mother still make the best *bougatsa* in the world?

Was she sorry she'd screwed my groom five minutes before I was supposed to marry him?

"Look, I've got to get going," I said, longingly eyeing the

shopping aisles where it would be so easy to disappear. "It was . . ."

It was what? Good to see her? I couldn't say that because it wasn't good to see her. I hadn't even been able to think her name in five months, much less say it aloud. And I could easily have gone the rest of my life without seeing her again.

"Yeah," she said, as if echoing my thoughts.

I began to pass her.

She reached out a hand to stop me.

I stared at the unwanted limb as if I might check out why Muffy found biting so appealing.

"Listen, Sof, I've been meaning to call you for months . . ."

"For what? So we can compare notes on Thomas?"

I raised my brows, my heart beating loudly in my ears.

While my family had ceaselessly tried selling me on the line "boys will be boys" in regard to Thomas' behavior (except for Efi, whose friend the body piercer had offered to do interesting things to Thomas' anatomy while he slept), no one had really ever mentioned Kati. It was almost as if she'd been completely erased from our past. Like her sin had been so bad, her existence had been wiped from our hearts and minds. Pictures of her disappeared from photo albums, tucked away in the closet in boxes that were never touched.

Me? For purposes of self-preservation I'd removed myself from anything remotely connected to our friendship, including the circle of friends we'd once shared. The blow inflicted by her and my groom's betrayal had been enough for me to question everything in my life, not just my career path.

Besides, they'd all known what Thomas had been doing behind my back, and somebody should have had the balls to tell me.

Just not in the way Kati had.

Now she cleared her throat. "I guess what I'm trying to say is . . ."

I wasn't helping her out on this one. Not like I had throughout school when she'd gotten into trouble for talking in class and I'd taken the blame. Or when I allowed her to copy off my tests because she hadn't studied the night before. Or let her borrow my favorite sweater because she didn't want to be seen in the same thing twice.

She laughed without humor. "I don't really know how to say it, so I guess the best way is to just spit it out . . ."

I waited.

"I'm sorry."

Funny what impact two simple words could have on a person.

Honestly, I hadn't expected her to apologize. And would never have suspected that the action would have any affect on me whatsoever. But as we both stood in the front of the supermarket, me in my muddy jeans, her in her impeccable suit, I suddenly remembered all the good feelings that went along with the years we'd been friends. The secrets we'd shared. The astronomical number of nights we'd stayed at each other's houses mapping out our futures and griping about our lackluster pasts.

I managed a shrug. "Yeah, well . . ." I didn't know quite what to say. "That's okay," was so far from the truth that I didn't dare say it. So instead I mumbled, "I guess it could be said Thomas screwed us both on that day." I was having a hard time looking at her so I stared at a pyramid display of tampons instead. "I guess you're just as much of a victim as I was."

"Victim?" Kati repeated, blinking. "I'm not a victim. Thomas and I are still seeing each other."

I had a vision of shoving her into the tampons. Or the display of creamed corned next to them. I could see her with her legs up in the air, one of the cans teetering above her then smacking against her forehead even as tampons dangled from her hair.

Instead I managed a smile and said, "Well, then, you deserve what you get." I began walking away again, then turned. "As for your apology? I don't think I have to tell you what you can do with it."

I DON'T KNOW HOW MANY times I'd washed my hair or stood in the shower trying to scrub the mud from my skin. Mainly because that's not all I was trying to cleanse away.

I'd come so far in the past five months that I couldn't believe one accidental run-in could thrust me back to that day at St. Constantine's with the velocity of time travel. I felt outside myself, and no matter how hard I tried I couldn't rid my mind of the image of Kati with the skirt of her pink taffeta gown thrown up so my groom might get a little pre-wedding nookie from someone other than his bride.

What made me sicker yet is that I felt the incredible urge to cry.

Eventually, the water grew cold and I was forced to turn off the shower and rip open the curtain, nearly tearing it from its rings. Muffy sat on the bath mat, his tongue lolling out of the side of his mouth as he watched me. As I dried off, I realized that not only had I felt like crying, I was crying. Simply because I kept drying my face only to have it get all wet again.

"What?" I asked Muffy.

He cocked his head to the side and made a curious sound.

Then the smell I'd been detecting around him lately hit me full in the face. A big, noxious cloud of dog gas.

Ugh.

I shook my towel at him. "Go on, git," I told him, feeling like I needed another shower for fear that the stench had attached itself to my damp skin.

He growled then turned on his heels and left me blissfully alone. I sat on the closed commode with the towel wrapped around me, staring at the opposite wall and the other towels hanging there. For how long, I couldn't be sure. But by the time I blinked everything back into focus, my hair was nearly dry.

"Oh, get over yourself, Metro."

I swiped at my cheeks a final time and reasoned that it wouldn't be a good idea if I looked at myself directly in the mirror. So I fixed my hair as best I could, applied some makeup, and dressed without meeting the eyes of my own reflection. And what would I see if I did look? A sorry excuse for a woman destroyed by a chance meeting of someone who had betrayed her? A woman that had been my best friend but had thought so little of the friendship that she'd *shtupped* my groom on the very day she was supposed to stand up for me at my wedding?

What really stank was that I don't think seeing Thomas again had affected me with such fist-to-the-gut precision. No, I was still angry with him. Mostly because for the first few weeks after the wedding-that-wasn't, he'd called threatening to sue me for the cost of the engagement ring.

But Kati . . .

Pain panged deep inside me. Like one of those scalpels you read about being left inside people after surgery. The wound heals around it, but lean just so and the sharp blade cuts you all over again.

But in my case it felt like a meat cleaver.

How many times right after the event had I automatically reached for my cell to call Kati to tell her something or another? How many times had I found my car in her neighborhood without even realizing I was driving there?

Of course, I'd deleted her pre-programmed number from my cell to keep myself from accidentally calling. And I'd also cut off from the other friends we'd shared because, well, I'd given in once and went for coffee with Leta Hionis two weeks after returning from my solo honeymoon trip. I was shocked when she'd told me in so many words that I should have known something like this was coming and could I pay her for the gift she couldn't return on credit?

I didn't go to the same clubs I used to go to before. The restaurants we'd frequented I avoided like the plague. I'd even switched clothing stores for fear I'd run into the old crowd. I didn't think I could stand their tsking about what had happened. Or, worse yet, face their pity.

So on that day, my life had changed completely. Oh, I'd expected it would. Only I hadn't bargained for exactly how.

Five minutes later, I emerged from the building searching for my car keys in my purse when I heard Muffy growl again from where he stood next to me, having followed me without my realizing it. Only this time he wasn't directing his hostility toward me. Rather he was openly challenging Jake, who leaned against my car wiping engine grime from his hands.

Considering that I wasn't all that enthralled with the opposite sex just then, I told myself I wasn't happy to see him. Unfortunately, my body told me something different.

"Cheeky little bastard, isn't he?" he said about Muffy. "You know, considering I could crush him with one boot."

I was tempted to tell Muffy to sic him, only I didn't know if the mutt worked on command. Probably my asking him to attack would make him roll over and want his belly rubbed.

I opened the passenger's door, forcing Porter to move farther down the car, and told Muffy to get in. He did. Then he sat inside, his gaze fastened on Jake, his sharp little teeth bared in a growling sneer.

"Don't tell me. You heard about last night, too," I said, crossing my arms and facing off with Jake.

His blue eyes squinted as he took me in. It wouldn't surprise me in the least if he suspected I'd been crying. Jake Porter seemed to know far more about me than I would probably ever know about him. And right now that bothered me, too.

"Yeah. The attacking suit," he said quietly. He reached out and tucked a strand of hair behind my ear.

I moved it right back where it was.

"You okay, luv?" he asked softly.

No, I wasn't okay. I wanted to go back upstairs and disappear under the covers for the next month or so, or at least until the ache throbbing in the vicinity of my chest went away, whichever came first.

The problem was, I was afraid I'd never get out of bed again once I climbed in.

"Fine. I'm fine," I said. "Why wouldn't I be?"

He considered me for a long moment before saying, "Indeed. Why wouldn't you be?"

I sniffed.

His eyes narrowed further.

I made a face and gestured toward the car. "So, you've taken up tinkering with my Sheila again."

That got a grin out of him. "I came up with a part I was looking for."

"Ah. That's why you haven't been around for, oh, about the past two months."

"Did you miss me?"

"You were never around long enough for me to get used to you."

He rubbed his thumb against something on my cheek. "Maybe that's something we should talk about working on."

I moved closer, only it wasn't him I was intent on touching. Instead I reached around him and slammed the hood to my traitorous Sheila shut.

"Maybe I have some work to do and should go do it."

He cocked a brow at me.

Not that I could blame him for being surprised. After all, hadn't it been me who had thrown myself at him no fewer than three times when our paths had crossed before?

Now it seemed I couldn't get rid of him soon enough.

Probably because I was afraid if I stuck around I'd end up hitting him, taking out all of my pent up anger toward my ex-groom and my ex-best friend on him, or kissing him.

And right now I couldn't decide which was worse.

"This work . . . it wouldn't happen to have anything to do with the DiPiazzas now, would it?"

It was my turn to raise my brows. "What, do you have my phone bugged?"

He grinned. "I don't have to bug your phone, luv. Your movements are pretty much out there for everyone to see."

Was that like wearing my heart on my sleeve?

It was then that I realized there was no sign of my new

friends in their sedan. They'd followed me to See Foods, that much I was sure of because I'd wanted to toss a brick through their windshield when I'd come out, right after my run-in with Kati and everything.

"Who you looking for?" Porter asked.

I blinked at him and smiled. "Nobody. Who do you think I would be looking for?"

"I don't know. Maybe that black sedan that's been following you all morning."

"And its not being here now . . . would that have anything to do with you?"

He shrugged and crossed his arms. "Maybe. Maybe not."

I gave him an eye roll and rounded the car.

"I don't need protection, Jake."

He pushed from the car to face me over the hood. "Who said you did?"

"You just did."

I climbed in and slammed the door, my destination the DiPiazzas.

Of course, first I'd have to find out where they were.

Nine

A COUPLE OF PHONE CALLS netted me the info I needed: Tony DiPiazza operated out of the anchor of three dance clubs he owned in Queens on the other side of the Boulevard of Death aka Queens Boulevard. I searched for a parking spot, ignoring that I was already drenched in sweat and that my mind was firmly on Jake Porter and not the job at hand. I supposed I could be thankful for him in that he'd managed to push my reaction to Kati onto the back burner—mostly because my attraction to him had switched from a low simmer to a rolling boil.

I just didn't get him. Two months ago I could have thrown myself naked, spread-eagle at his feet, and he probably would have stepped over me to get to where he wanted to go. Now he seemed to be asking me for a date.

Or at least I think that was the gist of what he'd said back at my place.

Then again, maybe all he was interested in was a quick sack session. Something I was more amenable to now given my recent track record with relationships that lasted longer than a night.

Besides, there could be no more than a night of hot monkey sex between the two of us. Mostly because he wasn't Greek.

Yikes, now I was sounding like my mother.

I found a spot in the shade and climbed out of my car, quickly closing the door after myself to shut Muffy in, though I left the windows open slightly. I made a note not to leave him in there too long because, hey, while the dog and I had some issues, I didn't want him suffocating in my car.

The instant I rounded the corner I spotted the sedan that had been noticeably missing from my street while Porter was there. Okay, so if I'd had any doubts that the goons were with DiPiazza, those had just vanished.

I came to a stop in front of the club in question. Why was it that in the light of day clubs always looked like shabby movie sets with one too many sequins and coats of garish paint? The paint in question was purple and the name "Strobe" was spelled out in silver discs that moved in the wind. I was reminded of a really cheap Halloween outfit my mother had made for me when I was fourteen and I'd known everything there was to know. By the end of the night, not a sequin remained on my backside and, unfortunately, the material that had held them was transparent when I stood with the light behind me. I'd heard about it for weeks at school.

The sign on the door said the club was closed but I reached for the door handle anyway, the presence of the sedan enough to tell me that probably there were people inside. But as I moved to step in, someone else moved to step out.

I immediately understood that the Tony DiPiazza I'd known at AHS was indeed one and the same as the Tony DiPiazza that caused Rosie to cross herself every time she said his name.

"Oh . . . my . . . God," I couldn't help myself from saying. "Tony, is that you?"

Generally, that was the response I got, not one that I gave. But the truth of the matter was that the past ten years had been good to Tony. Very good. Where he'd once been a short, skinny teen who'd spent too much time on his hair, now he was tall and built, and his hair was close-cropped and probably didn't even need a comb.

And that grin . . .

"Sofie. Long time."

I wasn't sure what to make out of his putting his arm around my shoulders and kissing both my cheeks. The last time we'd met, he'd upset the stack of books I'd been holding and I was late for third period as I scrambled to pick them up from the hall floor.

His grin seemed to glint in the sun. "Hey, I saw you on that show a few months back. You looked good."

I doubted his sincerity if only because I knew a person could only look so good with bug legs stuck in her teeth.

"In fact, you look even better in person." He gave me an open perusal. "The years have been good to you."

I shivered, ignoring that I'd just thought the same about him.

"So, what brings you to my neck of the woods?" he asked.

His neck of the woods . . . Was that mafia speak for "his territory"? By crossing Queens Boulevard, had I passed a demarcation line of sorts?

"I've got a couple questions I want to ask you."

"Questions?" he asked, although I was fairly certain he knew what I was talking about, if only because that sedan sat a few car-lengths away.

"Mmm. About Uncle Tolly. You know, Apostolis Pappas?

He's the dry cleaner over near Steinway and Ditmars?"

"Ah," he said, nodding his head several times. "I'd heard somewhere that he was missing."

I'd guess he'd heard a lot more than that and more than just in passing, as well.

"So it's true then? You're a PI?"

"It's true."

"But aren't matters like missing persons something for the boys in blue?"

The same boys he probably owned?

Okay, I vowed not to watch another mafia movie again. Or the news for that matter.

"Mrs. Pappas hired me," I told him.

"So she can bury him."

"So she can sell his car."

"Ah."

I squinted at him. "Who said he was dead?"

Tony rubbed the tip of his index finger against a smooth brow. "You did."

"No, I didn't. I said he was missing. Actually, you said he was missing and I said I'd been hired to find him." Or something like that. Still, I was pretty sure I hadn't said anything about Tolly's being dead.

Did Tony know something I didn't?

"You know," he said, grinning at me again, "you and me should maybe have some pasta together sometime."

The way he said "pasta" made me think of spaghetti not at all. Rather he seemed to be using it in place of the word "sex." And something responded in me that wasn't all that turned off by the idea.

"Pasta . . . yeah."

My grandpa Kosmos didn't think much of Italians. He called them thieves. Everything Roman had once been everything Greek. From mythology to politics, they'd "borrowed" the very structure of their civilization from the ancient Greeks, then tried to take all the credit for coming up with it. Even most Greek architecture was called Greco-Roman. Grandpa Kosmos hated that.

They'd stolen everything except for the fountains, he said. But they could keep those. Who needed naked cherubs pissing water on your head, anyway?

Tony smelled good. Not too-much-expensive-cologne good. Rather, he smelled clean and fresh and, well, okay I'll admit it, inviting.

I didn't know what bothered me about that more: that I was more than a little attracted to a guy who might have hung Uncle Tolly on a meat hook, or that I was attracted to a guy who used the word "pasta" for "sex."

"When's the last time you talked to Uncle Tolly?" I asked after clearing my throat and pushing all thought of pasta from my mind.

"Hmm. I don't know. A month or so ago maybe."

"And the nature of that meeting?"

Was it me or did his grin look a little different? More challenging? "I had some . . . things to be cleaned, of course."

Ask a stupid question.

Since I didn't think it was a good idea to ask if those "things" were American dollars, and how many of them he'd laundered, I smiled.

"Do you know where he might be now?"

"Me?" He shook his head and pursed his lips. "Nope. Not a clue."

I looked over my shoulder at the sedan. "That yours?"

He stared at the car, then looked back at me. "It belongs to some associates of mine. Why?"

Two guys came around the back of the club. One of them had the same type of close-cropped haircut Tony had but it somehow didn't look the same because of his receding hairline. In fact, the guy looked pretty much how I would have expected Tony to turn out. Short. Wiry. Cocky.

And the way he stared at me said that if I'd been carrying any books he would have liked to knock them out of my hands.

The two guys headed toward the sedan, and the one with the receding hairline unlocked the driver's side.

"Who are they?" I motioned toward the sedan. "The associates in question?"

"Who, Rokko and Dozer?"

The name Rokko rang a bell; the name Dozer made me lift a brow. "Yeah."

He grinned. "Yeah."

"Hmm, interesting. You would know why they've been following me then."

"Following you? Of course I wouldn't know that. Hey, up until now, I hadn't thought about you in a good ten years or so. Well, except for that worm-shake thing." He raised his arm. "Hey, Rokko! You been following Sofie?"

The driver said, "Why would we be following Sofie?"

Then it hit me. I knew the driver as well. He'd been Tony's best friend in school. Panayiotis Rokkos.

My throat tightened. Probably because I remembered something else about him. Namely that he and another guy had held me down in the second grade to get a look up my skirt at my white panties.

Tony said, "Maybe you're mistaken."

"Maybe I'm not. Those two were definitely following me."

He scratched his eyebrow again. "I don't know how that could be. They were here with me all morning."

Now I understood how the police had such a hard time nailing the mob for anything. Tony lied as smoothly as he rubbed his brow.

"You don't mind if I call you, do you?" I asked. "You know, in case I have any other questions?"

"Nah. Not at all. You got my number?"

I didn't have his number.

He took a business card from his back pocket, motioned for me to turn around, then used my back as a table on which to write a couple additional numbers on the card.

"Here. Call me any time, Sof." He handed me the card.

"Thanks." I took it and began tracking back to my car.

"Hey, how does Thursday sound?" Tony called out.

"For what?"

His grin very definitely glinted in the sun. "That . . . pasta."

"Thursday's bad for me," I said. "I have to go to the doctor to see about this really nasty rash I have."

He chuckled. "Good luck finding Uncle Tolly."

I rounded the corner and fought the urge to stop and catch my breath although I'd done nothing physical. Tony's wish could mean one of two things: that I'd need all the luck in the world to keep myself out of trouble while looking for Uncle Tolly, or that I stood absolutely no chance in hell of finding him.

Or possibly it meant both.

Whichever it was, I determined I wasn't going to be having pasta or anything else with Tony in the near or faraway future. Not if I could help it, anyway . . .

Ten

TRUTH WAS, I DIDN'T KNOW quite what to make of my sidewalk meeting with Tony DiPiazza. I mean, aside from the pasta part. If he was, indeed, a component of the New Generation Mafia, well, I think he had his work cut out for him.

The New Generation Mafia, it was said, resembled the Old Mafia very little. Whereas the bosses of the various families were still either from or had a tight connection to the homeland—in this case Italy, or worse, Sicily—this new bunch of underlings probably couldn't point Europe out on a map, much less speak Italian beyond uttering the occasional curse word or "paisan," which probably came from watching too many Pacino movies. And much of their income came from white-collar crime instead of prostitution and drugs, although I understood that gambling was going stronger than ever, what with *The World Series of Poker* show going into nationwide syndication and half-wit B-list stars making it look cool.

At any rate, Tony had nothing on say the Teflon Don, John Gotti.

Then again, it was probably a good idea if I didn't underestimate either Tony or the New Generation Mafia right now. Better I should keep my wits about me. Even if Tony's henchman Rokko was no longer following me.

I let Muffy and myself into my apartment then stared at the business card Tony had given me. I put it down on the hall table along with my cell phone.

One question that stuck out in my mind was what a Greek—namely Panayiotis Rokkos—was doing associating himself with the Italian element—namely Tony DiPiazza.

I'd have to have a conversation with my grandpa Kosmos. See if he knew anything about about a possible Greek-Italian connection. The problem lay in that even if he knew nothing, he would probably pretend to know something. And that was the high-wire act most Greek-Americans performed every day. Trying to distinguish myth from truth. Unfortunately, the words "I don't know" weren't part of the Grenglish language.

It was past six P.M., Rosie had closed up the agency, and there really wasn't all that much I could do anyway, so I decided a veg session with my new roommate was in order. I put together a couch picnic to rival all couch picnics with a delivery from the Chirping Chicken, souvlaki from the cart on Broadway near thirty-first, a few selections of *pasta* (not Tony's idea of pasta but rather Greek sweets, what they call petit fours in English), from Omonia Bakery (they'd made the cake for *My Big Fat Greek Wedding*, and for my wedding—the top of mine was still in my freezer).

Muffy seemed pleased with my idea and ran around the living room a few times to show his appreciation. So long as he didn't lift his leg on anything I was okay with his display, even if he was probably scratching the wood portions of the floor that weren't covered by rugs.

I'd ordered a plain souvlaki for him, just grilled pork and pita, and put it on the floor in the foil it came in. He gobbled it up, making sounds I preferred over his constant growling, while I alternated between chicken and souvlaki. I figured since I hadn't really eaten anything since yesterday—aside from my most important food group: frappé—I could indulge without worrying too much about it going straight to my hips.

Truth was, I hadn't had much of an appetite lately. Not since seeing my father being a little too friendly with Magda. And not since I'd made a pretty solid connection between Uncle Tolly and the mob.

Of course, the unbearable heat was also largely to blame. I caught myself scratching my knee and stopped, then I crossed my legs on the couch and picked up a triple-chocolate *pasta* in the shape of a mouse. The greatest thing about living on your own was that no one was around to tell you that you couldn't eat dessert first. Or in the middle of the rest of your meal. Oh, and absolute power over the remote control was another plus. I had the DVD of the first season of *Seinfeld* in my player, figuring I could pretty much pass the rest of the night in bliss so long as no one interrupted me.

I forked a healthy portion of mouse into my mouth, making much the same sounds of satisfaction as Muffy.

At least until a familiar, rancid smell assaulted me.

"Oh, God."

I put my plate down and plugged my nose, glaring at Muffy full on.

I almost asked what he'd eaten then spotted the pork. But surely the meat couldn't have gotten through his system that quickly. Could it?

"You and me, we need to make an appointment with the vet," I told him.

He seemed to realize what I'd said and cocked his head to the side.

I put some chicken sans skin down on his licked clean foil. "Enjoy this while you can because I have a feeling this may be your last supper."

Or at least the last supper of that nature, anyway.

Probably I should be feeding him only dog food. But since the faux meat rock pellets supposedly soaked in gravy made me wrinkle my nose, I figured he probably didn't think much of them either.

A knock at my door.

I froze, my mouth full of mouse.

Aw, hell. Don't tell me my mother had caught up with me.

Since I had the volume up high enough to hear from the hall, and since I'd just been talking to the dog, it was pretty hard for me to pretend I wasn't there.

I went to answer the door.

"Hi, Mrs. Nebitz."

"Sorry to bother you, Sofie, but I wondered if you knew that nice Mr. Porter is working on your car again."

Twice in one day. I pondered what I did to get in the gods' good favor.

"Thanks, Mrs. Nebitz," I said. "Oh, and wait a minute. I have something for you."

I collected the box of two other *pastas*, closed it, and handed it to her. "These are for you."

"Oh. Thank you, dear," she said, although she clearly didn't know what to make of the sweets or my giving them to her.

Simply, my appetite had changed from wanting all things sweet to craving all things naughty. Mostly in the shape of one sexy Aussie named Jake Porter.

After I closed the door, I shut off the DVD player, changed into a clean pair of jeans and clingy black top, and primped myself up a bit. Finally, I stood in the living room staring at Muffy.

"If . . . when I bring Mr. Porter up here, you're to be on your best behavior."

He growled.

And another noxious cloud reached my nose.

"*Toof.*" I picked him up, opened the window, and put him out on the fire escape. "Then again, maybe you should just stay on the roof until after he leaves."

I brushed my hands against one another then stared down at where Porter was bent over the open hood of my Mustang. The denim of his jeans hugged his backside just so, making my mouth water.

Mmm . . . definitely better than anything a bakery could offer.

And, after all, I did owe him an apology for my sour attitude earlier.

I closed the window at a barking Muffy then went down to see if there wasn't some way I could tempt the sexy Aussie into my room to see my sketches.

Okay, maybe not my sketches. But all the unopened wedding gifts that still lined the back wall might do the trick. I recognized where that could be a buzz kill and thought that maybe we should just stay in the living room . . .

OKAY, SO I COULDN'T HELP myself. Jake didn't seem to know I was behind him, and his backside was just a tad too sexy to resist. I reached out and gave a pinch.

He nearly hit his head on the car hood.

"Bloody hell," he said, rubbing the top of his head as he turned to face me. By then I'd clasped my hands behind my back and looked around as if I hadn't a clue what had happened. Although I was pretty sure my grin gave me away.

"Imagine my surprising you."

"Oh, I knew you were there: it's your actions that caught me off guard."

"Find another part?" I asked, motioning toward the car.

Dusk was beginning to fall, coloring the sky and everything else in a warm, golden, purplish glow. The cement beneath my feet was so hot it felt like someone was blowing at coals under it with the intention of cooking me. But the sweltering temperatures weren't what I currently had my mind on. Rather, I was more concentrated on the heat generated by Porter's return.

He wiped his hands on a rag, his gaze taking in my fresh change of clothes and the extra swipe of mascara I'd put on. "Mmm . . . something like that."

"You know, some people just ring the bell when they want to talk to somebody."

He grinned. "Well, now, that would be a bit boring, wouldn't it?"

I admitted that it would. But then again if Mrs. Nebitz hadn't alerted me to his presence, I might never have known he was outside looking to have a word or two.

"I see your new friends are back," he said, gesturing with his head toward the opposite side of the street.

My good mood took a nosedive when I spotted the sedan parked up the block, with Rokko definitely behind the wheel.

"The DiPiazzas are nobody to mess with, Sof."

I wasn't aware I had messed with anybody, much less the DiPiazzas. I just wanted to find Uncle Tolly. I didn't care where or how he got to be wherever I found him. I was hired to do a job and I was doing it.

Unfortunately, I was afraid the sedan that had followed me all day, which was sitting outside my house again, was proof of the DiPiazzas doing *their* job.

I gave Porter a smile that was minus much of the sexy bounciness of my previous smile. "I don't have anything to be afraid of. I have you, remember?"

He grimaced. "I can't be here twenty-four/seven."

Even the mention of his being around for longer than it took for him to fiddle around under my hood made my blood race.

"I'd settle for a solid hour," I told him, wiping pretend lint from his tight-fitting white T-shirt.

God, the guy felt like he was made of granite.

He caught my hand. "I'm not joking around here, Sofie."

I met his gaze square on. "I'm not joking around either, Jake."

He struck me as the type of guy who didn't need to have things spelled out for him. And as I watched his eyes darken, I knew he knew what I was talking about.

"Why don't you come upstairs so we can start that 'getting to know each other a little better' stuff you talked about earlier?"

He seemed to consider my suggestion. "How about you go back upstairs and I'll see what I can't do to get rid of those two thugs up the road?"

"And then you'll come up?"

"Then I'll trust you not to go around poking a stick into a pit of snakes again."

I sighed deeply and took my hand from his grip. "You know something, Porter, you're making me work just a little too hard for this."

I was slightly surprised to find myself saying what I was thinking. While I'd never exactly been called a wuss before, I was used to getting what I wanted when I put my mind to something. And Porter's playing hard to get was bringing out a side of me with which I wasn't very familiar.

"Tell you what. You do whatever it is you feel you have to do. I'll go upstairs. And you don't come back again until it's my personal Sheila you want to tinker around with. What do you think of that?"

His grin returned and he looked like he was an arch away from waggling his brows at me.

Instead he cleared his throat and crossed his arms over his wide chest. "So it's going to be like that, is it, luv?"

I gave him an eye roll. "It's going to be exactly like that. And don't call me luv anymore, all right? It makes it hard to sleep at night."

Since I wasn't particularly interested in seeing his reaction to that, I turned on my heel and climbed the stairs to the building, aware of Muffy's loud barking from the fire escape.

A COUPLE HOURS LATER, I stood at the dining room window staring down at the quiet street. Porter had managed to get rid of Rokko. I don't know how, but he had. Probably he had told him I wouldn't be going anywhere for the rest of the night.

I only wished that had more to do with Porter's being up here with me than lack of anything else to do.

Muffy had taken up residence on Thomas's Barcalounger and was snoring away, smells I didn't want anything to do with emanating from his furry body. My picnic was sitting in the refrigerator and I . . . well I was wondering what it was going to take to get laid in a city where it usually wasn't a problem.

I picked up my cell phone, scrolled through the address book, and called Rosie.

"Sofie? Sofie is that you?"

The voice that asked the question didn't sound like Rosie at all. Well, it did—there was no way to completely disguise her high-pitched voice—but it was obvious she was trying not to sound like herself.

"Yeah, it's me. Why are you whispering?"

"I'm not whispering," she said again in a whisper.

"Yes you are."

"Where are you?"

"At home? Why? Where did you expect me to be?"

Silence then, "I dunno. At the bottom of the East River, maybe?"

I made a face. "I don't think reception would be all that great down there."

"Yeah. Maybe you're right." There was some shifting around. "What do you want?"

"What are you doing?"

"I'm in bed."

I glanced at the clock. She was in bed at nine o'clock?

"Well get up and get dressed."

"Why?"

"Because you and I are going to do some ferret hunting."

Eleven

I PARKED DOWN THE STREET from Jennifer Lopez's cousin's house, you know, in case I hadn't completely shaken Rokko. I approached a vintage Trans Am (read, it was in just as bad shape as my Mustang with the addition of a few rust spots I didn't think any amount of bondo would be able to fix) and knocked on the window. Rosie jumped at the same time I did.

"Geez, scare the crap out of a body already," she said, climbing out of the car. "I think I swallowed my gum. Oh, wait." She began chewing, apparently having salvaged it.

"What?" she asked, clearly irritated.

Her question was inspired by the open way I stared at her. Aside from the cutesy little pink pj's and fluffy pink mules she had on, she wore some sort of thick green gook on her face and a blue liquid-filled eye mask.

She put a hand to her hair, which was the least startling of her beauty care treatments. Namely, she had Diet Coke cans fastened like curlers on the top.

"You know, you should have worn that when we visited the vampire's nephew. He may have been the one who bolted in the other direction."

I could laugh now at the memory of Rosie hovering by the front gate of the Romanovs' place then taking off like a shot down the street the instant Vladimir said good evening without my even being aware the door had opened. But back then it hadn't been the least bit funny.

"Ha, ha. Don't remind me. I'm still not convinced that 'dog bite' you said you had wasn't actually a vampire bite."

"I go out in daylight."

We both looked at the lengthening dusk.

I gestured her away. "Did you bring the peach?"

Out of the two of us, the only thing fruit-wise either of us could scare up was a peach that Rosie said had been sitting in her refrigerator for Lord only knew how long.

She handed it to me.

It made an icky smooshy sound.

"This is rotten."

"I told you I had it for a while."

I made a face and took the napkin she offered. "Yes, well, let's hope Fred isn't picky." I led the way toward the darkened house.

She looked up and down the street. "You still being followed by DiPiazza's goons?"

I hadn't spotted the sedan, but I was coming to understand that meant little. "No," I told her anyway.

A disguise. That's what Rosie's get-up was. It was a disguise. It had to be because I couldn't imagine anyone going to bed looking the way she did. I mean, how did you keep that green goop off your pillow? And how did you roll over with Coke cans in your hair without crushing them to your scalp?

I don't care if you promised me I'd look like Pamela Anderson pre-breast surgery in the morning, I wouldn't do it in a million years.

Now, throw in the breasts . . .

"So, we gonna do this or what?"

I motioned for Rosie to precede me into the gated yard.

"Oh, no, after you. I'm not getting bit by that thing."

"It bites?" Great, that's all I needed to know. I had so many marks from being bitten by Muffy and a Muffy look-alike you could play connect-the-scars on my person.

Rosie shrugged as if to say, "Of course. It's an animal, it bites."

I entered the gate. "You would have to say that now, wouldn't you?"

"Well excuse me for living already." She passed me. "Let's just find this stupid thing."

"Okay, I'll go this way around the house, you go the other way. We'll meet back here."

Rosie nodded and started walking away.

"Oh, wait." I pulled off a piece of the rotten peach and slapped it into her hand.

"Eeew. What did you go and do that for?"

"Hey, you're the one wearing avocado dip on your face. Actually, maybe you can try to feed him that."

She drew her head back as if wondering whether Fred would try to eat it off her.

"Don't worry. Just don't put your face too close to any bushes or anything."

"Some help you are."

"Hey, anything I can do. Oh, and look for some sort of nest or something."

"Nest?"

I nodded, not sure what that entailed either. But I was pretty sure it wouldn't look like a bird's nest.

We split up.

I took the same route I'd taken before. Were ferrets nocturnal? I didn't know. I did know they spent the majority of their time sleeping and that a call to a vet that kept night hours—whom I'd called to schedule an appointment for gassy Muffy—told me the best opportunities to find the ferret would be around sunset and a couple hours before sunrise. Since I wasn't about to get up at five in the morning to ferret hunt, I was here now. And I figured it was only fair that I'd gotten Rosie out of bed to help me. After all, she'd been instrumental in talking me into taking the case, calling me 'cruel' to even consider turning Lopez and her crippled cousin away. At least I was getting paid for the job.

I held the peach out at arm level. "Here, Fred, Fred, Fred."

Did ferrets respond on command? I cleared my throat and looked at the neighboring house hoping no one could see me. I felt stupid bent over, holding out half a peach, and calling a ferret's name.

I met Rosie in the back. We shared some head shaking then moved around the other side of the house.

Five minutes later, we were back in front, peach juice running from our hands, no Fred the Ferret to show for our efforts.

"I think it's too dark," Rosie said, putting her peach at the top of the porch steps then staring at her hands as if she didn't know what to do with them.

I was forced to agree. "Maybe we should have come a little earlier."

"Maybe."

I was reluctant to admit that the next window of opportunity was at five in the morning. But I did.

"What? You got me out of bed and now you're telling me you want to take away even more of my beauty sleep?" Rosie protested.

"It's your fault I even took the case."

"Yeah, but I didn't agree to look for that smelly, furry thing. I don't even like ferrets. Anyway, you're the expert."

"Expert on being a sucker," I mumbled.

I caught movement out of the corner of my eye. "Shhh."

"What do mean, 'shhh'?"

Were there that many meanings to "shhh"?

Then again, considering the way Rosie was backing up as if expecting Vladimir the vampire or DiPiazza the wanna-be-mafia-don to leap from the bushes, I understood that shushing Rosie was akin to scaring the crap out of her.

I slowly turned my head.

Fred the Ferret was on the porch eating Rosie's peach.

"It's him! It's got to be!" Rosie cried.

The long-bodied weasel-type animal snapped alert at the sound of Rosie's voice.

I resisted the urge to shush her again as I held out my hand with the rest of the peach in it.

"Come here, Fred, Fred, Fred," I said quietly, inching my way toward him. Only what I was going to do if I got my hand anywhere near him was a mystery to me. After all, it . . . he bit.

My hand was a few inches away. He dropped his food, put his little long-clawed paws on my fingers, sniffed the peach, then took it from my hand.

Then he darted around the side of the house before I could grab him.

"Damn!"

"What did you do?" Rosie practically shrieked at me. She stomped a mule-shod foot. "He was right there in your friggin' hand! And you let him get away."

"Hey, I didn't see you trying to help."

"You didn't tell me you needed help."

The porch light went on and the front door opened.

"What the hell is going on out here?" Jennifer Lopez's aunt asked, hands on hips.

I brushed my hands together. "Well, at least we know it's alive."

"And that he's eaten," Rosie agreed, joining with me in the face of the angry aunt.

I began backing toward the gate.

Rosie did the same, then both of us were bolting for our cars.

MUFFY SEEMED OVERLY INTERESTED IN my hand even though I'd scrubbed it no fewer than three times since returning home. Thankfully the sedan was nowhere to be seen. Then again, neither was Porter. I checked my cell phone to find my mother had called three times. Shocker. I put it back on the coffee table then did a bit of channel surfing, regretting I'd given Mrs. Nebitz my *pastas*. My sweet tooth was aching something terrible.

I got up from the couch, Muffy's eyes following me from where he was curled up on the Barcalounger.

"You're not getting anything but dog food from here on out," I told him. "Doctor's orders."

Of course, when the vet had asked what Muffy was eating that might cause him gas, I'd lied and told her only dog food. If she'd suspected otherwise, she didn't say so. Instead, she suggested I might change brands and gave me the name of one. I stopped by to pick up a bag on my way back from the ferret hunt, but Muffy hadn't even given the food a sniff before walking away from it.

You'll eat it if you're hungry, I thought, walking to my bedroom and switching on the light.

My king-size sleigh bed was pretty but would also be forever marred. Not by the fact that I was supposed to be sharing it with my no good, cheating ex-groom. But because it was rumored my Aunt Sotiria, who owned a funeral home, had one of her coffin suppliers make it special for me.

I guess it put a whole new spin on the saying "Sleep like the dead." I *did* sleep well in the bed. Well, at least when wet dreams of Porter didn't intrude.

My stomach growled and my craving for something sweet increased.

Sex . . . sweets. Same thing.

Okay, maybe not the same thing, but sweets were what helped me out when thoughts of Porter reached a feverish pitch.

Lining the opposite wall were the wrapped wedding presents that had been sitting there since my would-be wedding five months ago. During her last visit, my mother had mentioned in passing that she hoped there wasn't anything perishable in any of them. I'd told her I'd smell it if there was.

But it wasn't the gifts I was interested in tonight. Rather I went for one of the boxes to the right of the gifts. I opened the lid of the top one and stared down at the *boubounieras* that had never been given out to wedding guests as they left the church. *Boubounieras* were little white net bags of Jordan almonds tied with a white ribbon. I pulled one of them out and opened it. The almonds were covered with white, shiny sugar that was hard even when freshly made. Since five months had passed, they were probably inedible. Probably they would break my teeth.

I hesitantly put one into my mouth, catching it between my back teeth. I gave an experimental crunch. Mmm. Okay. Not bad. Hard as a rock, but once you broke the outside coating it was smooth sailing from there.

I picked up five or six of the *boubounieras* and headed back out to put my *Seinfeld* DVD back in the player.

Tomorrow had to be better, no?

I encountered one of the worst toxic clouds yet as I entered the living room.

"Muffy!"

He lifted his head and whined at me as if to say he wasn't enjoying the experience either.

I sighed and switched the thermostat lower so that the air-conditioning would hopefully dissipate the smell.

Ah, yes. Old Jordan almonds and dog farts. Welcome to my life.

Twelve

OKAY, MAYBE I WAS IN over my head.

Truth was, I didn't really think the Uncle Tolly case through before deciding to take it on. Deciding to take it on? That made it sound as if Aglaia Pappas had approached me begging for me to find her husband. Instead, I was the one who had gone there offering my services . . . for a quarter of the going rate.

There was a time not so long ago that I would have welcomed a paying gig that had nothing to do with cheating spouses. Now I was complaining. Go figure.

At any rate, I'd thought Uncle Tolly had gone for a walk, maybe he'd fallen down and hit his head and was even now wandering around somewhere in Queens asking people if they knew him.

Of course, that left out the fact that a lot of people knew him. He probably would have been taken home the first day.

"I'm going to quit," Rosie whispered.

I looked up from my desk where I was piecing together some

of my notes on the case. Rosie looked a "boo!" away from catapulting from her chair. It was only nine in the morning and she'd been extraordinarily quiet when I came in twenty minutes ago. No mention of Fred the Ferret. No reference to how she'd gotten little beauty sleep the night before. She'd merely looked at me with her big, dark eyes as if she'd been visited by the ghost of Astoria past and he'd shown her a future sans nail decals and push-up bras.

But somehow I didn't think her threatening to quit had anything to do with surface matters. Rather I suspected something else, something more serious, was to blame.

"I'm not being followed," I pointed out, happy that I hadn't spotted the sedan when I left the house this morning.

However, I was curious to find that my car was running a little strangely. Almost like she wanted to stall out every time I pressed the accelerator. When Porter worked on her before, she ran like a dream. Today, I'd left Lucille at home and walked to the agency.

Rosie stared at me again, all big eyes and no explanation. "Pete's in back."

I raised my brows. Not exactly a rare occurrence and certainly not enough to put the fear of a vengeful Puerto Rican god into Rosie.

Pete is my cousin, my uncle Spyros' son from his first marriage. Sometimes he drops in—mostly when he needs money, which is often—and pretends he's seriously considering taking over where my uncle left off. I think my uncle would like it if his son actually was serious about following in his footsteps. But experience told me that the only thing Pete was serious about was being a handsome loser.

He was a little younger than me. Still lived at home with his mother. Had never held a real job as far as I could tell. And forever blamed my uncle for everything bad that had ever happened in his life because he'd divorced his mother. (Actually, his mother had divorced my uncle Spyros, but that didn't seem to matter.)

Usually, he showed up for an hour or two every now and again, taking over my uncle's office. I figured that's probably how long it took him to find some cash stashed somewhere. Cash I suspected my uncle planted for him, this being his way of making him work a little at finding it.

Of course, I fully expected the money train to pull into the station empty any day now. And what happened then? Did Pete go from playing PI to actually being one?

I made a face. Right now I had bigger fish to fry.

"And . . . and . . ."

I blinked at Rosie again.

"Jesus, Rosie, just spit it out already. What's going on?"

Her gaze moved from me to the closed door to Lenny Nash's office.

Lenny Nash was my uncle's silent partner. He was so silent that most times I even forgot he was there. Of course, that had something to do with that fact that he wasn't there a lot of the time, and neither Rosie nor I knew how to contact him outside the office even if we'd wanted to.

I had no idea what he did. He never took clients. He never met with clients. I only knew that occasionally an unexplained entry would pop up on the income sheet with nothing but Lenny's name next to it. A very large entry.

"What?" I asked Rosie again. "Is something going on?"

Even if she could have told me, I figured everything out when the door opened and Tony DiPiazza's henchman Rokko stepped out.

I was pretty sure my eyes went as big and vacant as Rosie's.

Silence.

Rokko disappeared through the outer door with barely a look at either of us, then out onto the street. Lenny's office door closed. And Rosie and I sat like we'd been grabbed by our lapels and given the hearty mafia kiss of death.

"That's it. I quit."

Rosie got up and started collecting things from her desk drawers.

"Whoa, hold up a minute." I halted her hands as she searched for a place to put her many nail files and her fingernail polish, along with perfume bottles, tampons, and a romance novel boasting a hulking, bare-chested man dressed as a pirate on the cover. "What's going on?"

"What do you mean, what's going on?" She pointed a black-painted nail toward the window. "That's what's going on."

"How long was he in there?"

The best I could figure is he must have been in there before I arrived twenty minutes ago, because I didn't think his arrival was something I'd overlook.

And that would certainly explain Rosie's strange behavior.

Okay, so Rosie's behavior was always strange, but . . .

"You just don't get it, do you?" she asked, dumping the contents she crowded against her stomach into the cavernous depths of her purse. "What does it matter how long he's been in there? The fact that he was in there at all is what I'm worried about."

I agreed.

She shook her head so that her silver hoops swayed against

her curly hair. "I knew your messing with the mob would get me into trouble."

"I'm not messing with the mob. I'm trying to find a missing person."

"A person the mob made missing." She shook her head again. "Uh-uh. Spyros doesn't pay me enough for this."

I stayed her hands with one of mine. "Let me go talk to Lenny."

We stared at each other.

Up until now, the most words I'd exchanged with Lenny Nash had to do with the morning being good or a general comment on the coming night. And those were only on my end.

Even Rosie seemed uninformed when it came to what kind of role he played in the agency and interacted with him as little as possible.

"Stay here," I said.

I began to release my hold on her hands, afraid she'd continue packing her stuff.

"Promise me you won't move a muscle until I get done."

She nodded, but said nothing. "Okay. But be quick about it. I mean I've heard the thing about women's biological clocks ticking, but I swear I hear the sound of my life clock."

That was Rosie for you. All exaggeration.

Problem was, she was beginning to scare the crap out of me.

With my gaze locked to Rosie's, I knocked on Nash's door then opened it. "Lenny? May I have a word with you?"

I'D SNUCK A PEEK INSIDE Lenny Nash's office before. It had been my thirteenth day at the agency and I'd been more than a little curious what was beyond the constantly closed door. (Okay, so I'd tried to get inside a couple of times before then, but the door had always been locked and I hadn't honed my lock-picking skills yet.) Lenny had gone to the bathroom and the instant the door closed behind him, I'd slipped inside his office, surprised to find the light off. (Who turned off the light when they were going to be right back?) I'd seen little outside an antique desk—strangely clear of any papers, folders, or an in-out box—a good-sized safe that took up a corner of the room, and a framed movie poster of Bogart in *The Maltese Falcon*. I'd snickered at the last part. Lenny Nash fancying himself as Sam Spade. Right. First, he'd have to expand his vocabulary beyond the two words I'd ever heard him utter. Second, he'd have to grow at least two feet and undergo a complete makeover, although full-body plastic surgery would probably be more the ticket.

Now, as I stood there gripping the door I'd just knocked on and opened, I saw little more than what my peek had given me before. Except now Lenny Nash was sitting behind his desk, an unlit pipe clenched between his teeth as he read something in a file in front of him, the safe door propped slightly open.

If he knew I was standing there, watching him, he didn't indicate.

"Lenny, might I have a few moments?"

He didn't respond and I wondered if he could hear me at all. Then he closed the file, put it in the safe, and closed the door.

The moment his sharp, intelligent gaze fell on me, I realized he'd never really looked at me before. At least not so as I noticed. If he had, I would have remembered what it felt like to be a kid about to confess to stealing cookies from the cookie jar.

He moved his cold pipe from one side of his mouth to the other, then gestured to the single chair in front of his desk.

"That's okay, this shouldn't take long," I said. "Do you mind if I ask what Panayiotis Rokkos was just doing here?"

Mind or not, I'd just asked the question.

And although there was no sign that he found my query strange or unwelcome, it occurred to me he might not answer.

"You know he's one of DiPiazza's goons, don't you?" I realized I'd spoken before he'd answered and made a face. "Did it have anything to do with Uncle Tolly?"

He maintained that stare that made me want to confess all my sins, real and imagined. He'd have made a great Greek priest.

"No."

That's it. Nothing more. Nothing less.

He turned away, retrieved another file from the safe, then opened it on his desk, his teeth clicking against his pipe as he moved it to the other side of his mouth. An indication that my visit was over? Probably.

I cleared my throat. Considering it had taken every ounce of false courage to walk through that door, I wasn't all that eager to walk back through it without something I could use.

"You understand that I'm a little concerned. I mean, ever since I've taken on Uncle Tolly's case, Rokko has been pretty much tailing me." I crossed my arms. "Then this morning, I see the same man who has been hanging over me like an unspoken threat coming out of your office."

There was nothing but the sound of papers being turned in the file he was browsing through for long moments. I stepped closer, trying to get a look at the file. Rather than shifting his pipe, he removed it from his mouth altogether, fixing me with that unsettling gaze of his.

"It's nothing that concerns you."

I blinked. The way I saw it, the entire situation concerned me a little too much.

The pipe went back into his mouth and his attention went back to his file.

"Okay, then," I said, not really knowing where to go from there. "Thanks."

I closed the door behind me to find Rosie standing and staring at me in exactly the position I'd left her.

"So?"

I twisted my lips. "So I think we're okay."

LATER THAT AFTERNOON, I WAS still mulling over that "word" I'd had with Nash.

"You mean he didn't tell you to stop working the Uncle Tolly case?" Rosie had whispered.

I'd shaken my head, as surprised by his reaction as she'd been.

"It's nothing that concerns you."

That had been all Nash had said as he stared at me.

Nothing that concerned me . . .

Correct me if I'm wrong, but having DiPiazza's henchman meeting with what was essentially one of my bosses was my concern, wasn't it? Seeing as that same henchman had been tailing me for the past two days. And seeing as I was working a case that seemed to be tightly connected to the henchman's boss.

Nothing that concerned me . . .

Rosie had immediately started packing the rest of her things.

I convinced her to wait until I talked with Uncle Spyros. The only problem was, it looked like I wouldn't be able to do that anytime soon. It seemed Rosie didn't have a number for my uncle on the remote unnamed island in the Aegean where he was currently staying.

"What?" she'd asked at my surprised stare. "He always calls me."

Only he hadn't been in contact for the past three days.

"I'll call in sick," Rosie had said.

"For how long?"

She'd given me an eye roll. "For however long it takes for this . . . thing to be over."

This . . . thing. Now there was a description.

Anyway, I stuck around the office all day to make sure Rosie wouldn't disappear on me. (I figured the longer I kept her there, the better the chance I'd convince her that nothing bad was going to happen.) I let her go at five on the dot, long after my cousin Pete and Nash had silently vacated the premises, and watched as she launched herself like a shot through the front door.

Of course, the last thing I wanted to do after a long day of cheating spouse paperwork, billing, and staring at the papers I had yet to serve, was talk to my mother. But if my cell phone kept vibrating the way it was from her constant phone calls, my battery would be dead inside an hour.

I still had no idea what I was going to say to her.

I'd walked to work that morning so that meant I also had to walk to my parents' place. I passed my apartment building and stared at Muffy barking at me from the fire escape. I nearly tripped over the bike of Etta Munson's daughter, evil incarnate Lola; the sound of the business school students' stereo was nearly deafening.

I crossed to the other side of the street and felt a chill creep up my spine. Although I hadn't spotted Rokko since his mysterious meeting with Nash, I had the intense sensation that I was being watched by someone interested in more than my choice of hairstyle or lip gloss.

I fished out a couple of Jordan almonds from my pocket and crunched on them as I hurried along the sidewalk, past what used to be Mrs. K's place, and let myself into my parents' house.

As usual, my grandfather and father were sitting in the living room reading rival city newspapers in their rival recliners. I kissed them both, this time my grandfather first, my father second, although I didn't want to acknowledge why. (This brought a curious stare from my father.) There was an unfamiliar man seated by himself on the couch with a glass of water, a Greek coffee, and a plate of *koulourakia*. I said hi only because I wanted to snatch one of the cookies. He answered me in Greek.

It wasn't all that long ago that I would have thought the man had been handpicked for me, you know, part of the matchmaking effort on behalf of my mother that managed to chase all kinds of interesting characters from out of the woodwork. Now I knew the men my mother had coming over every other day were for my younger sister Efi, who was all of nineteen and prime marriage material. In the old country.

"You can never start too soon," was my mother's motto.

As I crunched on the cookie, I took him in. This guy wasn't bad. About ten to fifteen years older than my sister, but at least he didn't have too much hair or too little. And he didn't seem to mind sitting by himself on the couch while everybody ignored him.

I went into the kitchen where it seemed my mother and grandmother were always cooking something. Today it was *gemista*—rice-stuffed tomatoes and peppers.

I got a look from my mother that could have turned goat's milk into feta.

"I'm sorry I couldn't pick up your calls," I said, kissing her cheek after I finished swallowing the cookie. "I haven't had a minute to myself all day."

"What's this I hear you're in trouble with the mob?"

I snuck a piece of roasted potato and earned a whack on the hand with a wooden spoon. "Mom, you're the one who asked me to look into Uncle Tolly's disappearance."

"Yes, but I had no idea it had anything to do with the mob."

"There is no mob anymore, Ma." Right.

This even earned a stare from my grandmother, who most of the time pretended she didn't understand a word of English.

"So, who's the guy in the other room?" I asked.

My mother gestured vaguely. "A friend of a friend's brother-in-law's cousin. Just moved here from a town near Patras."

Patras, Greece. Not that far from where my father's family was from, which meant it was a definite plus in his column.

I caught myself. What was I thinking? I wasn't possibly hoping to match my sister up with someone obviously too old for her just because of where the guy came from, was I?

My mother moved closer to me.

"So?" she asked with a fierce whisper.

"So what?" I blinked innocently.

My grandmother leaned closer from the other side. My mother pushed me in order to push her farther away. I felt like a human bumper car.

"It's all your imagination," I said.

I held my mother's gaze without blinking.

I hadn't known what I was going to say until the moment I said it.

Truth was, my mother was looking a little rough around the edges. Not how I was used to seeing her. She was the glue that held the family together. The rock everyone clutched to when the rising tide threatened to sweep you away. And while I suspected that she might be right about my father's . . . extracurricular activities, I found I couldn't tell her that.

Footsteps sounded on the second staircase in the kitchen leading to the bedrooms upstairs. I looked up to find my sister Efi bouncing into the room. I blinked. At least I thought it was Efi.

For one thing, Efi never bounced. For another, she looked nothing like the sister I knew and loved.

Efi was an endless source of exasperation for my mother. Thalia was constantly on me to talk to my sister about her latest body piercing or tattoo. If I was a little miffed because at her age my parents probably would have locked me in my room had I gotten my ears double pierced . . . well, I wasn't sharing.

Had my sister's behavior been strictly rebellious, intended only to shock my parents, I probably would have given the talks I was asked to have with her a bit more effort. But the truth was that with Efi, what you saw was what you got. She might not have a lot to say on a lot of subjects, but when she did speak, it was to the point. And all her marbles were firmly in place, despite all the holes she insisted on putting in her head.

But now . . .

Last Sunday, her short, spiked hair had been tinted with purple, and she'd worn enough metal to make the Terminator envious.

Now her hair was a solid shade of brown. Instead of spiking it up she had skipped the hurricane-strength gel and blown it dry so it was all soft and feathery. Aside from a simple pair of pink rhinestones at her lobes, she was metal free. And she wore a nice pink T-shirt, minus any offensive sayings (one of my favorites was "Practice Safe Sex: Go Screw Yourself"), and a stylish pair of jeans with low heels.

My mother slapped her hand to her heart. "Finally, my baby wakes up."

The look my sister gave her was pure, unadulterated Efi.

My mother took her by the shoulders and pushed her toward the door. "Go . . . go. Meet Constantinos."

Efi dug in her heels, although it seemed to take her a moment. Probably because she wasn't used to high heels. Her normal footwear consisted of black combat boots. "Who's Constantinos?" She gave an exasperated sigh. "Never mind. I don't want to know."

So, if my sister hadn't changed into Efi-the-Reformed for Constantinos, for whom had she altered her look?

I remembered one of the last times we talked about her love life. (We couldn't talk about mine because, well, we've established that I don't have a love life.) She had been e-mailing or instant messaging or chatting on-line or whatever you call it with a guy who'd had no idea what she looked like. She'd been contemplating sending him a picture of a pretty blonde instead of herself and I'd talked her out of it.

I took her by the arm. "What's going on?" I whispered, realizing that with this change she'd completely destroyed my chance to live vicariously through her. "This doesn't have anything to do with . . . oh, what's his name?"

"Jeremy," she supplied.

"Yes! Jeremy."

"Jeremy?" my mother said from across the room. "Who's this Jeremy?"

Efi rolled her eyes then grinned at me. An impish grin that managed to make her look even younger than her age. "He finally asked me out. We're going for pizza."

My sister going out for pizza.

I couldn't help smiling at her, she was so excited.

"Wish me luck," she said, checking a cute little pink XOXO knockoff and heading toward the back door.

"Good luck," I said, even as my mother descended on me to find out what I knew.

I hardly heard her as I stared at the empty air that had moments before held my sister but now only held the scent of some kind of fruity body spray instead. This wasn't good, was it? My sister changing herself in order to be what she thought some guy wanted?

Or was Efi evolving into who she was meant to be all along?

I scratched my head, wondering why life had to be so damn complicated all the time.

"Stick a sock in it, Ma," I said then turned around and smiled. "When do we eat?"

Thirteen

OKAY, MRS. PAPPAS WAS ON DRUGS.

I stood at the door to her apartment just after nine that night, ringing her bell with no response. The best I could figure is she got up so early in the morning, she must turn in just as early at night. And in order for her not to hear a doorbell even I could hear on the sidewalk from the second floor . . . well, she must be indulging in some serious sleep aids.

I sighed and rubbed the back of my neck.

After an awkward dinner with my parents and grandparents, I'd gone home to my apartment wishing I'd taken a doggie bag and been done with it. My mother kept giving my father what my sister and I referred to as "the Look"; my father either ignored her or appeared not to notice; and my grandfather kept taking cheap shots at my father. All of this in front of our guest Constantinos, who had been a nice enough guy but seemed to have been forgotten after seeing a transformed Efi leave for a date with Jeremy.

After a quick drive over to Woodhaven for another failed round of Find Fred, I'd fed and watered my own pet—although he'd barely touched his new dog food—and thought about taking him for a walk. I decided against it when he essentially gassed me out of the place. (How could he produce farts like that if he wasn't eating?) So instead I went for a walk by myself, then decided to stop by the dry cleaners to try to collect a couple more pieces of the puzzle I hoped would help me find Uncle Tolly.

I stepped back to glimpse the upstairs apartment windows. Dark.

The way I figured it, if Uncle Tolly had been laundering money for the DiPiazzas, well, then, the DiPiazzas or one of their legally owned subsidiaries would have to be part, half, or even full owners of the dry cleaners in order to collect the money. I mean, what was the point of laundering money, writing down that you charged fifteen dollars to clean a dress when you really charged ten, if you couldn't legally lay claim to that same "cleaned" money?

It probably wouldn't be a bad idea if I checked out the tax forms for the past couple years to compare numbers either.

"And if I see anything suspicious, I'll take it to the police," I said aloud.

Actually, if I'd had half a brain, I'd probably back off and leave the entire case to the police right now. But something kept me on it. Something I couldn't put my finger on propelled me forward.

I heard a sound far enough away to not concern me too much, but near and suspicious enough to catch my attention. While the butcher shop was on the right side, a small parking lot was on the left, with houses from there on up. I craned my neck to see that the lot was empty.

Another sound.

It appeared to be coming from the alley behind the cleaners. Yeesh.

I wasn't a big fan of enclosed dark places. There really wasn't any one reason for this, just a lot of small ones.

I eyed the Pappas apartment again, then looked at the Mercedes, not realizing I was looking for the car I'd left at home until I wanted my gun. I wasn't a big fan of guns either . . . until I needed one anyway. And at just after dusk in a dark alley, I figured my Glock and I could form a bond worthy of note.

I'll just go take a peek . . .

Sounded like famous last words to me. After all, curiosity had killed the cat. Nine times, if you believe in that stuff. And while I really didn't buy into it, I checked to make sure the Greek eye that had pretty much always been on my person in one way or another since the day I was born was firmly attached to my bracelet.

Now what, exactly, the eye was supposed to do to protect me, I don't know. Generally, it was supposed to ward off those complimenting you too much, bringing on bad luck, or those talking behind your back, which often resulted in physical illness. Feeling a bit under the weather with a headache or an upset stomach? Someone had given you the *mati*, or evil eye, is what the Greeks said.

Me, I figured either I'd eaten something bad or I was PMS-ing.

Anyway, in extreme cases, an exorcism of sorts was performed. No, not the Linda Blair type of Catholic possession exorcism, but if you thought you were cursed—given an extreme case of the evil eye—then you went to a Greek seer in order to have the curse or "eye" removed.

"Oh, shut up," I told myself, exasperated by my own nervous mental babbling.

I picked up my step, putting some backbone into my stride. I might not have my gun, but there was no reason for the other guy to know that. I bunched up my T-shirt near the back waist of my jeans and tucked my fingers there as if reaching for my firearm even as I flanked the side of the building and peeked around the corner.

Another sound so close I jumped.

Oh, yeah, good show, mate.

Porter sprung to mind and I quickly shook him away.

The alley was dark—as most alleys were—and I could barely see five feet ahead of me, much less to the source of the sound. But the good thing about darkness was that I couldn't be seen either.

I edged around the side of the building into the shadows, paying particular attention to the back door to the cleaners. Two shadows lurked there, but whether they were caused by humans or—

A shadow moved and my throat choked off air.

Okay, they were human.

And I was essentially stuck there in the shadows, unable to move for fear of being spotted.

Oh, for cripes sake. I wasn't going to sit there for Lord knew how long waiting for something to happen.

"Hey, what are you doing there?" I said in my best deep, manly sounding voice.

The shadows froze and seemed to stare at each other . . .

Then they bolted full out in my direction.

That was the thing about alleys. Sounds tended to bounce off neighboring walls so it was impossible to tell where they had come from.

As the shadows began to pass, I stuck my foot out and stopped one's progress. It fell flat onto the cracked cement in front of me while the other one kept on running.

"What the hell were you doing back there?" I said.

"Fuck off," the shadow said.

Only it wasn't really a shadow anymore. The words told me it was a kid. A teen to be more exact. I grabbed the back of his shirt and pulled him up until I was face to face with him.

"Vaggeli?" I asked, staring at a kid I knew.

"Jesus Christ, Sofie, you scared the shit out of me."

I wasn't about to admit that he'd done basically the same to me. I released his shirt.

"Yanni, come out. It's only Sofie."

The other shadow popped out a couple buildings up, out of breath and resting his hands against his knees.

I crossed my arms. "What in the hell were you doing in the back of Uncle Tolly's place?"

Vaggeli looked over his shoulder. "That was Uncle Tolly's?" He shrugged. "I didn't know it was his place. We saw somebody messing around back there and decided to go have a look. The guy took off, but we saw the lock was busted. Only there are more locks on the inside door."

"Uh-huh," I said. "Of course you wouldn't have anything to do with busting that lock, would you?"

He held his hands up. "Do you see any lock cutters around?

I told you we saw someone else messing around back there. Actually, he kind of looked like Uncle Tolly, now that I think about it."

The other kid came over. "He's telling you the truth, Sof." He squinted at me in the semi-darkness of the parking lot. "Hey, aren't you a PI now?"

I nodded. "Yeah."

Vaggeli snickered. "A PI who knocks back worm shakes like they made 'em at McDonald's."

"Hey, that shake was a far sight better than those boogers you used to suck back when I used to baby-sit you and your sister."

Yanni pointed at his friend and laughed.

"Shut up," Vaggeli told him.

"Actually, I think you both should probably get on home. Your mothers are probably wondering where you are."

"Not mine," Vaggeli said. "She's at the church getting ready for the bake sale this weekend."

"Mine, too."

"Then go home because I said so."

"What are you gonna do if we don't? Shoot us in the knee?" Vaggeli asked.

Cute. Real cute.

They seemed to consider my silence for a few moments, then their shoulders dropped in an "aw shucks" kind of way they never did when I used to look after them. Maybe the shooting-in-the-knee bit had gained me a bit of respect.

"Oh, come on, Sofie. We didn't mean any harm."

"Right." I pushed them both toward the street well away from the alley. "Sounds like famous last words to me."

Thankfully, my own brand of famous last words had netted

me a couple of teenagers with too much time on their hands instead of another bout with the Suit.

"Now go on before I call your mothers and tell them what you've been up to."

They shuffled a few feet, then as soon as they hit the sidewalk they took off in opposite directions, both of them heading for home.

I shook my head and backtracked to the alley and the cleaners. Vaggeli was right. The lock had been cut. But the inside door was locked tighter than a virgin's cedar chest.

Could it have been Uncle Tolly, as Vaggeli had suggested? Then again, Uncle Tolly would have keys.

So who else would be trying to gain access to a dry cleaners? Not a random burglar, certainly. Unless sniffing glue wasn't doing anything for some druggie anymore and he was looking for something else to shove up his nose. Namely cleaning solution.

Of course, I was purposely ignoring the DiPiazza connection to the cleaners. Mainly for self-preservation purposes. But so long as I didn't have to go inside again and risk another run-in with plastic-covered clothes, hey, I wasn't going to argue with myself.

On the walk home, I debated whether or not I should call in the lock break to the NYPD. But I really didn't want to take the chance that it would be Pimply Pino showing up on my doorstep. He took too much pleasure in torturing me, and I knew it was only a matter of time before he hauled me in on some sort of trumped up charge. You know, just to see me sweat it out a little while in a holding cell. I suppose it would be one way to pay me back for all the tricks I'd played on him when we were kids. But just the same, I would prefer things stay the way they were. Namely me as the bully, him as the victim instead of the other way around.

I took in a deep breath of the summer air. Ahead of me was Thirty-first Street. To my right was Broadway. To my left Ditmars. Even though it was a Tuesday, the neighborhood was alive with activity. Cars cranking out tunes cruised by. Corner cafes were packed with customers. Everywhere you smelled the scent of something cooking. I wasn't hungry, but you didn't have to be hungry to enjoy the smell of a good souvlaki cooking. Or a thick steak. Or . . . was that sweet bread?

I used to ride my bike up and down the streets like it was the safest thing to do. If I had a kid now, however, I probably wouldn't buy them a bike for fear that they'd be hit by a car jockeying for a parking space.

Kids. Huh. The closest thing I had and would have for the foreseeable future was Muffy the Mutt.

I let myself into my apartment building, hearing the sound of a sitcom coming from Etta Munson's place in 2A, music from the business school students in 2B. I paused outside Mrs. Nebitz's door but didn't hear anything. Sometimes her grandson Seth took her out. Or maybe something was going on at the Jewish Community Center. Either way, I was pretty sure she wasn't home.

I unlocked the door to my own apartment and stepped in . . . and immediately became aware of something wrong.

I halted my movements although the hall light probably silhouetted me like the sun. I reached out and switched on the light inside. Nothing was out of place. Everything was exactly where I'd left it, including the *boubouniera* wrappings from the Jordan almonds I'd eaten the night before.

Still, something wasn't quite right.

I sniffed. It was the scent of a man's expensive cologne. I stepped back into the hall. Nothing but the scent of stuffed cabbages, probably Mrs. Nebitz's. Into the apartment again. The unmistakable scent of cologne.

My heart beating a million miles a minute, I picked up that crystal vase I'd left near the door the other night, then exchanged it for another that had been a wedding gift from Thomas' cousin—a butt ugly one that matched nothing but made me feel good when I looked at it. Besides, there was the added advantage of its potential to leave a good-size dent in the back of an intruder's head.

I crept forward, craning my neck to see both into the kitchen and the dining room. Nothing.

It's then that it hit me: Muffy was nowhere in sight.

I glanced quickly behind me into the hall and back again. I'd left the window open as I always did. Was he having business problems again up on the roof? Then again, I couldn't remember leaving the window open so wide. After all, there was that whole air-conditioning-the-outside thing to think about.

I heard a whimper behind me and whipped around. I'd left the door open, you know, just in case I had to make a quick run for it. But the sound hadn't come from there. Rather, it seemed to come from the direction of the bathroom.

I crept slowly forward, despite the fact that my throwing the switch pretty much revealed I was home. The scent of cologne was stronger here. I whipped around the corner to my bedroom and flicked the switch there. Empty.

Same with the second bedroom.

I curved my fingers around the bathroom doorknob and took a deep breath.

There was no one in there.

Only Muffy, taped to the toilet with duct tape, a good amount of it swirled around his snout.

My heart pitched to my feet.

He was so pitiful sitting there looking at me with his big watery eyes. I put the vase on the sink and dropped to my knees, working at the tape until I'd freed him from the toilet.

"Oh, baby. What did they do to you?"

Through the narrow opening of his mouth his tongue dipped out and licked my chin.

I'd always wondered what Mrs. K had found so appealing about the little fur ball. Since he'd bitten me so many times, I had good reason not to like him then. But now . . .

Now my heart melted as I gently tried to remove the tape from his snout. A piece pulled a good chunk of fur from his skin and he whimpered.

I held him close. "I'm sorry, Muffster. I'm sorry. But we have to get this off you."

My mother had employed the "grin and bear it" brand of childrearing with us kids. Cut? Peroxide directly on the wound. A hard to remove Band-Aid? Hold tight while she ripped it off.

Only I didn't have the heart to employ the Thalia approach to medicine on the dog. (Why hadn't I noticed how small he was before?) Instead, I carried him into the kitchen and retrieved a pair of blunt edge scissors from a drawer. I eyed them, then eyed him. He stared at me, not a growl to be heard as his little tail wagged resolutely against the counter where I held him.

"Okay, boy. The sooner we do this, the better off both of us will be."

And I began slowly, methodically cutting the strips of tape, not stopping until every last piece was off his little body. His thanks came by way of a full-face bath. Wads of fur were missing from him, and he looked like he'd survived either a really bad fight or a bout with my grandmother and her knife. I wondered if I should give him a bath to remove whatever residue remained from the tape.

I held his head against my neck. "No. We don't like that one little bit, do we? Not one little bit."

His tail was going a million miles a minute and I couldn't seem to hold him close enough.

Then my front door slammed shut and both of us froze.

Fourteen

I HAD A NEW GOAL in life: to keep Pimply Pino as far away from my apartment as physically possible.

From experience and, okay, television, I thought most NYPD officers had partners. But not Pino. After two squad cars had responded to my break-in call, Pino was the one who—shocker!—remained after the others had left.

"So your dog was duct taped to the toilet," he said, using the end of a pencil to push open the bathroom door.

I was reasonably sure he couldn't see me, so I gave in to an eye roll.

The instant company arrived, Muffy had refused to be held anymore, even though I felt compelled to squeeze the little fur ball to my chest until . . . well, until my need to do so passed. His skin where he was missing tufts of fur was red and irritated; he looked like he'd been spattered with hot grease or something.

I idly wondered how long it would take for the fur to grow back.

"Yes," I finally answered Pino.

I looked up to find he had a clear view of my face in the bathroom mirror and had probably seen my eye roll.

Chalk up another point in the negative column. Yeesh. At the rate I was going, Pino would make it his full-time ambition to make my life a prolonged living hell.

"You say the apartment door was locked?"

I followed him back into the living room. "Yes. It took my usual three keys to gain entrance."

He noted this on his ever-present pad. "And the window?"

I glanced toward the item in question. "The window I leave open for Muffy."

"Muffy?"

"Mmm. He uses the roof for his business."

"Business?"

I stared at him.

"Oh." He scratched his head. "There's probably a law or something against that."

"I clean it up once a day." Or every two or three days. No one went up to the roof but Muffy and me anyway. And unless it rained, increasing the risk of clogging up the rain gutters with doggie poo, I figured we were okay.

"You really should walk him like normal people do."

Pino had stepped so that he stood in the doorway to the kitchen. Muffy's undisputed territory. The Jack Russell terrier's body tensed as he growled at Pino full out. Take anything you want, but don't go near his food.

Hey, I was with him on that one.

Of course, it would help if he actually ate the new food I'd gotten him.

"So, they probably gained access through the window."

"Probably," I agreed, resisting the urge to stare at my watch.

"And the only things missing . . ."

"Are Uncle Tolly's books."

It didn't take a rocket scientist to come up with a list of suspects interested in those books: Tony DiPiazza. But I wasn't about to say the name. And, so it appeared, neither was Pino.

I really wanted to give him credit for his astuteness. If only I wasn't afraid that the idea hadn't occurred to him.

One of Muffy's toxic clouds rose from the floor and enveloped us. I tried my best to hold my ground. Pino sniffed a couple times then gaped at me as if I'd just vomited on his shoes. I raised my brows, completely okay with him thinking I was the guilty party. And also willing to suffer through it if just to watch the horrified look on his face.

Muffy, however, couldn't seem to stand the smell of his own creation. He whimpered and ran to the window to jump out onto the fire escape.

Pino followed, of course, having no idea the mutt was the cause of the stench.

He stuck his head out the window and I heard Muffy's loud growl. It was all I could do not to pray the dog would bite him.

Pino looked up, then down.

"The lower ladder's still up."

"Mmm. I noticed that too," I said.

I'd pretty much figured out that they had gained access via the roof.

While it was my belief that New York roofs were the most

under-appreciated aspect of the city (the view from my roof was to-die-for gorgeous, what with the Manhattan skyline to the east and the East River between here and there), they were also dangerous. Most apartment buildings and houses were crowded together with little or no room between them, so the roofs created a path all the way to the end of the block. Gain access to one roof and you had access to all the buildings in the row, sometimes even the row behind, depending on whether there was an alley or yard space. And the original owner of my building must have gotten a deal on fire escapes because the steps of mine ran all the way to the roof.

Of course I hadn't considered that when I decided to leave the window open for Muffy.

A cousin of mine from Greece had barely slept during her visit a couple of years ago. She couldn't believe that most New York apartments didn't have bars or shutters like they did in Greece. She'd felt unsafe the entire time, and I didn't think she would be back again anytime soon.

My parents did have white wrought-iron bars over their ground-floor windows. They were designed to look stylish, but there was no mistaking their true purpose.

Pino pulled back in. I was standing closer than I realized and had to step back to keep him from bumping into me.

"I'd recommend you keep your windows closed and locked from here on out."

I sighed. "Come on, Pino. Open or not, if someone wants to gain access, they will."

"Yes, but broken glass has a way of getting people's attention."

"Not if they have one of those round magnetic glass-cutting things."

He stared at me.

Okay, so I'd browsed through some of my uncle Spyros' detective supply catalogs.

But if I closed my windows, that'd mean I'd actually have to walk Muffy.

I remembered the smell of cologne I'd detected earlier and decided the sacrifice would be worth it.

Besides, maybe not air-conditioning the outside would help keep my electric costs down.

"Fine," I said.

There was a loud, insistent knocking on my door. "Sofie? Sofie, you in there?"

Rosie.

I wasn't entirely sure why, but the second person I'd thought to call after NYPD was Rosie. If it had anything to do with seeing her with that green goop all over her face again, I wasn't talking.

I opened the door. Only Rosie wasn't wearing Coke cans as curlers or dripping avocado sauce from her face. She looked drop-dead gorgeous.

She barreled into the room. "Oh . . . my . . . God, I can't believe this happened. No, wait. Yes, I can. I told you this is what messing with the DiPiazzas would get you. First they break into your house, then torture you, then you're swimming with the fishes in the East River."

Pino's ears perked up after he got over the shock of the red number Rosie had on that very definitely showed off her breasts to "their utmost flattering degree."

"Where were you?" I asked her.

"At a club. Where else would I be?"

"Getting that much-needed beauty rest?"

She briefly stopped chewing her gum. "Why do you think I spend at least three nights a week doing that? So I have a reason to look beautiful." She batted her heavily made up eyes. "You okay?"

The question caught me off guard, simply because I'd been so busy since my apartment had been broken into that I hadn't had a chance to think about what it meant.

Someone had invaded my space.

Muffy jumped in through the window looking pleased with himself. I guess maybe he'd literally had the crap scared out of him. Nothing like being duct taped to the commode to get those ole bowels a-moving. He rushed around my legs then jumped on top of his favorite recliner and did his circle bit before lying down where he could watch the action.

"Yeah, I guess I'm okay," I said. "Thanks."

"Sofie? Is everything all right?" Mrs. Nebitz stuck her head through the open door.

Pino slid his pad into his belt and held his hand out. "Back away from the door, ma'am. This is a crime scene."

Mrs. Nebitz's body followed her head. She looked a blink away from swatting him with the umbrella she held.

I said, "It's all right. This is my neighbor Mrs. Nebitz."

A great-looking young man stepped up behind her. He was tall, blond, and cute enough to eat with a spoon.

"And this is my grandson Seth," Mrs. Nebitz said.

Time for their monthly trip into the city for a nice Jewish meal, I deducted.

"This is Rosie," I said. "And this here is Pino Karras, our local neighborhood police officer."

Pino looked none too happy to see people trampling over what he called a "crime scene."

"What happened?" Mrs. Nebitz asked. "I hope no one was hurt."

My gaze automatically went to Muffy, who looked much the worse for wear but seemed to be taking the ordeal in stride.

"I could have you all arrested," Pino said.

I stared at him. "Listen, Pino, I can tell you exactly who did this."

He pulled up his pants and everyone watching gave a sympathetic wince, including Mrs. Nebitz.

"Who?"

"A guy who wears expensive cologne and who's sporting a dog bite."

Muffy barked.

Considering all the scars I bore, and the fact that Muffy looked like a walking commercial for Rogaine, it stood to reason that he'd probably taken a pretty good chunk out of whoever had broken in.

"That's a big help," Pino said.

Rosie snapped her gum even as she openly eyed Mrs. Nebitz's grandson in much the same way he was eyeing her. "Oh, and he works for the DiPiazza crime family."

"That's a pretty serious charge there, young lady."

Pino probably had all of two years on Rosie. She poked her long-nailed finger into his chest. "Look, mister, I'm not anybody's young lady and I'm not stupid. If I say the DiPiazza family is behind this, then the DiPiazza family is behind this. You think I go around saying stuff like that unless I know what I'm talking about?"

I hid my smile behind my hand.

The radio transmitter pinned to Pino's shoulder issued a burst of static. He quickly moved to adjust the sound level.

"All officers in the vicinity of Ditmars and Shore, please

respond," a woman's voice said, naming some sort of code or another that I probably should have known but didn't.

Whatever it was, Pino's spine snapped straight and his attention appeared no longer on us. He produced a cell phone from a holder on his belt then turned his back as he spoke to someone. I leaned closer to try to make out the words of the other speaker so that when Pino whipped back around we nearly bumped noses.

He stared at me.

"What is it?" I asked as he hurried toward the door.

"Looks like our Uncle Tolly has washed up from the East River."

Fifteen

EVEN THE BREEZE BLOWING IN from the East River seemed to be hot, as if the current was a cauldron of churning lava instead of water fed from the bay and the Atlantic beyond. Everywhere red lights flashed, bathing everyone and everything in an eerie glow.

At first Pino had been reluctant to let me ride along with him, but since I'd planted myself in the passenger's seat of his squad car, he'd had little choice (although I did see a shadow in his eyes that said he wouldn't mind shoving me out).

Rosie had stayed behind at my place, along with Mrs. Nebitz's yummy grandson Seth, to "hold down the fort" as she put it and take care of Muffy, while Mrs. Nebitz herself had gone back to her place and probably rolled her china cabinet against the door.

It seemed the entire 114th Precinct had shown up for the event, along with a few cars from neighboring precincts judging

by the number of police cruisers on the scene. A few spectators
were gathered across the street nearer to Astoria Park, but for
the most part, neighbors watched from their windows. Despite
belief to the contrary, New Yorkers weren't used to violent
crime. Not even things like bodies washing up on the shores of
the East River. Astoria was as safe as it had ever been and crime
rates were low. In fact, the first time I'd ever seen a dead body
was at my Aunt Sotiria's funeral home.

At any rate, the locals probably figured they'd get a better
view on the eleven o'clock news later on.

"Maybe you can help identify the body," Pino had said, after
telling me to stay put near the street.

A long cement embankment and a railing separated the
rocky riverbank from the general public and next to that was a
wide sidewalk that runners and walkers used at all times of day.
Then there was Shore Boulevard and Astoria Park. Above me,
a train went over the Gothic-style Hellgate Bridge, named for
this stretch of the river whose strong currents and riptides had
clutched many unsuspecting ships in her lethal grasp.

Uncle Tolly was dead.

Of course the possibility had always existed but the news
made my stomach feel tight. I absently watched as Pino walked
down the sidewalk about a hundred feet where the jump over the
railing to the bank wasn't as steep as it was here. I gripped the
top rung and peered over the side. Rocks ranging in size from
grapefruits to my fist made up the shoreline. I remembered when
I was five or six and my mother used to bring my brother and me
to the park to run off some of our excess energy—usually after
gorging ourselves on Greek sweets. I'd heard what sounded like
wind chimes and asked my mother where they were.

"They're not chimes, Sofia. That's the sound of the tide rolling over the broken glass. That's why you can't go swimming in the river."

That and you'd probably come down with some awful flesh-eating disease.

In the light, you could see shards of different-colored glass that had been broken against the rocks. When the tide rolled in over the rocks and glass, the sound it made was similar to wind chimes.

I wrapped my arms around myself, cold even though I was sweating.

Uncle Tolly hadn't played a large role in my life, but he had been a colorful thread in the tapestry that was Astoria. A thread that would leave a noticeable hole now that it had been taken away.

A spotlight shined on the area where the body had reportedly been spotted by a jogger. I couldn't see much given the number of people down there—from police officers to paramedics and someone from the medical examiner's office—but it didn't take a whole lot of imagination to know what they were seeing. During my brief stint at my Aunt Sotiria's, I'd gotten used to seeing dead bodies. Well, at least that's what I thought. Until I'd had to identify another floater found in pretty much the same place on the riverbank two months ago. (He'd turned out to be some kind of hitman hired to knock off my client's wife.)

Little did I know at the time that it had been my client who had taken out the contract.

Finally, movement.

A big black body bag was hoisted on top of a gurney and that gurney was passed along until the team could get it over the guardrail. I started backing away.

"What's the matter, luv," a familiar voice said softly. "Came here for the show but leaving before the main event?"

Jake Porter was right behind me. The moment he spoke I felt his heat emanating from his body to mine. It was all I could do not to lean into him for support.

"Do you think it's Uncle Tolly?"

I felt his hand on my shoulder. "Hard telling. The city and her boroughs have a rough population of ten million, give or take. And seeing as Apostolis Pappas is the only one who's gone missing in the past week, and the guy they found matches his description, you figure the odds."

I squinted up at him, but his gaze was on the scene in front of us. "How do you know this stuff?"

He grinned. "Anyone tell you that you ask too many questions?"

His just being there warmed me in a way I was unprepared to battle. "Is that the same thing as saying I talk too much?"

I wasn't sure what it was we were experiencing in that one moment, but whatever it was, I liked it. A lot. I no longer felt alone, but a part of something. Something perhaps even bigger than me.

"Sofie?" Pino called out from a couple dozen feet away.

I swallowed as I broke my gaze with Porter. "Duty calls."

His fingers tightened against my skin then he released me. "Put something over your nose."

I nodded and walked toward the group of people blocking my view of the gurney.

Finally, I was standing over the body, the bag unzipped so I could see inside.

The river did strange things to corpses, I was coming to understand. The fast-moving water tugged and pulled. The undercurrent wore away at features until they were almost unidentifiable.

I took a deep breath and immediately regretted it as I coughed at the smell that filled my nose. "It's not him," I choked out.

"You sure?" Pino asked.

I nodded. "One hundred percent."

As they rolled the body toward the waiting van, I wanted to say I felt relieved. But as I stood there in the midst of the red flashing lights, a part of yet apart from the people moving around me, I realized that while that man wasn't Aglaia Pappas' husband, he probably was somebody else's husband. Father. Brother. Son. And the knowledge nearly overwhelmed me.

I looked over to where Porter had been standing moments before.

Unsurprisingly, he was gone.

But I was awfully glad he'd come.

I turned to walk back home.

THE NEXT DAY IT WAS all I could do to put one foot in front of the other. I guess bloated dead bodies had that effect on a person. But since I'd seen dead bodies before, I couldn't place the blame entirely on my visit to the river last night.

Perhaps it was everything combined that had me down in the dumps. The break-in. Finding Muffy duct taped to the toilet. Being afraid the floater was Uncle Tolly.

At any rate, some days I almost wished I had nothing more serious to worry about than spilled coffee and bad tippers.

Almost.

All morning, Rosie had also seemed preoccupied, although

she hadn't really said anything about last night. By the time I'd gotten home, she had left with Seth, who apparently had agreed to see her home safely. Mrs. Nebitz was apparently in bed, and Muffy had looked up at me from the Barcalounger then followed me into my bedroom where he crawled up onto the foot of my bed. Usually, he pretty much stayed out of my bedroom, aside from waking me in the morning so I could let him out to do his business. But considering all that had happened, I let him stay there. And was rewarded with a constant gas leak that nearly choked me.

Nerves. Probably it was nerves. I'd called the vet that morning to tell her that the toxic clouds hadn't stopped and all he'd been eating for two solid days was the dog food she'd recommended.

She'd told me to bring him in. So I had first thing that morning. Thankfully, it didn't appear that anything physical was to blame (although Dr. Monica Zell's eyes had nearly popped out of her head at the pitiful sight of Muffy in all his molted glory). So she'd given me some salve for the reddest bald spots and asked me to fill her in on some of his psychological history. And I did, telling her about Mrs. K and the kidnapping and how I inherited him. The vet had nodded throughout, then told me that dogs suffered from stress just the same as we humans did. But I drew the line at having her prescribe doggie Prozac. Aside from the gas thing, well, Muffy seemed to be fine. Maybe Dr. Zell was onto something when she said that he just missed Mrs. K.

Hell, I missed Mrs. K and I hadn't even liked her much.

At any rate, after dropping Muffy off at home, I spent the morning in Flushing parked outside Charles McCutcheon's house watching him watching, well, nothing as he knocked back a six-pack from his favorite lawn chair on his porch. In between bathroom runs—his—I jotted down the numbers I could remember from the ledgers taken from my apartment last night. I had a call in to Mrs. Pappas and she promised to have the tax returns and ownership papers ready for me to pick up this afternoon, you know, when foot traffic lightened up. (Seemed everyone wanted the scoop on Uncle Tolly—especially after the news of the floater—and she was getting double her usual business.)

And no, I'd told her, she couldn't sell the Mercedes yet.

I twisted my lips as I drew circle after circle around one of the dollar amounts on my legal pad. Then again . . .

I called Aglaia again.

"Mrs. Pappas, this is Sofie again."

"Sofie who?"

It was nice to be remembered. "Sofie Metropolis?" You know, the woman who's going to find your husband so you can sell his car?

"You find Tolly?"

"No, that's not why—"

"What you want then?"

If she'd shut up for a minute maybe I could tell her.

"What did you say to me?"

God, had I said the words aloud? I lightly shook my head. I needed to get a tighter grip. "Nothing, Mrs. Pappas. I was just wondering . . . you wouldn't happen to know where the papers to the car are, would you?"

"No," she answered. "That's all you want?"

"You realize you're going to need them in order to sell it, don't you?"

She didn't say anything.

"Mrs. Pappas?"

"I talk to you later."

She hung up.

I stared at my cell for a moment then looked at my watch. Pressing the button for the office, I got Rosie and found out that nothing much had been happening around the office in my absence.

"Where you going next?" Rosie wanted to know.

I sighed and stared at Charlie, who was popping open the tab on another beer. "I'm meeting my sister Efi for lunch."

"You coming by the office after? If so, can you pick me up one of those gyro thingies on your way?"

She said "gyro" with a *j* rather than the soft *y*—"yero"—it was supposed to be said with. Then again, half the Greeks had thrown up their hands and begun pronouncing it that way, too, so who was I to argue? Even if hearing it said that way always made me think of gyrating and old Elvis movies.

"Has my uncle called in?"

"Spyros? Uh-uh. I guess he's not back from his fishing trip yet."

My uncle. Doing his Old Man and the Sea bit.

I signed off, then started the car. Charlie didn't seem to notice me parked up the street, which meant I could probably drive by without fear of being recognized, but I backed up to the neighboring street anyway, heading in the direction of Broadway and my father's restaurant.

What I really wanted to ask my Uncle Spyros was what connection his silent partner Lenny Nash had to the DiPiazza family. Of course, I was half afraid he'd blast me for having taken on Uncle Tolly's case, but I figured if that was the price, I was willing to pay it.

I just didn't want to pay with anything else. Namely my life.

I finally found a parking spot some blocks up from my father's place and climbed out of the car, stretching the kinks from my neck and legs.

Yesterday, I'd called my sister and asked her to meet me for lunch at the Metropolitan. I figured it was a good excuse to stop by and feel her out, as well as to see if Dad was still being a little too friendly with the help. I wasn't sure what I was going to do if he was, but I did know it probably wouldn't be pretty.

As usual, my Grandpa Kosmos was sitting across the street outside his Cosmopolitan Café. Rather than trying to avoid him, I walked on that side of the street to say hello. He and his friend Takis were playing backgammon on a set he'd had specially made in Athens. It was rich mahogany with mother-of-pearl insets.

It also held its share of dents from where one or the other of the present players upset the board when they lost, toppling it and the *tavli*—discs—so they flew all over the sidewalk and street. I don't know how many discs my grandfather had bought to replace lost ones over the years.

"Sofie!" he exclaimed, getting to his feet and hugging me as we kissed each other's cheeks.

There was something about hearing my name said in that way that boosted my mood. *"Yiasou, Papou. Ti kanies?"* I asked how he was doing in Greek.

"Kala, kala." He told me he was fine then waggled a gnarled finger at me. "Good you stopped this time. You and I would have to have words if you avoided me again."

"I'd never avoid you," I lied. I readjusted my hold on my purse and said hello to Takis. "Anyway, how did you know I was coming?"

"Efi just stopped by on her way to that place across the street."

"That place across the street" was my father's restaurant. I was just glad my grandfather hadn't spit off to the side the way he sometimes did when he mentioned my father's restaurant.

"You know," I said, "you and I have never talked about looking for that missing medal case of yours again."

I really didn't need to be chasing it down, but the words needed to be said.

He waved me away, indicating with a nod of his head that maybe I shouldn't have said anything in present company.

"Medal? What medal?" Takis asked, as if on cue.

I smiled an apology toward my grandfather then kissed his cheek again. "I've gotta run, *Papou,* or else Efi might leave before I get there."

He chuckled. "Maybe you come by for coffee afterward?"

"Maybe," I told him, but I didn't think I would. I had an appointment with Mrs. Pappas after lunch.

I walked across the street and let myself into the restaurant. I paused a moment to allow my eyes to adjust to the darkness, and my skin to the air-conditioning. The place was packed, as was usually the case with lunch . . . and dinner for that matter. What with everyone seemingly on the eat-all-the-meat-you-can-shovel-into-your-mouth diet, the steak house was doing phenomenally well.

I spotted Efi sitting at the end of the bar where the staff and family usually gathered when they stopped in. I smacked her slender back as I sat down and she nearly choked on her Coke.

I noticed immediately that the purple was back in her hair—pink, actually—the rings were back in her person, and the saying on her T-shirt was as offensive as always. "Men are pigs and I love pork." I smiled.

"Good to see you back to your old self," I told her.

She scowled at me. Uh-oh. While Efi wasn't known for smiling much—she barely smiled at all, even when she was happy—a scowl wasn't her MO either.

"Uh-oh. Don't tell me," I said, accepting my usual frappé from Nick. "Things didn't go well with Jeremy the other night."

"I don't want to talk about it."

Normally when Efi didn't want to talk about something, she didn't, well, talk about it.

"Okay, spill."

She could have seared the foam off my frappé with her glare.

"Oh, no. You forget who you're talking to here, little sister. You can't just roll your eyes and stomp away from me like you do with Mom."

Efi appeared more agitated than I could ever remember seeing her. "It just didn't go well, all right? You happy?"

No, I wasn't happy. But that she would think I would be bothered me.

I reached out and touched her arm.

Beyond casual gestures, it wasn't often when I made contact with others. And it never ceased to surprise me how much a simple hand against an arm could change the dynamics of a conversation. In this case, some of the tension seemed to ease from Efi's shoulders and her dark eyes softened.

"Was it that bad?" I asked quietly.

"Yes." I watched her swallow hard, apparently having a hard time putting her thoughts into words. "I mean, in the beginning, it wasn't. We went out for this great pizza . . ."

Great pizza. That was good.

"Then everything just kind of slid downhill from there."

"You're going to have to be a little more specific. Define 'downhill'?"

She grimaced. "What do you want to know first? About how we ran into a group of his friends, some of whom I also happen to know, and how they teased me for . . . well, for going girly girl for Jeremy?"

I was pretty sure I cringed. Partly because I'd been a bit thrown by my sister's transformation myself. But mostly because I knew my sister didn't take kindly to teasing, and when she was younger the outcome had usually involved someone getting hit.

"Or do you want to hear about how I walked three miles alone at midnight?"

I considered her for a long moment. "I think I'm more interested in how you feel."

Her brows rose slightly. "I don't know. Stupid about covers it."

"I mean about Jeremy."

She didn't blink. "Stupid about covers it."

"Meaning you're no longer interested in him?"

"Meaning he's a shallow, kowtowing coward who wouldn't recognize his own conscience if it grew teeth and bit him in the butt."

I tried to keep from cracking a smile. "Ah."

I failed at suppressing the smile. To my surprise, Efi returned it.

"Sounds harsh, doesn't it?" she asked.

"Not if he deserves it."

She took a deep breath then blew it out. "Yeah, well, that's the problem, you know? I'm not sure if he does. Deserve it, I mean." She gestured with her hands. "I was so . . . I don't know, consumed with responding to the other guys that I . . ."

She trailed off. "That you didn't stop to consider how he might feel about what was happening?" I suggested.

She looked sheepish. "Yeah. I, um, just kind of told him that if those were the type of people he called friends, then they deserved each other."

"And you walked home."

"And I walked home."

The messes we Metropolis women got ourselves into. If life weren't difficult enough, we had to go creating additional problems.

"Have you talked to him since?" I asked.

"What do you think?"

"I think no."

"Duh."

She shifted on her stool, but this time I got the impression it wasn't because she was agitated with the circumstances, but bothered by something else.

"What?" I asked.

"He did call me that night. Left a message on my cell. Well, two, actually. The first he wanted to know where I was so he could pick me up. The second to find out if I'd made it home okay."

I decided that I might like Jeremy.

"But you didn't talk to him?"

Silence was my answer.

I sipped at my iced coffee. "Mmm. I think you should at least return his call. Thank him for his concern."

She didn't say anything and I could tell by the look on her pretty face that I'd lost her for a few moments while she let everything sink in.

I looked around for my father but couldn't make him out through the window in the kitchen.

"Have you seen Dad?" I asked.

Efi flicked a thumb over her shoulder.

I scanned the tables thinking he must be making the rounds with the customers, asking them if they were enjoying their meals, chatting them up. For a guy who normally didn't say two words at home, he was amazingly talkative to customers here.

I couldn't spot him. "Where?"

"Corner booth."

I raised my brows. Dad never sat down on the job.

I looked over at the booth Efi indicated. Dad was indeed sitting at the booth. And he wasn't alone. But instead of it being Magda a little close to his elbow, one of my mother's best friends was flush against him as they talked.

My father threw back his head and laughed in a way I hadn't seen him do in a long time.

Not since Magda anyway.

Oh . . . my . . . God. It appeared my father was nailing everything that moved . . .

Sixteen

"WHAT ARE YOU TALKING ABOUT?" Efi stared at me when I apparently said the words I'd been thinking aloud. I'm not all that clear on what I'd said, but the gist of it was that our father was knocking boots with others not our mother.

I blinked at my sister, not sure where to take this. Or if indeed I should take it anywhere at all.

I shook my head. "Nothing. I didn't say anything." I pretended an interest in the bar menu although I already knew everything on it. "At least nothing that makes any sense."

"You're right there." Efi looked over at our father, then back at me. "He's talking to Aunt Aliki."

He was doing more than talking with her. He was laughing with her. Sitting too close to her. All without the presence of our mother. Who was right this minute probably at home slaving away scrubbing the kitchen floor . . . or cooking his dinner . . . or ironing his shirts . . . or folding his underwear.

Efi looked at me and I looked quickly away. I called Nick over and gave him my order of steak sandwich and fries.

"Grilled chicken salad for me," Efi said.

I wanted to hit her. "What? Are you dieting? You're already skinny enough to see through when you stand in the light."

She rolled her eyes. "I happen to like chicken salad."

"Nobody likes chicken salad."

She stared at me.

"Okay, maybe you like chicken salad. But chicken salad to me is diet food."

Efi sipped on her Coke and pointed at me. "That's why one of these days your bad eating habits are going to catch up with you."

One of my mother's favorite stories had to do with a cousin of hers back in Greece who had been thin as a rail growing up. She ate whatever she wanted, whenever she wanted, and never gained an ounce.

Until she turned twenty-five, that is. The day after her twenty-fifth birthday (I'm sure that's not the way it went down, but it lent the story a certain umph), she ballooned to over two hundred pounds. To this day, she is still a virgin and a *yerotokori,* which literally means "old daughter" in Greek but is the equivalent of an old maid in English.

I was twenty-six.

I gulped down half my coffee, hoping the caffeine would burn a few extra calories. Maybe I would eat only half the sandwich and take the other half home to Muffy. Then again, Muffy couldn't eat it. Even Muffy was on a diet.

"Do you really think Dad is having an affair?" Efi asked.

She'd said the sentence as casually as if asking what else I liked on the menu. Absolutely no sense of the dramatic at all.

"Shh," I said, looking around, although it didn't appear anyone had heard her.

"Shush, what? It's stupid and I want to make you see what a stupid idea it is."

"It's not stupid. It's . . . possible."

"Look, Sofie." I toyed with my straw until Efi leaned closer. "I know these past few months have been hard on you. But just because your ex-idiot-fiancé didn't know the meaning of the word monogamy doesn't mean all men are getting a little on the side. Especially not Dad."

"Especially not Dad what?" my father asked, coming to stand behind us.

I nearly catapulted from my stool.

"Hey, Daddy," Efi said, kissing his cheek and returning his half hug.

I kissed and greeted him as well, staring at my sister over his shoulder. "Not a word," I mouthed, locking my lips with an imaginary key then tossing it away.

I smiled at my father. "I'd ask how's business but I can see it's good."

"Good? It's great. Have you both ordered?"

We said we had.

He glanced at his watch. "Good, good. I have a few things I need to do in the kitchen. Let me know if you need anything."

We both said we would.

"Insane," Efi whispered when he was out of earshot.

"Possible."

"No, you just have cheating men on the brain."

That one stung. "And Mom?"

Efi stared at me.

"That's right. Mom's the one who put the idea into my head in the first place. Asked me to look into it."

"And of course you agreed."

"No." I fidgeted on the stool. "I didn't want to touch it with a souvlaki skewer. But you know how Mom is."

"She can never talk me into doing something I don't want to do."

"That's because she doesn't need to. She has me."

Efi leaned back as our meals were delivered. I thanked Nick and asked for a refill of frappé. At this rate, I'd probably vibrate out the door.

"Is she going through 'the change'?" Efi asked.

"Is who going through what?"

"You know," she gestured with a forkful of lettuce. "Is Mom experiencing menopause?"

I nearly choked on my bite of sandwich. I hurried to chew and swallow then wiped sauce from the side of my mouth. "You know, I never thought to ask."

"Maybe you should. Because if there's one thing I'm sure of, it's that Dad would never be unfaithful to Mom."

I stared at her for long moments, really hoping she was right.

DURING MY HEATED DEBATE WITH my sister over lunch, I'd forgotten I was only going to eat half of my sandwich and gobbled the whole thing down, along with every last French fry. Hey, there were starving children in Africa, as Yiayia had been fond of saying when we were kids.

If only I didn't feel like the Austin Powers character Fat Bastard as I waddled from the restaurant and up three blocks, headed for my appointment with Mrs. Pappas. The walk wouldn't be nearly as much as I needed to feel normal again. In fact, a nice long nap in my nice cool apartment sounded perfect right about now.

Truth was, my overstuffing myself wasn't solely to blame for my irritation. While Efi and I had moved onto other topics—like who was screwing up at the restaurant, who might be fired, and who the new hires were—what she'd said to me about my seeing all men as lowdown cheaters really hit home.

Could she be right? Was my own personal experience, combined with the number of cheating spouse cases I handled, contributing to a sour view on relationships? To the point where I saw my own father in a different, unflattering light?

I rounded the corner and instantly slowed my step as Uncle Tolly's new Mercedes came into view. But it wasn't so much the car itself that caught my attention as the broken passenger's side window and the glass littering the sidewalk.

What now?

Mrs. Pappas came out of the store and began sweeping up the glass.

"What happened?" I asked.

She looked like she didn't recognize me for a moment then looked to the sky. "Funniest thing. A bird flew into it and broke it."

I raised my brows, looking at where a mallet lay against the door to the dry cleaners and the butcher stood shaking his head next door.

"A bird," I repeated dubiously.

"Yes, yes, one of those big ones. A hawk or something. Or maybe a pigeon. I don't know. I just saw it limping away."

"Limping away?"

"Yes. It barely could fly."

Coincidence that I had mentioned to Mrs. Pappas that she couldn't sell the car without the papers and not even an hour later a bird broke the window?

"Do you have the tax returns?" I asked.

"Yes. They're on the counter. Go and get them." She thrust the broom at me. "Better yet, you sweep, let me go and get them."

I stood leaning against the broom in the midday heat, not in any kind of shape to be sweeping. Then I heard a small *beep-beep* and a boy of about three or so ran his tricycle through the glass.

I swept.

Conveniently, Mrs. Pappas found the returns and the deed to the cleaners at the same time I finished scooping the glass into a garbage can.

"Here."

I accepted the papers and handed her back the broom. "Thanks."

I began walking away.

"Oh, and no. Even though you have the papers you cannot sell the car yet," I called over my shoulder.

I PUT IN AN APPEARANCE at the agency but circumstances conspired against my going over the items I'd picked up from Aglaia. I'd given Rosie her gyro, which left me in charge of the telephones. Of course, it only stood to reason that they would pick then to start ringing off the hook. Three more cheating spouse cases. (It had to be the heat.) Also, a visit from my brother's old classmate Debbie Matenopoulos, whom I'd given a job out of the goodness of my heart even though

Porter occasionally used her as a decoy (long story). She'd heard I'd given Pamela Coe a promotion of sorts and she wanted one too. I'd told her no out of the blackness of my heart. My cousin Pete popped in again, spent a couple hours in my uncle's office, apparently couldn't find the money he was looking for, and hit me up for a hundred.

And Pino dropped by to follow up on last night's break-in.

Rosie had long since finished her gyro, so she sat in the opposite side of the room, popping her gum, with her arms crossed under her generous chest, watching the police officer with barely concealed contempt.

Pino seemed to cringe at every pop of her gum. "Did you take an inventory? Did you find anything else missing?"

Probably Pino didn't have anything better to do with his time than harass me. Especially since I was pretty sure a uniform wouldn't be in charge of my case. Someone from the detective squad would be. "No. Just the ledgers."

I glanced toward the papers I'd gotten from Mrs. Pappas on my desk, wondering if I should lock them in Uncle Spyros' safe for the night.

"You talk to DiPiazza?" Rosie asked.

I gave her a warning look. Pino was hard enough to deal with on a normal day. I didn't want to see him actually irritated. He might run me in for having my place broken into.

I looked at him. "Well?" I couldn't resist asking.

"No."

Rosie threw her hands up in the air, causing her bracelets to jangle. "What the fuck is it with you guys?"

"Be careful with your words, miss."

"Or what?" Rosie's eyes bulged. "You gonna arrest me for

cussing?" She shook her head and re-crossed her arms. "That really bugs me. You let a burglar go, yet arrest me for cussing. That's why nobody likes the NYPD."

That wasn't entirely true. In the wake of 9/11 the FDNY and NYPD had become untouchable heroes. There wasn't a thing they could do wrong. But with the passage of time, the pedestals we'd put them up on began crumbling, until they were once again just average citizens like the rest of us, prone to the same weaknesses and susceptible to the same dangers that went along with power.

Targets for Rosie's frustration with this case and life in general.

Pino sniffed. "I didn't question DiPiazza because there wasn't enough evidence to suggest his involvement."

"You didn't even collect prints or nothing," Rosie said.

"That's because you and your friends contaminated the crime scene."

"No, that's because you're in DiPiazza's pocket along with everybody else."

I couldn't be sure, but I think my eyes were bulging as much as Rosie's were, but for an entirely different reason. I couldn't believe she was saying these things. What happened to the woman who was going to quit because I had Uncle Tolly's books in the office? The woman who was ready to crawl under her desk at a moment's notice to hide from possible gunfire? Was she really trying to provoke Pino and, by extension, the mob?

"Rosie? Can I handle this, please?" I calmly asked her.

She stared at me and I was half afraid she was going to blast me. Instead she sighed and threw up her hands again. "Go ahead. But I don't know how far it's going to get you."

"Thanks," I said.

I stopped shy of sharing a "what was that about?" look with Pino and waited for him to continue.

"Anyway, that's not why I stopped by."

Hmmm . . . my house was broken into, items stolen, my dog duct taped to the toilet, yet that's not the reason he was stopping by . . .

"Remember that floater they fished out of the river last night?"

"Oh my God," I heard Rosie whisper, then she crossed herself several times.

"The body that wasn't Uncle Tolly?" I made a point of saying.

"Yeah. That one."

I didn't think I'd be forgetting it anytime soon.

"Anyway, the medical examiner took a preliminary look at the body this morning and he came up with something strange."

"Yeah, he was dead," Rosie said.

I stared at her.

"Sorry," she muttered and continued popping her gum with her mouth closed.

"He found two puncture wounds on his person and it looked like the body's been drained of blood."

Rosie turned white as a ghost and I was pretty sure I was probably the same ashen shade.

"What does someone being bit on the neck have to do with me?" I asked, my hand going to my own neck.

"Who said he was bit on the neck? The puncture marks were on the inside of his arm." Rosie and I shared a glance. "Anyway, I heard you were doing some investigating of the Romanov house a couple months back."

Rosie went from rock still to a virtual whirling dervish. I glanced over to find her looking for her perfume bottles of holy water and garlic, rushing this way and that, as if her very life depended on what she did in the next five minutes.

"So?" I asked Pino.

"Do you . . . I mean, is there a possibility that they're . . ."

He couldn't seem to get the words out.

"Vampires?" I asked.

He snapped upright, hiked up his pants and nodded.

"There's no such thing as vampires," I said.

The only problem is it wasn't all that long ago that I'd jokingly said, "There's no such thing as the mob," and look where that had gotten me.

I had to wonder if there was anything else that could happen to me in such a short span of time, but I didn't want to tempt the gods . . .

Seventeen

THE MAFIA, VAMPIRES, AND SEXY Australians, oh my.

When I called it a day at around six and walked home from the agency, my head was spinning. I couldn't quite understand why things worked the way they did. Weeks, sometimes months could go by with nothing much happening. When it was all I could do not to bang my forehead against the steering wheel waiting for the money shot in a cheating spouse case.

Then there were times like these when everything seemed to happen at once. So much so that I could do little to control what was going on. I could merely hang on for the ride and hope I wouldn't end up on the losing end of whatever grand design was playing out before me.

Or wake up in the East River with fishes swimming around my head.

I let myself into my apartment building. A bike and toys littered the hall and first floor of steps, compliments of Lola.

(I swear, sometimes I was tempted to check the back of the nine-year-old's head for a 666 tattoo.) A broken toy was in the middle of the first flight of stairs. Probably one of the business school students had stepped on it. I picked up the pieces and, with no other place to put them, stuck them in my purse, thinking about asking the woman who cleaned the halls once a week to maybe come by every five days instead.

Even though the building had been a generous wedding gift from my parents, owning my own place had both its perks and its setbacks. One definite plus was that I'd never have to wonder where I was going to live. A minus was that I'm not particularly good about collecting the rent. An unexpected plus is that Mrs. Nebitz had taken it upon herself to start collecting it for me. And she fed me knishes. Both of which more than made up for the fact that because of New York's rent control laws, she'd lived in the apartment for over a century and paid little more than she had forty years ago.

I reached the hall outside my door and heard Mrs. Nebitz open hers.

"Hi, Mrs. Nebitz. How are you tonight?"

"Fine, fine. You?"

I wasn't fine once, much less twice, but told her I was anyway.

"I just wanted to give you these," she said, going back inside her apartment.

I expected a knish or noodle kugel or another yummy Jewish delicacy, other than gefilte fish, that is. Or that liver pâté stuff she made.

Instead she brought out what looked like an entire garden's worth of flowers.

I blinked.

"The nice delivery man rang my bell an hour ago when you didn't answer yours. I didn't think you'd mind if I accepted them for you."

Mind? The arrangement of roses and daisies and lilies was breathtaking. I took them from her before she dropped them and the large crystal vase they were in.

"Thank you, Mrs. Nebitz."

I took them inside my place and turned to close the door. She was still waiting in the hall.

"I was hoping you could tell me if they're from that nice Mr. Porter."

The thought hadn't occurred to me. Okay, maybe it had. If only because outside Porter I couldn't think of a single person who would want to send me flowers.

I searched around in the arrangement for the card, deciding that if there was anything naughty in it, I wouldn't read that part to Mrs. Nebitz.

"Sofie," I read. "Great seeing you again. We really need to do that pasta together."

It was unsigned and I turned the card over.

"Oh, that's nice," Mrs. Nebitz said.

Only my easy smile had turned into a tight one. Namely because it had dawned on me who'd sent the beautiful bouquet. And it wasn't Jake Porter.

"DIPIAZZA SENT YOU FLOWERS?" ROSIE asked when we met up outside Jennifer Lopez's cousin's house again a couple hours later.

I nodded.

"Not good."

I suppose I should be glad she didn't cross herself, but she might as well have because I was feeling the exact opposite of what a girl should be feeling when she received such a pretty gift. Rather than thinking of romantic pasta dinners with soft lighting and Chianti, I was seeing funerals.

Muffy barked at my heels as if agreeing with my thoughts.

Rosie planted her fist on her hip and tsked. "Why'd you bring him? He might . . . eat Fred or something."

Honestly, I hadn't had much choice in the matter. I still felt bad about his being taped to the commode and my general neglect of him lately. And it was still so damn hot, despite the time of day, that I didn't have the heart to leave his partially bald self in the car.

"Did you stop to think maybe he'll protect us?"

"From a ferret?"

"Hey, you're the one who said the rat bites."

She pointed a finger at Muffy. "So does he."

Muffy growled at her, his little body vibrating backward from the passion he put into it.

"Oh, would you two stop it already?" I sighed. "Come on. Let's get this ferret hunt out of the way and be done with it."

Rosie made a face. "Yeah. You might have a date or something."

"Yes, well, I don't see you doing cartwheels over your own love life."

Her dimples popped out as she smiled.

"What?" I asked, inexplicably irritated.

"Turns out I've met somebody."

Great. Rosie had met somebody. That must have been the reason she was in such a good mood today and the motivation behind challenging Pino, no matter the risk to her health.

Love, especially new love, had a way of making you feel all-powerful, as though you were immune to normal dangers. Kind of like when Super Mario ate one of those floating stars.

Only I wasn't in love and there were no stars hovering around me anywhere.

I heard a flapping sound.

Rosie and I ducked at the same time then stood staring at each other.

She hugged herself and I could swear her teeth were chattering. "Did you see that?"

Truth was, I hadn't seen anything. But I had heard it. "Probably it's a pigeon or something."

Not that a pigeon flying at night was any better than a possible vampire bat. The Greeks believed a pigeon flying at night meant someone close to you was going to die. Or perhaps even you personally were at risk.

Rosie fumbled for something inside her bag. I realized it was one of her blessed bottles of perfume.

Muffy made a curious sound and I rolled my eyes. "Oh, come on already."

We entered the yard via the squeaky gate, and suddenly everything seeming darker somehow. More sinister. I'd brought two flashlights and turned them on, handing one of them to Rosie along with a banana.

"I don't know," Rosie said, whispering. "I don't like this. I feel like something bad is going to happen."

"We're looking for a ferret, Rosie, not going on the hunt for Dracula himself."

She tsked. "Why'd you go and have to bring him up for?"

"Because that's what you were thinking."

"Was not."

"Was too."

"Was not."

I recognized the juvenile silliness of the exchange and stopped myself. "You go around the right side, I'll go around the left."

"I think we should stay together."

"Okay," I readily agreed.

Rosie had called Jennifer's aunt earlier and learned that Delores and Michaela would be out for the night, some sort of birthday party or other for one of Michaela's classmates. They wouldn't be back until late. That meant the house was empty. And dark.

And it meant if something were to happen to us, our bodies probably wouldn't be found until morning.

Rosie latched on to my arm. I walked carefully forward, my flashlight trained on the perimeter of the house while Rosie shined hers above us.

"Fred isn't going to be in the trees," I told her.

"Who said I was looking for Fred?"

I adjusted the aim of her flashlight so it covered the fence end of the yard.

Was it my imagination or was Muffy even on guard, his growling low and tentative as he moved as slowly as we did?

I gave myself an eye roll and peeled the banana as best I could while holding the flashlight.

"Here, Fred," I said, crouching slightly over so I could wave the piece of fruit.

Muffy smelled my hand and the fruit, then continued onward.

"I don't think we should be doing this now," Rosie said, and

I was now positive her teeth were chattering because I could hear them. "I think we should come back tomorrow or something. When the sun's out."

"The vet told me now is the time ferrets come out to play."

Actually, given the information Dr. Zell had given me about the glorified rat, I wondered why in the world anyone would think them good pets. They slept like twenty-two hours a day. And they smelled.

I glanced at Muffy, thinking the description fit him a little too snugly.

He barked and darted ahead of us.

"Where is he going?" Rosie asked.

"Maybe he's onto Fred's scent." I picked up my step, nearly causing Rosie to trip as she fought to keep up with me.

"Maybe the vampire is distracting him so he can swoop down and bite us."

"Shut up, Rosie."

Even as I said the words, I glanced toward the sky.

Muffy had disappeared behind a small shed. I swallowed hard and followed, even though Rosie had dug in her heels and finally released the steel grip she had on my arm.

"Uh-uh. I ain't going back there."

"Fine. I'll go myself."

"And leave me here alone? I don't think so."

Rosie followed on my heels.

I could hear Muffy sniffing up a storm. I shined the flashlight around the back of the shed only to have it flicker. I smacked it on the side and it went back to full beam.

"That ain't good."

I found Muffy and illuminated him. He was panting and looking back and forth between me and whatever it was he had found behind a trashcan. Huh. It looked like a nest of sorts put together with twigs and bits of newspaper. Just like Monica had described.

Only Fred was nowhere in sight. Of course. Now was the window of time when he actually left his nest.

Muffy barked and Rosie and I jumped.

"Hush," I told him.

There was a rattling sound from the garbage can. I looked at Rosie, but she was shining her flashlight everywhere but behind the shed.

"Do you think he's inside there?" I asked her.

"Who?"

Her teeth chattering had expanded so that she seemed to be shaking from head to foot.

I neared the garbage can, holding the flashlight up high. Hey, in case Fred was in there, I didn't want to be close enough for him to bite.

"Here, Fred," I whispered, dangling the banana from my other hand.

There was a loud screech and something much larger than the rat I'd seen the other night pounced from the can.

Rosie screamed, causing me to scream, then we both ran around the shed, down the side of the house, Muffy on our heels barking his head off, not stopping until the gate swung on its squeaky hinges.

"A cat," I said, resting my hands against my knees and trying to catch my breath.

Even as my mind registered what we'd seen, my body was still alive with adrenaline.

The sound of Rosie and me and Muffy panting was all that could be heard. Well, at least until Rosie giggled.

Without really wanting to, I giggled as well.

Until the two of us stood in the middle of the street laughing full out, Muffy barking along with us.

"That was a cat?" Rosie repeated. "That was an awfully big cat."

"Probably a Tom looking for something to eat."

"Maybe it ate Fred."

"Maybe." But I doubted it. From what I understood, cats and ferrets pretty much steered clear of each other. And dogs didn't have much use for the animal either. "At least we found the nest."

"Is that what that thing was? I thought the yard needed to be cleaned."

"We should probably have checked to see if it was warm."

Rosie stared at me.

"Then again, maybe not."

I chucked my banana over the side of the fence into the yard.

"What did you go and do that for?"

"I figure if we didn't find him, at least we should feed him."

"I think we should make him starve. Then he'd come to us."

She had a point, but one I couldn't bring myself to live with. Cruelty to animals wasn't in my blood, no matter what people thought I'd done to Muffy.

"Come on, let's go."

"I'm with you there."

We heard another flapping sound above us just as a pair of headlights caught us in their high beam, a familiar car peeling to a halt mere inches from us. As if to punctuate the happenings, my cell phone gave a shrill ring.

"Oh, God, it's DiPiazza's heavy," Rosie whispered to me, back to clutching my arm.

I looked at the phone display to find an unrecognized caller.

Muffy barked at the grill of the dark sedan, his furry body lifting about an inch off the ground with each bark until he fastened his teeth to the side of the license plate.

I stared at the phone, the car, then nudged Rosie until we were both moving sideways out of the road.

"Muffy, come here," I said quietly.

He made another valiant attempt at relieving the car of its plate, then came to stand next to me.

The car's tires squealed as it continued down the road at the same time the phone stopped ringing.

I had the icky feeling that I just been given a warning of sorts. That the next time, it would be me under those tires instead of asphalt.

"Not good," Rosie said.

I had to agree with her one hundred and ten percent . . .

Eighteen

THE FOLLOWING MORNING, I CLOSED myself in Uncle Spyros' office. The reason for this was two-fold. First, between the imagined vampire bats hovering overhead and the Rokko incident last night, Rosie was insufferable. If she wasn't dousing herself with holy water perfume, she was checking into life insurance policies, you know, in case next time Rokko's car didn't stop. (Of course, she'd also told me I was on my own across the board from here on in. She absolutely refused to be seen with me, and that included any Fred-hunting excursions.)

Second, I honestly didn't feel comfortable going through Uncle Tolly's tax returns and business papers in the open lobby where my desk and Rosie's were located, with God and everyone watching me.

So I'd taken over my uncle Spyros' office, closed the door and hoped my cousin Pete wouldn't happen by, maybe having remembered somewhere he hadn't looked for stashed cash.

It was strange somehow, being in here. I'd gotten used to my desk outside, the one with no privacy where the phones were ringing constantly, people were coming and going, and with Rosie supplying inexhaustible entertainment. In here . . . in here I could actually think. Oh, I still heard a lot of what was going on on the other side of the door; but I was no longer included in it.

I sipped my second frappé of the morning as I pored over the papers spread across the desk.

What caught my interest was that the numbers I remembered and jotted down from the stolen ledgers matched the numbers recorded on the tax return. That was fine. The problem lay in that the numbers on the tax returns weren't the numbers I was expecting. Right there in black and white, the smaller numbers in what I guessed were the real books were posted.

If Uncle Tolly had been laundering money for DiPiazza, wouldn't the larger numbers be listed?

Second, the business papers showed Apostolis and Aglaia Pappas as the sole owners. Nary a DiPiazza, a DiPiazza subsidiary, or a DiPiazza family friend to be found, either on the ownership papers, or any sham loans that needed to be paid back.

I scratched my head and sat back in the plush leather chair, putting my feet up on the desk for good measure. That didn't make any sense, did it? I mean DiPiazza's—and by extension Rokko's—interest in Uncle Tolly's case and me proved that there was a connection between them. If it wasn't the laundering of money—as indicated by that second set of books—then what was it? And was it enough for DiPiazza to have Uncle Tolly whacked?

Of course, I wasn't exactly a pro when it came to laundering money, so probably there was something I was missing. I drank my frappé and looked at the nice, framed licenses and diplomas on the wall behind me, then the bookshelves that lined the wall to my right. Uncle Spyros had a comfortable office. Unlike the outer lobby, which was in dire need of a paint job, new office furniture and equipment, he kept this room tidy and up to date. The latest model computer sat on the corner of the desk. The chair didn't squeak. And two nice Queen Anne–style visitors chairs sat facing the desk.

I put my coffee down and picked up the previous year's tax returns again, reaching for the telephone at the same time.

". . . and I'll be damned if that little son-of-a-brother's mother didn't latch onto that license plate and rip it clean off the friggin' car . . ." Rosie's voice came over the line.

I immediately pressed the button for an open line and dialed my father at his restaurant.

"Hi, Dad, it's Sofie."

"Sofia. How are you doing?"

I heard voices in the background, indicating the restaurant was gearing up for the lunch crowd.

"Fine, I'm fine." Well, mostly anyway. But I'd be infinitely better if I could erase thoughts of the possibility of his infidelity from my mind. "You?"

"Fine. Can you hold on a second?"

I began to say sure, but it was apparent he was no longer listening as he spoke to someone else.

"No, you can't make reservations for that night. Remember, the restaurant will be closed." Then he must have covered the receiver with his hand because the rest came through muffled in bits and pieces. ". . . the last one we want knowing . . . my wife . . . you'll be there . . . I need you."

I was pretty sure my mouth was hanging open. I was not hearing what I thought I was. The only day my father ever closed his restaurant was Sunday. And I don't think that's what he was talking about. His staff would know that, so there would be no question about making reservations on that night of the week.

Suddenly, I had a headache. Which could have been as a result of just sucking down the rest of my iced coffee in one long pull.

"You still there, Sofie?"

I hung up. On my own father.

I sat for a long moment staring at the phone, unable to believe I'd done what I had.

I immediately picked up the receiver and dialed again.

"What happened?" he asked.

"I'm sorry. We must have gotten cut off."

Cut off. Yeah, that was a good one. But thankfully, he appeared to buy it.

"So did you want something in particular?"

I shrugged, having completely forgotten why I had called in the first place.

Hearing your father set up a date for a rendezvous had that effect on a person.

Oh, yeah, the books.

"If someone was going to launder money through their business, how would they do it?"

"What?"

I repeated myself and waited for his answer, my mind still firmly stuck on what I'd overhead during the first go-round.

"You're not still working that Pappas case, are you?"

"Since Uncle Tolly hasn't popped up yet," I cringed, thinking of the floater from the other night, "yes, I am."

"Okay. But just be careful, you hear?"

"Careful is my middle name."

Actually, my middle name was something Greek and unpronounceable and seemed to rhyme with "trouble," but I was drifting off-topic, all because I wondered who my dad was closing his restaurant for in order to fool around with someone not my mother.

"Can you help me?" I asked.

"Sorry, sweetheart, but I don't have the faintest idea how you would go about laundering money. But Costas Gounaris might. He's in the restaurant now. If you want to stop by, I'm sure he wouldn't mind talking to you."

I was bending the corner of the top page on my notepad back and forth, wondering how hard it would be to find out which night my father intended to close the restaurant and how difficult it would be for me to catch him in the act.

"Huh? Oh. No, no, that's okay. I just thought you might know something."

There was a brief knock at the door, then Rosie opened it and stood with her hands on her hips.

"It's that rude cop for you on line one." She popped her gum for added emphasis.

Had she really just knocked?

"Look, Dad, I've got to go."

"See you later at the house?"

"Yeah. Maybe."

I hung up again and stared at Rosie. "Pino's on the phone?"

"Yeah." She gave me an eye roll and turned and closed the door again.

I might have enjoyed the moment of feeling like the boss. If only I wasn't pondering how I might stop my father from having the affair he apparently was already having.

I wrote a note to myself on an empty space on the pad. "Call and try to book reservations for every night at Met," it said. There. That was one way to find out which night he planned to close the restaurant for nefarious reasons. I'd keep calling, using different names, and when I got to the night I couldn't get reservations for . . . well, I'd cross that damn bridge when I got to it.

I picked up the phone again.

"And to what do I owe this displeasure?" I asked Pino.

A pause as he apparently digested my words, then a curt, "Aglaia Pappas has just been arrested."

I nearly launched myself right over the desk I got up so fast. "Get out of town."

"And she's insisting on talking to you."

"INSISTING ON TALKING TO YOU," essentially meant that Aglaia Pappas was shouting at the top of her lungs to see me, driving everyone at the 114th Precinct crazy until I got there, my Mustang sputtering and coughing all the way.

I stepped out of the one-story brick building on Astoria Boulevard and nearly bummed a cigarette from a cop smoking nearby. Oh, I didn't smoke. I had for a while when I was a teen. Until Alex Nyktas, my sweetheart throughout high school, told me kissing me was like licking an ashtray and I stopped cold turkey. No one wanted to taste like an ashtray. Especially when she was being licked.

"Out of here, you got to get me," Aglaia had said, her pale, stubby fingers gripping the fence of the holding cell, her eyes wide and wild.

I explained to her that I had a call in to the agency's bail-bondsman, Fedor Petenka, and that he was working in concert with the attorney the agency kept on retainer to spring her as soon as possible. (I'd used both connections to spring Grandpa Kosmos from the hoosegow a couple months ago after he'd broken Thomas-the-Toad's nose.)

I'd expected her to demand that I get her out now, right that moment. I know that's how I would have felt.

Instead, all she'd said was, "Okay. Then put a closed sign on the shop."

Getting anyone to give me any information on what evidence they'd arrested her on had been futile beyond one word: homicide. Pino aside, my activities since becoming a PI had earned me a bit of a rep around the precinct. While the head detective had been nice, I couldn't help thinking he wanted to pat me on the head and offer me a piece of candy—or worse, ask if I intended to shoot him in the knee if he didn't cooperate—instead of share anything of importance.

Not that I could have done anything with the info anyway. It was the principle of the thing.

The hazy midday sun glinted off something and I blinked to find Rokko's sedan across the street.

Damn. They were even following me to the police station now.

I squinted at him. Then again, was it possible he'd already been at the precinct? That it was Rokko—or more importantly DiPiazza—who was responsible for a little old lady being locked up for a crime she didn't commit?

Don't ask me how, but I was convinced Aglaia didn't off her husband because of an argument over who was going to get the last of the macaroni and cheese. (I'd read that had actually happened a few years ago and the story had stuck with me if only because it had been so ridiculous.) And it wasn't because I was convinced DiPiazza and his henchmen had done something to Uncle Tolly either.

I climbed into my car and turned the key in the ignition. Nothing. I stared at the dusty dash and the glove box that held my Glock and tried again. The same result.

I smacked my forehead against the steering wheel, immediately regretting the action when the old leather practically burned a stripe across my skin since it was sitting in the direct sun.

The last time Porter had tinkered around with Lucille, she'd run like a dream. Why was it this time I was having more problems with her than I'd ever had?

I tried starting her up a couple of more times, then got out of the car and popped the hood. I stood staring at what could have been an alien spaceship for all I understood about cars. I'd heard it said that the older ones were easier to figure out, what without all the computerization and fuel injections and the like. But it might as well have had directions stamped on it in Japanese for all I understood of it beyond the oil dipstick and the air filter.

I turned my attention toward my cell phone, thumbing through the numbers in my address book. When I came to Porter's entry, I hesitated.

Okay, I'll admit it. I'd called him once about a month ago when the weather had been hot and after I'd chugged down half of one of the champagne bottles left over from the wedding reception that never was. Only when he'd answered, I'd hung up.

Not smart, I'd realized even in my intoxicated state. I mean with caller ID he'd surely known it was me. And for a couple of days afterward, I sworn I'd seen his black pick-up following me.

But soon enough the pick-up had disappeared and I'd forgotten about it and went back to life as usual.

"Hey, he's the one to blame for the car," I said, pressing my thumb against the call button firmly.

To be honest, he was to blame for a whole lot more, but I wasn't going to go there now.

I listened to the line ring. It went over to a generic voice mail system that listed nothing but the number. I rubbed my forehead and thought of something to say.

"Hey." Oh, that was swift. "This is Sofie. My car conked out right in front of the 114th. I'm going to walk back to the agency, but if you could undo whatever it is you did to her when you get the chance . . . well, I'll think about talking to you again."

Yep, that was my car and me. First time around, Porter had made us hum like a couple of happy Sheilas. Now . . . well, now we were having trouble running at all.

I snapped the phone closed, got my purse from the front seat, then locked up the car with the gun still stashed in the glove box, readying myself for the hot walk back to the agency with a pit stop at the cleaners along the way.

Aglaia had been arrested for Uncle Tolly's murder . . . I tried wrapping my brain around that as I walked the few blocks to his place of business. Correct me if I'm wrong, but didn't you need to have a body before you could actually charge someone for killing it?

I hung a right on Steinway and headed south, the sidewalk

feeling like the largest frying pan in the world under my feet. I could swear the bottom of my K-Swiss were sticking to the cement. Add a little olive oil and there would be one medium-well Sofie Metropolis for whoever wanted it.

The problem lay in that no one seemed to want Sofie Metropolis, medium-well, medium, or even rare.

I made a face. I was so not the self-pitying type. Oh, I might bemoan the fact that I couldn't seem to tempt Porter into my bed, but I knew that all it would take was a spritz of hairspray, a swipe of mascara, and a tight skirt and I could have a man in bed that night.

Only I knew I'd wake up in the morning and not want him there anymore.

While Porter . . .

I caught myself scratching my arm and stopped. The heat was really starting to get to me on more levels than I could count. But while I couldn't do anything about the constant itch, I could do something about my body temperature. I eyed the restaurants and storefronts I passed, looking for something interesting that preferably served frappés.

I stopped cold in front of one I didn't recognize. Even better. A *zaharoplastio*—a Greek sweets shop—and my own personal mirage. Not only would they probably have my frappé, they would have sweets.

My stomach growled, reminding me I had yet to eat anything aside from a piece of melba toast that morning.

I pulled the door open and stepped into the blessed air-conditioning. Normally, I went to the two sweets shops—one on Broadway, the other on thirty-first—that I knew. But this one looked just as inviting. I salivated over the tortes in the display. Oh, yes.

"Sofie? Sofie, is that you?"

I tensed, really not up for any casual conversation just then. My client was in jail, my car was kaput, and I'd probably sweated every ounce of liquid in my body and smelled like it.

I looked up to stare into the grinning face of the guy on the other side of the counter. Someone who looked oddly familiar, but who I couldn't place.

"It's Dino," he said in a nicely accented voice. "You know, Constantinos? I had dinner at your house the other night."

I raised my brows. I'd definitely remember if I'd had dinner at my place with a great-looking guy. Especially given that itch I couldn't seem to reach no matter how much I scratched.

Then it dawned on me. "Oh! You're talking about my parents'." The guy my mother had tried to fix Efi up with. My nineteen-year-old sister who had run out the door for a date with another guy.

Dino gestured with his hands. "Welcome to my place."

I looked around, although I'd already taken a full inventory of the shop. "This is yours?"

He nodded. "Yes. Well, right now it's the bank's, but I hope to own it outright in five years."

A man with a plan. What wasn't there to like about that?

"Well, then, *kalo riziko*." I wished him good fortune.

There was a sitting area in the back that appeared to over-look a garden of sorts where he had those mist thingies set up around tables with umbrellas. There were a handful of people there, sipping iced coffees and smoking.

Hmmm . . . it wouldn't be a bad idea at all to have a guy who owned a bakery in the family.

A small voice told me I sounded an awful lot like Thalia, but I refused to listen to it. Dino was a nice-looking guy (Did I say nice? He was fantastic looking, with big dark eyes and a dimpled grin that was just a little lopsided), and anyone who could weather a dinner with my family and still want to see any of us again was okay in my book.

I smiled at him then set about ordering just about one of everything in the place. I justified myself by thinking that since he might become my brother-in-law, I was pitching in for a good cause.

Nineteen

AT FIVE I WAS AT the agency by myself. Rosie had taken off early to do some last-minute prep for her sister's baby shower the following day. I'd spent pretty much the entire afternoon following up on what Petenka and the lawyer were doing to spring Aglaia Pappas (who was bonded out a little while ago), eating the dreamy creations I'd picked up at the bakery, and trying to connect the dots between Uncle Tolly and DiPiazza even as his henchmen waited on the street outside.

Honestly, I didn't know what they hoped to accomplish. Was Rokko waiting for some kind of word to come down? Something from DiPiazza telling him what to do with me?

I crumpled up a note and threw it in the garbage bin under my desk. It was already pretty full with the packings from the bakery, so I had to push the rest of it down before I could fit the note in. I got chocolate frosting all over my hand for the effort because the items had been half melted by the time I stopped by the cleaners and made it back to the agency.

Ah, the cleaners. I'd asked Plato the butcher for help, and he'd given me one of his CLOSED signs and a marker with which to write "until further notice." I doubted there was anyone out there who hadn't heard that Aglaia had been arrested already—probably they would cover it on the eleven o'clock news. If not the eleven o'clock, then the morning papers would surely have something on it—but it made me feel better to know my note would stop anyone from continually coming back to get their clothes only to find the place still closed.

Of course, that was a short-term fix. What was going to happen to the place if Aglaia was indicted and forced to go to trial . . . well, that was just one more thing I didn't have time to think about right now.

That and the FOR SALE sign I'd seen in the back window of the Mercedes.

The phone rang and I picked it up.

"Metropolis Detective Agency," I said.

"It's about time you answered the phone," my mother said, sounding none too happy with me. My shoulders sank down a couple of inches and I closed me eyes. Not that I could blame her. I'd been ignoring her calls all day.

"Hi, Mom."

"Don't 'hi, Mom,' me. I've been going crazy over here wondering what you've come up with on your father."

I was crashing from my sugar high and considering I hadn't had anything else to eat but that piece of melba toast and sweets . . . well, I'd landed with a loud smack.

I propped my elbow on the desk and rubbed my forehead. "The reason I haven't called is I have nothing to report," I lied. Or semi-lied anyway. After all, I didn't have solid proof of anything, only suspicions. While I may have seen my father flirting with Magda, and saw him sitting too close to Aunt Aliki, and overheard him talking about meeting a mysterious someone at the restaurant on a night he planned to close it . . . well, I hadn't actually seen anything.

Yeah, and the police hadn't needed a body in order to arrest Aglaia either.

"You're lying. I can always tell when you're lying."

I sighed heavily, mostly because she was right. When I was sixteen and snuck out on a school night to go partying with my friends, I'd gotten back into the house at around two A.M. with no one the wiser. Until the next morning at breakfast, when my mom had asked how I'd slept. I blurted everything out to her and ended up grounded for a month.

I guess that's the reason why I'm so transparent when I lie. Because I hardly ever do it. I fingered the papers for Eugene Waters I had yet to serve. Well, except when it came to business. And, unfortunately, I didn't think I did a good job of it then either.

"I'm not lying, Mom." I wondered if there was any cold water left in the tiny, dilapidated fridge so I could make myself another frappé. "Look, I've got to go. A client just came in."

"It's a sin to lie."

"I'll call you later."

"A sin."

I hung up.

What was it with that woman?

She thinks her husband is cheating on her, a voice answered.

Yeah, but that husband is also my father.

The phone rang again. I snatched it up.

"Mom, I told you I'd call you later."

A pause then a voice very definitely not belonging to my mother said, "That's all right with me, luv. But I thought you might like your car now."

"Porter."

The one word seemed to purge all the polluted feelings from my body with one simple exhale.

"Where are you?"

"Turn around."

My chair squeaked as I swiveled it around to face the window and the street beyond. There Porter stood leaning against my Mustang, his booted legs crossed at the ankles as he took the cell phone from his ear and closed it.

While I hadn't exactly forgotten about my car breaking down outside the police precinct, I wasn't sure what would come from the message I'd left for Porter. Since I hadn't heard anything, I'd suspected nothing would come of it.

Now . . .

Well, now the sugar high I'd been on returned full force as I grabbed my purse, shut off the lights, then closed the agency down for the night.

Despite the late afternoon hour, the day was still hotter than hot. I could virtually feel my bangs growing limp as I stood staring at Porter. But I couldn't bring myself to care.

Damn, he looked good. Good enough to eat. Better than the sweets I'd picked up earlier and devoured.

He gave me one of his naughty grins and I accepted it, giving him one of my own in return.

"If I didn't know better, I'd think you purposely did something to my car so she wouldn't run."

"Oh?" He tipped the leather cowboy hat he wore back a bit.

We New Yorkers don't get to see many cowboy hats on men on which they belonged. Especially not leather ones attached to really sexy Australians.

"Mmm. You see, I get the feeling you really don't want me to work this Uncle Tolly case, and I figured you fixed it so I couldn't do much without my car and all."

He merely grinned.

I cleared my throat, noticing he'd also washed Lucille. She looked good. Well, in between patches of bondo.

"So what was the matter with her?"

"Nothing."

I squinted at him. "She wouldn't start."

"I suspect you may have flooded her."

"I didn't have a chance to flood her. When I turned the key, she did nothing." I cocked my head. "By the way, how did you get into her without a key?"

He ran his hand down her side. I found myself watching the movement, my throat going dry as I imagined that same hand touching me that way. "Lucille here's just being a bit temperamental, is my guess."

"Cars aren't human. They're not allowed to be temperamental."

He stepped forward as if to keep the Mustang from hearing us. "I'd be careful if I were you."

"Oh?" I crossed my arms, the subtle scent of limes drifting over me. Mmm . . .

"She might just up and quit on you altogether."

Now that was something I wasn't going to chance. Given that my only paying client had just been thrown in jail, and I couldn't even seem to serve stupid court papers, my value to the agency had plummeted somewhat in the past week.

Which means I'd probably have to start taking on more of those cheating spouse cases.

"Actually, I think the biggest problem is that she just needs to be run a bit."

"Run?"

"Uh-huh." Porter's eyes shifted as he took me in from head to foot, making no move to hide his slow perusal. "Get in."

LUCILLE'S ENGINE GROWLED HAPPILY AS I fed her a little extra gas in order to pass a SUV on the Cross Island Parkway. It had been an hour since Porter had handed me into the car and directed me to get on the highway, destination unknown. The top was down. The warm air whipped my hair around my face. And I wore a silly grin that would track all sorts of dead insects if not for the windshield, not caring that Porter appeared amused with me and my reaction to being in control of my car.

In control of my life.

I'd taken Lucille out for rides before. But not for any this long for pleasure. Maybe Porter was right. Maybe she needed more than the short drives I'd been giving her. The more I pressed on the accelerator, the more she seemed to want, the engine vibrating under me like a hungry beast long overdue for a good, solid meal.

I'd bought the car for looks (or at least my idea of how I thought she could look).

I was now enjoying her for her power.

I followed the highways up the Long Island Sound past Whitestone and edged halfway around Little Neck Bay. The view from the island was different here. More open. Manhattan's skyline well behind me to the west, the sinking sun nearly blinding me in the rearview mirror. I'd perched my shades on my nose and gripped the steering wheel with joy.

Given Lucille's greedy growl and the wind, conversation was all but impossible. Of course, the fact that I had the radio tuned into WSOU and had the volume up nearly as far as it could go didn't lend to conversation either. Heart's "Straight On" came on and I pressed the accelerator down even farther, resisting the urge to sing along with the song, no matter how much it seemed to parallel my undefined relationship with Porter. Or in so much as my speed-fed adrenaline rush led me to believe, anyway.

I spotted an exit I was familiar with, switched on my blinker, then exited the highway, following the signs for public beach access to Little Neck Bay. Five minutes later, I parked in the deserted back section of a parking lot on a bit of a knoll. I switched off the engine, turned down the radio, then looked at Porter. He squinted against the sun setting over the bay.

"Never been here," he said.

My body still felt like it was vibrating from the power of the engine. Or was it Jake's presence that was affecting me that way? Whatever the cause, I felt invigorated and very much alive. And focused like a laser beam on the man next to me.

"Do you realize I don't even know where you live?" I asked quietly, taking in the slight wrinkles at the corners of his blue, blue eyes, the tanned roughness of his skin. "I don't even know how old you are."

And how old was he? Thirty? Thirty-five? I couldn't be sure.

He looked at me. "Does it matter where I live? Or how old I am?"

I pushed from the seat and climbed into the back of the car and sat on the top that was flush with the trunk, my feet on the seat below. "I don't know. Sometimes I think it does. At others, no."

I took a deep breath, noticing it was cooler here. Not much, but enough to notice. Around us, people were packing up their things and leaving the beach. Pretty girls in bikinis. Buff guys whose teeth flashed white against their dark faces. Families with picnic baskets. Somehow I'd forgotten it was still summer, a time for barbeques and family outings and moonlit strolls along the beach. Actually, for the past five months I'd forgotten a lot about the little details of life, period. It could have been winter, spring, it didn't make a difference. I had been so focused on my job and on making it through one day, then the next, and then the day after that, that I'd forgotten somewhere along the line to stop living that way and to resume, well, just living.

Porter joined me in the back of the car. We both sat staring quietly at the sparkling waters of the bay.

"Where are you from in Australia?" I asked.

"Just about all over."

I looked at him. I'd grown up knowing nearly everything there was to know about the people in my life. Where they came from. Who they were related to. Which neighborhood they lived in. Yet this one man was such a mystery. Though I hadn't asked him many questions about himself, those I had always got a vague, uncommitted answer.

"Family?"

He looked back at me, no sign of a grin about to break out. "How do you mean?"

"Parents? Siblings?"

Even as I said the words, it occurred to me that he might have thought I'd been asking about a wife, even kids. His follow-up question told me that perhaps he'd had a wife at some point, although I was pretty sure he didn't now. In fact, a couple months ago he'd told me he wasn't married. But that didn't mean that he had never been. At any rate, a guy like Jake struck me as being loyal to the bone. If he were married, he would never have kissed me.

And he certainly wouldn't be sitting in the back of my Mustang with me watching the sun set.

"All back in Australia," he said.

"So your parents are alive, then."

He gave a brief nod.

He'd taken his hat off at the beginning of our trip and his longish, dark blond hair was feathery in some places, damp and clinging to his head in others. I reached out and fingered the coarse strands.

"How many brothers? Sisters?"

He caught my hand in his grasp. "You always ask so many questions?"

I blinked to look into his eyes. Was that humor or a warning I saw in their seductive depths? A little of both, maybe.

"Always," I whispered.

I didn't know why I was so low on breath until Porter leaned in and kissed me.

Sweet. That's the first word that came to mind. His mouth on mine was gentle and considerate and sweet. I stared at him from under my lashes, thinking he was even sexier close up. There was a magnetism about this guy. Something undeniable that made my toes curl in my K-Swiss.

Curiously, that itch I'd been experiencing lately melted into a warm glow. Maybe it was the magic of the setting sun. Perhaps it was the light breeze off the bay. Probably it was because finally kissing Porter with both of us clearly wanting the kiss was like exhaling a breath I'd been holding for far too long.

I leisurely pushed my tongue past his lips. He tasted like toothpaste and tobacco, though he'd never smoked around me. My actions must have triggered something within him because he groaned and curved his hand under my hair and against the back of my neck, pulling me closer.

And suddenly I was filled with a heart pounding urgency for more, much more, than just his kiss.

My cell phone vibrated in my jeans pocket.

I ignored it. I didn't want anything interrupting this moment.

I scooted closer to Jake, running my hands over his shoulders and biceps then around to his back, not happy until I felt his rock hard chest pressed against my soft one through our T-shirts.

I hadn't felt this way since I was a teenager on my first beach outing with a guy. The anticipation. The fear of the unknown. The rush of desire and complete and utter lack of control.

My cell phone began vibrating again.

I groaned this time. Probably it was my mother. And I didn't want to talk to her right now. I didn't want to talk, period. I merely wanted to feel.

"Sof?"

I blinked my eyes open. Jake was still kissing me, but he was also talking. "What?"

"I think we'd better stop now."

I closed my eyes again and molded myself against him. "Why?"

"Because if we don't, I'm afraid I won't be able to."

His admission sent bliss spiraling through me.

He wanted me.

Up until now, I hadn't been entirely sure. Oh, we'd kissed before. But every time things got hot and heavy, he pushed me away. I'd thought it was because he'd had a change of heart mid-motion. I'd wondered if maybe what I thought existed between us in spades wasn't enough for him.

His fingers found the back waist of my jeans and dipped inside.

Oh, how very wrong I'd been.

My cell began vibrating. Then began again. And again.

Jake's fingers found the edge of my panties and tunneled under the slick silk. I shifted to give him easier access, my skin where he touched me on fire.

His movements ceased.

"What's that?" he asked.

I realized he must have felt my cell phone vibrating. I remembered my wet dream about him the other night, and the growling that had woken me up, and wondered if there was ever going to come a time when he and I would finally get this thing together on either plane.

Damn it.

I pulled away and fished the phone out of my pocket.

The display read "Rosie."

Probably it was about that stupid ferret.

Probably I should answer it because it might not be about that stupid ferret.

"What?" I practically shouted into the phone.

"Geez, bite a person's head off, why doncha?" came her lightning-fast response. "Pamela Coe's been trying to call you for fifteen minutes." A pause. "Where in the hell are you?"

"A long way away from home."

"Yeah, well, you better get your skinny butt back here cause Pamela had some kind of family emergency and that leaves you in charge of tailing Johnson."

A cheating spouse case.

I was pretty sure I cringed.

"It can wait until tomorrow."

"Uh-uh. Pamela says she overheard the target talking about a meeting tonight at ten. That means the money shot."

The money shot was the incriminating photograph taken of a cheating spouse meeting with his or her lover.

"You do it, then."

"What, do I look stupid to you or somethin'?"

There she went again, calling me stupid.

I glanced over to find Porter watching me.

I made a face. "Come on, Rosie. All you have to do is get one of those disposable cameras and snap a few pics. What's so hard about that?"

"Oh, I don't know. Maybe that I'll have to see disgusting things in order to do that? Uh-uh. I told Spyros when I hired on that I don't do disgusting."

"Sex is not disgusting."

Porter hiked a brow at me, his expression no less than powerfully suggestive.

"I don't mean when you have it yourself," Rosie said and I imagined her doing an eye roll. "It's watching other people do it—live—that gives me the creeps."

"It's not like you're going to be there for hours."

"I don't even like hearing people on the other side of hotel room walls. Uh-uh. You're going to have to do it."

Yes, I realized, that's what it was looking like I was going to have to do.

But it didn't mean I had to be happy about it.

Porter had climbed back into the front passenger's seat and had put his hat on. I put the cell into my pocket, then climbed into the driver's seat, reluctant to start the car.

"Problems?" Porter asked, staring out at the bay.

"Yeah. I got a cheating spouse to tail."

"Why don't you send Debbie to do it?"

Debbie would be, of course, Debbie Matenopoulos, Porter's sometime decoy.

I stared at Porter, not sure what bothered me more: that he was in contact with Debbie, or that he was suggesting her for a job.

"I can handle it," I said.

It wasn't until the words were out of my mouth that I realized that I'd just let a spurt of jealousy get between me and possibly the best sex of my life.

Twenty

I SAT IN MY CAR by myself outside the motel on Northern Boulevard sulking. I'd started my bout of self-punishment with repeatedly hitting my forehead against the steering wheel, beginning the minute Porter climbed out of the car back at the agency and continuing until my skin felt bruised, I started getting strange looks from others, and I was pretty sure the wheel felt a little loose from my abuse.

It was just like me to screw up what could have been a very good night because Porter had brought up Debbie Matenopoulos. What made it doubly bad was that Porter seemed to know exactly why I'd refused to send the other woman on the job. And when I'd leaned over to kiss him good-bye, to ask him if he maybe wanted to come to my place later, he'd kissed my forehead instead.

My forehead.

I rubbed at the spot in question, then stared at the red mark I'd made in the rearview mirror.

"Shit."

I sat back in the bucket seat and sighed. What time had Rosie said this rendezvous was supposed to go down? Ten, I thought. I stared at the clock on my cell. It was five till.

I reached for my camera on the floor behind my seat and adjusted the zoom. I really should have Uncle Spyros reimburse me for the cost of replacing the camera I'd borrowed—more like stolen—from my brother. Rosie had said there used to be a camera at the agency, but I half suspected my cousin Pete had hocked it at Antypas' pawnshop for some quick cash.

My uncle really needed to get a handle on that kid.

Then again, in order to do that, my uncle would actually have to be in town.

I adjusted the settings of the camera, fiddled with the focus so that the parking lot was in clear view, then put it down in my lap.

My target tonight was one Mr. Don Johnson, uncommitted husband of one Julie Johnson. I'd picked up the file at the agency. Not a bad-looking guy, really. For a pig, that is. If you had to worry about what a guy named Johnson was doing with his, well, Johnson, you knew you had a problem. I noted that he drove a black Chevy SUV and memorized the first three numbers of the license plate.

And there it was now.

I lifted the camera and snapped off shots of the vehicle in question pulling into the motel parking lot. Plate, back end of it parking. And of Johnson getting out.

Once, just once, I'd like to go out on one of these money shot runs and not actually find any damaging evidence.

Another car pulled into the parking lot. I squinted through

the zoom lens, not snapping any shots until it pulled up next to the SUV.

And none other than my own personal favorite serial cheater Lisa Laturno got out.

I dropped the camera to my lap again. Jesus, did the woman have an ounce of self-respect?

She seemed to spot me across the highway at the same time I spotted her. She waved, then kissed the husband that wasn't hers. I snapped the needed picture, honked twice, then was on my way.

And that's when it struck me. Instead of offering services to catch suspected cheating spouses in the act, why not bait them into acts of unfaithfulness? I mean, if the spouse already suspected that their husband or wife was doing the tube-snake boogie with someone else, it was a pretty good bet they'd be open to other offers.

Debbie Matenopoulos came to mind for the cheating husbands, which easily comprised seventy-five percent of the cases.

And the cheating wives?

The cheating wives we would probably have to tail for now. Unless I could talk my cousin Pete into finally working.

I made a mental note to follow up on the idea with Rosie and my uncle Spyros.

Bait . . .

The word caught and held in my mind even as I drove back toward Astoria.

I picked up my phone and called Rosie. Only she didn't pick up. Probably she knew it was me and thought I was going to try to get her to do something disgusting again.

While what I had in mind wasn't exactly sex with Porter, it

wasn't disgusting either. And hopefully it would be successful in finally finding Fred . . .

"IT'S TOO LATE."

I stared at Delores Lopez even as I wheeled Michaela out to the front porch.

"I can do it," the girl complained, putting her hands on the wheels to stop my progress.

I let go of the chair and she positioned herself so she was off to the side of the porch, likely where she usually sat when she went outside. Which given her over-protective mother probably wasn't often lately what with the heat wave and all.

Not that I could say I blamed Delores. I mean that metal probably got mighty warm in the direct sunlight.

"Here," I said, handing her one of the bananas I'd picked up from a fruit stand on Ditmars on my way over.

"No, it's not for you, honey," Delores said when Michaela took a bite of the peeled fruit.

The girl glared at her mother.

"Okay, this is where you and me act scarce," I said to Delores.

The pretty Latina crossed her arms and stood her ground. "I'm not leaving my daughter out here by herself."

"Mom, he won't come with you here," Michaela complained.

"She's probably right," I said. "Anyway, he probably won't come with me anywhere within touching distance either. Come on. We'll be right inside. You don't even have to close the door."

Delores reluctantly allowed herself to be led inside after she scoured the street with her gaze. Thankfully, Rokko was nowhere to be seen. And hadn't been ever since Porter had appeared outside the agency in Lucille.

"No, don't stand where he can see you," I said.

"The damn thing's been living in my house for over a year. He knows me."

I tugged her off to the side where we could look through a window. "Yeah, and he probably knows what kind of mood you're in too. He'll get one look at you and run flat out in the opposite direction."

"Yeah, well, he'd be smart. After hurting my baby like that by running away, I want to fry him up for dinner."

We looked at each other then both shook our heads in unison.

Fried ferret didn't sound particularly appetizing. Which was a good thing for them. Else they might be Thursday night dinner instead of a crippled girl's pet.

Minutes ticked by like hours as we stood inside the window watching Michaela. As I'd requested, she quietly called out to Fred, but not in a persistent, panicky, or impatient way. She merely called him then pretended an interest in the banana she was eating.

"This isn't going to work," Delores said.

I shushed her.

But after another twenty minutes, and with the clock edging toward eleven, I was beginning to agree with her. My plan to find Fred hadn't been such a good one anyway.

"It's pitch black out. I'm going to bring her inside."

Delores started for the door and I began to follow until I caught movement out of the corner of my eye.

"Wait," I whispered, grabbing her arm.

"What, what, what?" she whispered back, joining me back at the window.

We both watched as none other than Fred climbed up onto

the porch close to Michaela and made an inquisitive squeaky sound.

"Fred!" Michaela said, so obviously relieved I suddenly couldn't pull in a breath.

"Here, Fred. Do you want some banana? It's your favorite."

Take the banana, Fred, I silently ordered him.

Fred climbed on top of the back of a wicker chair and washed his face a couple of times with his paws.

"Take the friggin' banana," Delores said quietly from where she stood, next to me.

The ferret's head swiveled in our direction where we stood in the window.

I pulled Delores quickly back, hoping the curtains didn't move. Then I craned my neck to see if he was still looking.

"What's he doing now?" Delores asked.

But I couldn't respond. Namely because Fred had climbed up into Michaela's lap and was taking a piece of banana out of the little girl's mouth then putting it into his own.

"Oh, Fred," Michaela said, encircling the long-bodied animal in her hands and kissing the side of his neck. "I've been so worried about you."

"What's happening?" Delores demanded again.

I nodded toward the window.

She moved to it and I watched as her eyes flooded with tears. Which I'm pretty sure was what my own were doing just then.

"Come on, let's go inside," Michaela said.

And just like that she wheeled herself and Fred inside the house and closed the door.

Chalk up one Fred the Ferret found.

———

AS MUCH AS I BITCHED and complained about the pet-detecting component of my job, I also understood that it was the part that brought me the most pleasure.

I stared at Muffy, who licked his butt on the Barcalounger nearby.

Okay, *sometimes* the job brought me pleasure.

At least I hadn't had to bring Fred home with me.

Then again, the smelly glorified rat might be preferable to the smelly dog right now.

Three days into the new diet program and Muffy's farts were worse than ever. It was all I could do not to buy an oxygen tank and mask for when I had to be home. Or lock him outside on the fire escape. I'd have to call the vet in the morning to find out what the next step was in deodorizing Muffy. As it was, I'd been forced to shut off the air-conditioning and open all the windows instead, using the two portable fans to blow the hot air around.

I sat cross-legged on my sofa in a T-shirt and undies, going through the photos I'd taken earlier and had printed at a one-hour shop. The prints were eight by tens, and there in all his en-larged glory was the client's husband kissing Lisa Laturno like a man who'd been there before and would probably go there again.

I tossed the shots to the coffee table and picked up a bowl of Ben and Jerry's Karamel Sutra. The ice cream wasn't a treat for being good. It was a salve for being bad. I'd stopped and picked up a souvlaki on the way back to the apartment, grate-ful the corner stand didn't offer up French fries or else I'd have gotten an extra large order of those as well. But it was late and hot and the sliced onions and garlic sauce were burning a hole in my stomach. The dairy product helped sooth the feeling.

It also helped me forget that I could be having sex right now instead of ice cream.

I stared at Muffy, wondering if I should try giving him a spoonful of honey. To the Greeks, honey was a panacea for whatever ailed you. Coming down with a cold? Eat a spoonful of honey. Fever? Honey. Constipated, honey. I wondered if it was safe to give the Muffster a spoonful or two or ten. Then again, better I should wait to talk to the vet.

Truth was, I wasn't used to taking care of anyone or anything. Up until five months ago, I'd been the one being taken care of. Namely by my mother and grandmother and the rest of my family. I'd lived at home, had my laundry done for me, my T-shirts ironed, my food ready. Thalia had all but made my bed for me.

Now . . .

Well, now I was low on clean underpants, my T-shirts were wrinkled, and more often than not souvlaki was the main dish on my personal menu. And my body was letting me know that.

Well that and the *rugelach* Mrs. Nebitz had given me the other night.

I knew it was my own fault. Not because I didn't cook, but because of the ongoing thing with my father, I wasn't stopping by my parents' house as often as I usually did, which meant no neatly packed containers of leftovers with which to fill my refrigerator.

Maybe I should start cooking.

I paused as I ate the last spoonful of ice cream.

Then again, no.

While I might know how to serve food, I sucked at making it.

I put the bowl down on the table and pushed the money shots aside in order to pull forward my notes on Uncle Tolly's case. The news came on—delayed because of a Yankees double-header. I wondered if they'd mention Aglaia's arrest. It turned out to be the third lead story.

I cringed as I watched footage of her being released on bond and for the first time listened to her speak in rapid-fire Greek. Which was a good thing, because had she said what she had in English, there would have been a lot of electronic bleeping and she probably would have been charged with verbally attacking a police officer.

I spotted Pino standing in the background of the final shot. Shocker. Probably he had been the one to alert the media.

The man knew no loyalty.

I rested the back of my head against the sofa. Loyalty. Now that was a word. And just whom had I expected Pino to be loyal to? The Pappases? No. It wouldn't surprise me if his mother was the one who cleaned and pressed his uniforms. And since he always seemed to be on duty, he didn't need any other clothes, so he didn't have need for a dry cleaner.

Loyal to me?

I snorted at that one.

Muffy lifted his head from where he was still working on his butt and looked at me.

I cleared my throat.

I suppose maybe I thought he should show a little loyalty to the Greek community at large. Allowing Aglaia to be filmed that way . . . well, it didn't reflect well on her or the neighborhood. And probably fed into a shitload of ethnic misperceptions about the Greek-American community. A viewer likely wouldn't see beyond her bad behavior to the fact that there was virtually no evidence to support her original arrest.

Then again, what did I know? Maybe they'd found discarded

plastic bags in the basement with Uncle Tolly's blood all over them.

The telephone on the hall table next to my cell phone rang.

Who in the hell would be calling me at this time of night? I made a face at the idea that it might be my mother.

I checked the caller ID display. Not my mother. Not unless she'd figured out how to block her number, which was possible but not probable. The problem is I didn't know who it was.

"Hello."

Nothing but silence greeted me.

I swallowed thickly and tried again. Same response.

Then the line went dead.

Gripping the wireless receiver in my hand, I stepped toward the window, careful not to be seen. Parked up the street was that damn sedan again. And while I couldn't be sure, it looked like Rokko had a cell phone open, the blue glow from the keypad illuminating his creepy features, made creepier yet by the unnatural light.

His face went back into shadow as he apparently closed the cell. My own telephone nearly slipped from my sweaty-palmed grip.

A reminder that I was being watched?

Or was he checking to make sure I was home?

Either way, my illusion of being safe in my own apartment grew wings and flew out the window.

One of many windows I methodically closed and locked before turning the air conditioner back on.

Better I should suffer through Muffy's noxious clouds than tempt fate.

That night I positioned a chair under the knob of my bedroom door.

Twenty-one

THE FOLLOWING DAY, IT STRUCK me as odd that lately I seemed to be spending more time with Rosie than my own family.

"Come on." Rosie shoved me from behind, her hands full of wrapped baby shower gifts while I clutched a simple box that held a receiving blanket and a pacifier. It didn't matter that I'd never met Rosie's sister Lupe. Just as I'd been incapable of turning down the Fred the Ferret case, I'd been helpless to refuse her when she insisted I come.

So there I was at Rosie's mother's house, the smell of tamales in the air, and half the ten or so people there speaking in Spanish, which I really didn't understand, or Spanglish, which I understood better.

Ask me how I was doing, what my name was, and what I wanted to drink or eat and I was fine.

Ask me if I had kids or a husband and I was left shaking my head dumbly, because for all I knew, they were inquiring if a space ship had landed on the roof of my apartment and performed an anal probe on me the night before.

A smiling young woman took my gift with one hand and handed me a homemade margarita with the other.

Ah. Now we were speaking my language.

While I wasn't much for drinking more than wine with dinner at my parents', and an occasional beer here or there, margaritas and apple martinis had always been the exceptions to the rule. First off, they didn't taste like alcohol. Second, I liked the buzz they gave me. Just enough to take the edge off and make me comfortable in a roomful of strangers.

I glanced around, my gaze settling on what appeared to be the only guy present. A guy about my brother's age.

Guy . . .

It wasn't so much the presence of a male in a house full of females, it was that my mind was clicking with information. Rosie only had one brother and one sister. And her brother's name was Ricky and he happened to be the manicurist to the mob.

I took a deep sip of my margarita so it wouldn't spill as I oh-so-casually made my way across the room toward him.

". . . and that damn mutt grabbed hold of the car bumper and wouldn't let go. I swear!" Rosie appeared in the middle of telling her favorite story to a couple of women as I passed her. A story, I noticed, that was changing every time she told it. Before long, Muffy will have grown to mythical proportions and swallowed the car and the goons inside whole.

Not a bad idea, really.

I zeroed in on the guy just stepping away from another woman. "You must be Ricky," I said, thrusting my free hand forward. "I'm Sofie. Sofie Metropolis. I work with your sister."

"Ah. Yes. The infamous Sofie Metro."

Infamous? I wasn't sure I liked the sound of that. Then again, it depended on the context in which you were using the word.

Ricky wasn't at all what I expected. I suppose since he filed people's nails for a living and because Rosie had already told me he was gay, I'd thought he'd be more effeminate than he was. Instead, he was very male and tall, dark, and handsome in every sense of the cliché. And he had a drop-dead gorgeous Enrique Iglesias kind of grin.

I bet he got hit on by women trying to "reform" him all the time.

Given the way he was looking at me, I half guessed he'd "given in" to them once or twice as well.

"So, you work for DiPiazza . . ." I said, trying to appear uninterested.

"Mmm. And you're currently in Tony's sights," he returned, unfazed, his grin not dimming a wit.

This time I didn't repress my wince. "I'm not sure if I like how that sounds."

"Trust me, I don't like making it sound that way. But I'd give ten-to-one odds that there was a car behind you when you parked."

I eyed him. "Could you get in trouble for being in the same house as me?"

"No. I'm the only one who knows how to do his nails the way he likes without hurting him."

I felt Rosie's talons on my arm before I saw her. "Oh, no you don't."

Rosie was cute on a normal day. Given her petite size, she was even cuter angry. And she was definitely angry.

"It's all right, sis," Ricky said. "We're just conversating."

"Yes, well, that kind of conversating can get you killed."

Ricky rolled his eyes at the same time I did.

We both laughed until Rosie threw up her hands and huffed off into the kitchen.

"Is there anything you can share with me?" I asked Ricky point blank, now that we both knew where the other stood. "Anything on Uncle Tolly?"

"Unfortunately, no." He sipped his margarita, frozen to my salted. "But there is something going on around the place. I don't know what but I don't like it. I'm even trying to get close to one of the bigger bosses, you know, so I don't find myself caught in any kind of crossfire."

"This . . . something going on . . . does it have to do with me?"

He smiled. "No."

I knew a relief so profound, I was pretty sure my knees wobbled a bit.

"Why don't you get out?" I asked.

He tilted his head and stared at me from under lowered brows. "Surely you jest."

I knew the joke. "Surely you jest." "I'm not joking and my name's not Shirley."

"Everyone," Rosie said, clapping her hands near the coffee table. "Lupe's here."

I didn't miss the glare Rosie gave me as she said this. And it wouldn't surprise me if she'd overheard every word of my conversation with Ricky. But her expression switched to pure joy as a woman about my age, her belly seven months huge, walked in the front door.

"Thanks," I said over the sound of the warm welcome.

"Anytime." Ricky began to walk toward his sisters, then

stopped. "Oh, and if we ever happen to pass casually on the sidewalk somewhere? You don't know me."

Seemed to be the story of my life as of late.

My cell phone vibrated in my jeans pocket.

I slipped it out and read the display. I didn't recognize the number.

"Hello?" I said after stepping into the kitchen where one of Rosie's aunts prepared food.

When there wasn't an immediate response, I moved to disconnect the call even as I plucked up a tortilla chip and put it into my mouth.

"You want information on Uncle Tolly?" a muffled voice I didn't recognize said.

I suddenly found it difficult to swallow as I turned away from the aunt. "Yes."

"Meet me at the Hellgate Bridge tower in Astoria Park at midnight tonight. Alone."

The line cut off.

Yikes.

ALONE.

At eleven-thirty, well after I'd left the shower, and only a few clock ticks away from my meeting with a curious stranger, I sat in my car down the block from Astoria Park, my gaze drawn to where the floater had been fished out of the East River only a few days before.

I didn't know who the caller thought I might bring with me. Truth was, Rosie aside, there really wasn't anyone. I'd thought about calling my uncle's partner Lenny Nash, or even my cousin

Pete, to ride along as backup, but ultimately I accepted that I didn't want to chance that the caller might bolt, ruining what could be my first real break in the case.

Of course there was also Jake . . .

I stretched my neck. No. I was going to do this alone.

So I stared at what was essentially my partner for the night: my Glock.

And tried to convince myself that I had what it took to get through this.

First, however, I had to get past those things that terrified me most about this clandestine meeting.

Number one: I didn't like at all that it was taking place so near the spot where the body had been fished out of the river the other night.

Number two: I wasn't good with dark. Nighttime tended to make things sinister, turned shadows into monsters looming larger than life.

Number three: I'd got caught playing on the train tracks when I was ten and hadn't known better. My brother Kosmos and I had followed them, thinking it would be cool if we could cross all the way over to Randall's Island. What we hadn't counted on was a train. Not that there was a risk of us being hit since there were four tracks, but I'll never forget the way the train had vibrated the tracks; feeling its approach had put the very fear of God into both of us.

Of course, we'd been close enough to scramble down the tracks to safety before the train got anywhere near us.

But this . . .

This Gothic-style concrete tower and small stretch of track was the last stop before the arched steel bridge jutted out over the roiling black oil that was the East River at night.

I closed my eyes and took a deep breath, my watch telling me only a minute had passed since the last time I'd looked. If luck was on my side, I wouldn't have to go up the tower. The metal service door would be locked and the caller would be waiting for me in the shadows of the park.

Okay, that imagery wasn't helping my nerves any either.

When I'd left Rosie's, the sedan had been gone. Which could mean one of two things: that the caller had, in fact, been Rokko, who finally received his orders to whack me, or that he'd been genuinely taken off my detail.

But since I knew the only type of luck I had happened to be bad luck, well . . .

I forced a swallow through my sandpapery throat.

The night was quiet, even for a Friday. At a nearby corner restaurant, the usual outdoor customers had mostly gone home, leaving just a couple of staff. The park was completely deserted, even of teens, who were probably at home in the comfort of their air-conditioned rooms, playing video games.

I slowly got out of my car, scanning the area again from my new vantage point. Fifty yards and I would be at the tower door. I tucked my Glock into the back of my jeans and wiped my palms against the heavy denim. I heard a sound that hadn't been all that apparent inside the Mustang. The constant drone of a generator seemed to be coming from the other side of the tower. I walked on the path next to the river, craning my neck as I walked, spotting orange pylons and two men in hardhats and work vests with fluorescent stripes on the back. A little farther down, I saw the generator in question, powering a portable cement mixer.

Roadwork in the middle of a Friday night? Didn't make much sense to me. But in a city this size, you came to expect the unexpected. Sometimes, when I was sitting on my roof contemplating, the enormity of this city nearly overwhelmed me, how many people lived in such a small place and managed not only to function, but function so efficiently.

There was a sound to my left. I jumped, automatically reaching for the Glock. But I instantly recognized the sound. It was the sound of the metal security door slamming against the interior wall.

So much for its being locked.

What bothered me even more than the dark, was even darker places.

I rested my hand against the cement wall of the tower and peered inside at the steps leading to the bridge above.

"Hello?" I called up, although my voice came out as little more than a whisper.

I backed away from the door. I didn't like this. I didn't like this at all.

"Up here," came a somewhat familiar male voice. Or maybe it wasn't so much the voice itself that was familiar, but the heavy accent it spoke with.

A Greek.

Even as my heart slammed against my rib cage, I knew a bit of relief. Maybe my caller had been one of Uncle Tolly's friends.

"Where?" I called up the stairs.

"Up here."

I gulped and the sound echoed in the chamber.

"Come down where I can see you."

"You come up."

"I don't have a flashlight."

There was a click and a beam hit the stairwell, sending it into relief.

Damn.

My new shoes sounded against the gritty cement steps as I slowly climbed upward toward the bridge. The hollow tower had an eerie, canned quality, throwing sounds of my breathing and my footsteps back at me tenfold. But as I neared the top, I heard the subtle sounds of creaking, like the old bridge was settling, or someone was blowing on the top of an empty beer bottle.

"Where are you?" I asked, my fingers wrapped around the Glock in my waistband.

A figure stepped from the shadows. In the light from the half moon I noticed a man very much familiar to me.

"Uncle Plato," I not so much said as breathed.

The old butcher and Uncle Tolly's neighbor looked about as scared as I felt.

"Shhh. Don't say my name."

I looked around. There wasn't anyone there to overhear our conversation.

He paced a short ways away on the side catwalk that paralleled the far tracks. "I knew I shouldn't have called."

"Why? Do you know where Uncle Tolly is?"

He appeared not to hear me, so engrossed he was in whatever internal struggle he was having. "But I never expected Aglaia to be arrested."

I narrowed my gaze, trying to decipher what he could be saying. "Have you . . . did you kill Uncle Tolly?"

The dry cleaner who laundered more than clothes and the butcher who cut up more than pork chops.

He stopped and stared at me. "What? Of course, I didn't kill Tolly."

I blinked. "Then what did you call me up here to tell me?"

There was that sound again. The one I'd heard earlier. The crash of the tower door against the inside wall.

I swung to stare at the stairwell along with Plato, both of us probably looking like deer caught in headlights.

Or targets of assassins . . .

Twenty-two

AS I STOOD IN THE darkness on the bridge, I become aware of two things at once: that Plato and I were no longer alone; that Plato had an escape plan that didn't include me.

Damn it all to hell!

I backed away from the door to the tower, carefully stepping over tracks and supporting slats, my hand slick against my Glock as I held it steadfastly in front of me.

The minute a figure emerged from the door, I squeezed off a round . . . and found myself falling backward, ass-first to the slats between a set of tracks, my pistol bouncing away from me. I'd forgotten about the kick of the powerful firearm and hadn't had my feet solidly under me. Of course, it also didn't help that my knees were knocking together so loudly they nearly drowned out the scream of a man who'd obviously been hit.

"Fuck! She shot my fucking ear!"

Rokko? I was pretty sure it was his voice I heard as more footsteps followed his until the bridge was filled with at least five goons, all of them surrounding their superior, even as I tried to scurry backward, pretty sure nobody had seen me yet. Well, except for Rokko. But right now he was more concerned with the dark liquid running down his neck.

"Jesus, boss, she shot your fucking ear."

I scrambled to find my Glock, my heart beating so fast I was sure it would beat straight out of my chest. No need for Rokko to do whatever he had in mind. I'd take care of that by scaring myself to death.

I hit the edge of my gun with my fingertips when a flashlight beam hit me full in the face, blinding me. Then a booted foot was kicking the gun away and was knocking me back onto my butt.

Not good.

Rokko shot off a string of Greek curse words as another of the men shined a flashlight on him, revealing that I had, indeed, shot his fucking ear off. Well, I don't know about off. But I had shot him in a way that covered his right ear in blood.

Too bad I couldn't have shot a little farther to the left.

Then again, if I had, I was pretty sure I'd be lying dead right now. That Rokko's friends would have opened fire on me with the semi-automatic weapons each of them was holding like they were some sorry excuse for a militia group.

I stared wildly in the direction Plato had gone. Interestingly enough, I was pretty sure he had run in the direction of the river rather than toward land. What was he planning to do? Jump over the side? I shuddered at the thought as the end of an Uzi—or what I thought was an Uzi, I couldn't be sure because, hey, I'd never actually seen one before—was stuck into the middle of my forehead.

"You want I should whack her now, boss?" the gunman asked.

More Greek cuss words as someone handed Rokko what appeared to be a napkin or a handkerchief with which to stem the flow of blood. "No, idiot. That's not how Tony wants it to go down."

Tony.

Nice Tony DiPiazza, whose most serious crime back in high school had been getting a laugh out of knocking my books from my hands.

Nice Tony DiPiazza who wanted to have "pasta" with me and used the word in place of "sex."

Nice Tony DiPiazza who had apparently sent his guys to . . .

What had he sent his guys to do?

Inside my pocket my cell phone vibrated.

I knew a moment of stillness.

"Get that gun out of her face before it accidentally goes off, you moron."

The gunman removed the gun then was stepping aside. I found myself in partial darkness and I took full advantage of it, sliding my cell from my pocket and trying to blindly open it behind my back.

"You think you're so smart, don't you?" Rokko said, stepping in front of me. He looked kind of ridiculous with the wad of white fabric attached to his ear, but I didn't think it a good idea to tell him that just then.

"I don't think I'm so smart," I said. "If I'm so smart, what am I doing up here, alone, with you guys and no escape?"

That was true enough. And Rokko seemed to realize that as he grinned at me in a way that stole the heat from my blood.

I'd always known Rokko had an evil side. Something that went far beyond his desire to look up my skirt when I was eight. Actually, it wasn't so much the skirt thing that got to me, but the fact that he'd felt compelled to have his friends hold me down while he took a look. Little did he know that I'd probably have gladly flashed him. Then again, that likely would have taken the thrill out of it for him.

And if he'd been like that then, what did it take for him to get his rocks off now?

I told myself to shut up.

"Where's Plato?" Rokko asked me.

I blinked at him. "Plato? Plato who?"

"Don't try to fuck with me, Metro. I know you were here to meet Plato Kourkoulis."

"The butcher? Why in the hell would I be meeting the butcher? I want to see him, I go to his shop."

I wasn't sure how effective I was being, but I needed to try anyway. Bad enough I was in the trouble I was. I didn't want to pull Plato down with me.

Besides, on the off, off chance I managed to get out of this mess alive, I needed Plato to tell me what he'd called to tell me.

"Sure. And you usually take long, midnight walks on the train tracks, don't you, Sofie?"

The way he said my name made every hair on my body stand up in warning.

Yeah, I'd chance a guess and say Rokko had graduated from underpants gazing long ago.

I continued to toy with my cell phone behind my back. I had no idea who I was calling, or if I was indeed calling anyone at all, but I figured it was worth a try.

"What? Do you have my phone bugged?" I asked.

If he did, and someone out there was still intercepting my calls, then they'd know what I was doing.

911 . . .

I pressed disconnect then blindly tried to dial the digits. Then realized that my actions would be little more than a lesson in futility. If I couldn't talk to them, tell them where I was, then there was nothing they could do to help me. If they'd do anything at all.

My only wish was that I hadn't accidentally called my mother. I figured it was bad enough she'd have to bury her oldest daughter. To have to listen to her die too . . .

I shuddered down to my toes.

"Hellgate Bridge!" I screamed, hoping I had dialed 911. "Astoria Park!"

Rokko yanked me to my feet and reached behind me for the phone. He stared at the display, cursed, then closed the phone and pitched it over the side of the bridge. What seemed like a long time later, the sound of the plastic smashing to smithereens echoed back.

Had I just gulped? I was pretty sure I'd just gulped.

"Cute," Rokko said, his face entirely too close to mine for my liking. He smelled of garlic and strong cologne.

The last observation caught and held. Strong cologne . . .

"Tell me, Rokko, what are you doing hanging around with the Italians, anyway?"

His eyes narrowed. "What, you got something against Italians?"

"No. But you've got to know that you'll never be one of them. Not really. You'll always be the outsider, the Greek."

He didn't say anything.

"You know, you're really something else," I said after a long silence. I pretended no fear even though I was shaking in my shoes; I figured I wasn't going out looking like a coward. If this, indeed, was my moment of truth, I was going to go down swinging, damn it. The same adrenaline that had seen me through that stupid stint on that reality show during my solo honeymoon rushed through me, and I stuck my face closer to his. "It wasn't enough for you to bust into my place and duct tape my damn dog to the toilet, was it? It wasn't enough for you to take Uncle Tolly's ledgers? You've been hanging around, leering at me, peeping in my windows, waiting for the moment you could make your move, haven't you?"

"I peep at no one," he said with a sneer.

"Oh, yeah? I seem to recall you doing your fair share of peeping when we were kids."

"That was a long time ago."

Keep him talking, a small voice ordered. *Keep him talking until you can figure out what to do.*

If, in fact, there was anything I could do. Which I couldn't imagine. Not with him standing flush with my front, and with the five other goons blocking access to the door. Not that I thought I'd get very far. But I entertained the thought of turning into James Bond at the last minute and parachuting over the side of the bridge or something. Or at least running in the same direction Plato had.

Of course that was leaving out that I probably wouldn't get too far what with the weapons pointing at me. All they had to do was open fire and I would be Greek Swiss cheese within a matter of seconds.

"What would you like to do to me now, Rokko?" I asked, dropping my voice and looking him over. "Would you like to have some pasta with me?"

He looked an inch away from biting me. Which could be his way of getting off, who knows.

He grabbed me by the back of the neck and roughly pulled me even closer to him. "What I'd do to you, you wouldn't soon forget."

I had little doubt about that.

Then again, I'd have to be alive in order to remember so that inspired a small spark of hope in my chest.

Maybe he wasn't here to kill me. Or do some other kind of unspeakable something to my person. Maybe his job had been to interrupt my meeting with Plato. To keep me from finding out what he'd had to say.

"Rokko, get away from my girl."

Another voice.

Tony.

Oh, Jesus. Had he really just called me his girl? Okay, so the guy had mentioned having pasta with me. And he'd sent me flowers. Flowers, by the way, I hadn't thanked him for. But what was he doing on the bridge in the middle of the night when he had henchmen like Rokko and his goons to do his dirty work?

Maybe because he wanted to do the dirty work himself.

He limped to stand in front of me.

Why was he limping?

"Hey, Sof," Tony said, giving me the same grin he'd given me on the sidewalk outside his club a few days ago.

"Hey, Tony."

He reached out and fingered a strand of my hair, which gave me the creeps. "What you doing out here at this time of night by yourself, babe? You should be home in bed. Preferably with me."

I decided I like his pasta euphemism better.

But still somehow I managed a smile. "Why don't we go there now?"

Anywhere away from here where the wind was beginning to pick up, eerily whistling through the steel bridge supports.

Anywhere where I would have a better chance at escape.

And, hey, call me cheap, but the thought of having sex with Tony DiPiazza was much better than the alternative. Which I feared was death.

"Why are you limping, Tony?" I asked.

He narrowed his gaze, his grin taking on a menacing quality. "I hurt myself at the gym."

"More like my dog bit you," I said.

He leaned in and kissed me hard, his hand on the back of my head to hold me still. He pulled away, spittle briefly connecting us.

I couldn't help thinking I'd just been given the mafia kiss of death. Not a "both cheeks Fredo" kind of kiss, but an even more evil one that hinted at what might be done to my body before or after—or possibly both—the coming event.

He waved at one of the men that had followed him up. The guy moved to the side of the bridge and whistled below. I heard what sounded like the cement mixer power up.

It was then I realized that no one had been doing roadwork in the middle of a Friday night. Instead the guys on the street had been set up to look like a road crew but were instead connected to Tony.

My mouth went dryer than my grandmother's talcum powder.

My grandmother . . .

My mother . . .

My sister . . .

My heart hurt with the people I would never see again. Who would mourn my death.

Too soon, a voice said. *I'm not ready.*

Then again, who ever truly was?

I remembered one of my Aunt Sotiria's friends that she'd made me go to the hospital and visit when I was thirteen. I was at the age where I'd thought I'd known everything there was about life, give or take a few details—mostly of a sexual nature—and found out quickly that I hadn't known jack.

Bone cancer had eaten away at Fotini until she resembled a frail skeleton with skin laid over the top. (Not covering, because covering indicated some kind of shape. No, her skin had looked like it would slide off if she moved or if I touched it. Which I'd had no intention of doing.)

"Sofie," she'd said to me, pulling me to her bedside with an iron grip. "Live your life as best you can, as much as you can. Because it all slips away so quickly. It seems like yesterday I was your age with nothing to worry about but getting bobby pins at the drugstore to do my hair with. Then I blinked and here I am so close to death I can smell it."

I'd wanted to ask her what it smelled like, death. Because I was pretty sure that's what I was smelling now. And it stunk of musty old boards and iron and rotting vegetation to me.

I'm sure when Fotini had told me to live my life as best as I could that this wasn't what she'd had in mind. She'd probably expected me to live to a ripe old age. Own my own detective agency. Have a husband. Maybe children of my own.

She had been right about something, however. It all ended long before you were ready for it to end.

"Fuck! Open up the goddamn door," a man shouted. "These things weigh a ton."

I watched as two large containers that looked like ten-kilo olive oil tins were carried through the door and dropped to the tracks. Wet cement sloshed over the sides, spraying the front of Tony's pants.

"Watch it, you dimwit."

I only partially registered Tony's comment because I was too busy staring at what could only be my new pair of cement boots . . .

Twenty-three

LIKE MOST MOTHERS, THALIA HAD always told me to make sure I had on clean underwear, you know, on the off chance that I got in an accident or something and had to go to the hospital. Only I was pretty sure that when she'd said it, she hadn't been thinking about the medical examiner being the one to see what I had on underneath my clothes.

Still, I tried to remember what pair I'd put on this morning and whether or not they were embarrassing.

A purple thong.

I guess it depended on your definition of embarrassing.

I recognized the idiotic path of my thoughts, which seemed to indicate that this, indeed, was it. The end. I mean, how much was sense worth when you were about ten seconds from having your feet stuck into fast-drying cement and probably dropped off of Hellgate Bridge into the deep, churning waters of the East River below?

All I could seem to think about was that there went another pair of perfectly good shoes.

"Get her in there," Tony ordered.

I fought off the two guys who flanked my sides as best I could. I smacked one in the nose, I stomped on the instep of the other, but where was I supposed to go?

They grabbed my arms, hoisted me into the air, then tried to fit my K-Swiss into the cement-filled containers. I nearly toppled one of the containers over, and caught the rim with the other.

"Somebody hold her goddamn feet!" Rokko shouted.

Somebody not only held my feet, they held the containers as well. Within moments cement crept up inside the bottom of my jeans, the cold liquid that soon would turn solid, stealing the breath from my lungs.

Jesus . . .

The two guys continued to hold me, while another two made sure my feet stayed in the containers until the cement dried. I could already feel it adhering to my shins, heavy and unyielding. And was that a burning sensation I felt? How could cement burn? I didn't know, but I didn't like the feeling of it.

Tony stepped closer to me and grinned. How I ever thought that grin might have been a little bit handsome was beyond me just then. He was evil incarnate.

"You know, Sof, it really is too bad we didn't get to have that pasta. I'll bet you're a real spitfire between the sheets."

Neither of us had to point out that in a few minutes that "you are" would switch to "you were," mainly because I would no longer be in existence.

I could see the customers in my grandfather Kosmos' café

shaking their heads. "Real shame. It all began when she sucked back those bug shakes . . ."

Then again, the Greeks loved a good tragedy. Maybe one day they would change the name of the bridge from Hellgate to Sofiegate . . .

Or maybe not.

The henchmen released me and I nearly toppled over without my feet for balance. I tried to lift my right foot and fell backward.

"Whoa. We don't want you going over the side just yet," Tony said, grabbing my arm. "We've got to get you over the river first."

My throat tightened to the point of pain.

Going back to my stint on that stupid reality show, I remembered how, exactly, I'd missed out on winning that fifty grand. The third stunt had involved a water tank and my being stuck into it head first, my hands handcuffed behind me. They'd lowered me in and I'd immediately made the "uncle" gesture for them to pull me out.

The problem was I didn't think any amount of gesturing would find anyone pulling me out of the East River.

Out of worst ways you could possibly die, this rated at the top of my personal list.

"Tony," I said, fighting to keep the panic out of my voice. "Come on. I haven't done anything. There's nothing showing you had anything to do with Uncle Tolly's disappearance. His wife's already been arrested in connection with his death. Why do you want to implicate yourself in mine?"

He tapped my chin with his index finger. "Because no matter what I did, you wouldn't give up." He shook his head. "That's the problem with smart girls, wouldn't you say, Rokko?

They never give up. That's why I like the dumb ones. The dumb ones know when to shut up and when to realize the car that's been following them is a warning."

"A warning for what?"

"To butt out or risk having yourself butted out . . . permanently."

"I just wanted to find a body."

Tony chuckled. "See. She's about to be dumped into the river and she still don't give up." He tapped his finger against my temple. "You know what? I'm going to take back what I said. Because right now I'm not sure if it's because you're too smart, or too damn dumb."

Dumb. Definitely dumb, I decided.

He bent over and checked the cement.

"Done." He backed up and motioned to the goons on either side of me. "Carry her out and dump her. But don't do it until you're halfway over the bridge. We don't want her hitting the rocks."

I shuddered at the image and tried like hell to wiggle my toes. They weren't moving.

Oh, God . . .

The goons tried to lift me. "Jesus Christ. How much does this broad weigh?"

I wanted to tell them it was the cement but figured it was a moot point. I don't much think anyone cared what I weighed at that moment. Including me.

I should have eaten more ice cream . . .

I heard what sounded like a loud bird swoop overhead. A pigeon heralding my impending demise?

Only it wasn't a bird. It was a helicopter.

And I felt like it had lifted my heart from my body. Or at

least put hope where moments before there had been absolutely zero.

"Release the woman," an amplified voice I thought was
coming from the chopper said.

I looked up, my hair whipping around my face, trying to
make out the craft. I couldn't see it. Which was odd. Shouldn't
there have been spotlights or something? I heard the whoop-
whoop of the blades, but couldn't see the helicopter itself.

"Jesus, Mary, and Joseph, it's the cops," the goon to my right
shouted. "Let's get out of here."

The goon to my left yanked harder on my arm. "Not until we
get the job done."

"Fuck the job. What, you wanna be sent up for murder? Not
worth it to me."

The guy on the right released me and my cement boots hit
the planks with a loud thud.

"You're as good as dead anyway," Goon Two said to Goon
One.

The guy to my left for whatever godforsaken reason decided
he needed to continue.

I heard something whistle by my ear. The goon groaned. I
looked to find one of those dart things—a tranquilizer?—
embedded in his right shoulder. He took the dart out then
dropped to his knees, no longer any kind of threat.

The only problem was, I couldn't move in my new boots.

Doing a windmill move to keep myself upright, I looked
over my shoulder to find the bridge was deserted. Neither Tony
nor any of his goons were in sight. Probably he ran at the first
sound of the helicopter blades.

Coward.

I squinted up at the nearly invisible bird in question, or at least where I thought it might have been given the sound. There was movement, then I watched as two men clad in black slid on ropes to the bridge, a few feet in front of me.

But it was the voice behind me that got my attention.

"Hey, luv, imagine meeting you here."

I was so happy to see Porter I could have cried.

"I DIDN'T KNOW CEMENT BURNED. Did you know cement burned? No one ever writes about cement burning. I haven't even seen it in any movies."

I was babbling. I knew I was babbling. And slurring my words. But I couldn't seem to stop myself as I watched Porter trickle cold water over my reddened ankles as I sat on the side of my tub back at my apartment.

The last person I'd expected to see on that godforsaken bridge was Porter, large as life and twice as sexy. I think the combination of fear to the tenth power and relief had overloaded my system and I'd fainted dead away. I'd come to to find myself lying on the cool grass of Astoria Park while one of the men clad in black, his face eerily covered with a black mask even as he worked, maneuvered one of those small saws they used to cut casts from broken limbs on my cement boots. One by one the blocks of cement cracked in two: I'd felt like every bone in my ankles had shattered and I was pretty sure I screamed in pain.

Still, I'd felt the needle prick.

"A little something for the pain," Porter had said, taking a syringe from my arm.

A hazy visit to the hospital for x-rays and an hour long water flush of my ankles that the attendant told me was usually used for fire burn victims, and Porter was carrying me to my apartment, where Muffy barked and circled and barked again, probably wondering why I was being carried.

Porter had put me on the edge of my tub and was even now gently squeezing a washcloth full of cold water onto my ankles.

All told, I suppose I was doing okay. I was shaking from head to toe, not from the cold water, but from my experience, and my ankles looked red and raw. (The burn specialist had said I was lucky. I told her she had no idea just how lucky I was, but I think I slurred the words, unable to make my tongue work properly, so probably she didn't understand my explanation of what had happened on the bridge. Probably she thought I was a drug addict. Or maybe Porter had told her he'd given me a sedative of some sort. What he'd given me could have put down an elephant.)

Even now, I looked down to find my purple thong clearly visible, as was my white sports bra. I couldn't remember what happened to my jeans or top, but I was thinking that I should be trying to look sexy. After all, it wasn't every day I was in a bathtub with Jake Porter.

I glanced toward the bottle of salts on a shelf, then I slumped against Porter's back, thinking his white T-shirt smelled clean and slightly like bleach and that it was soft against my cheek. I was vaguely aware that Muffy was on the other side of me, his paws on the tub as he watched, his tongue lolling out of his mouth between growls and barks. I reached out to pet him, to reassure him I was okay, but I barely managed a pat to his head before my arm dropped to my side. I looked at the uncooperative limb.

Oh, but that was sexy.

Jake grinned at me, concern in his eyes. "How you feeling?"

It seemed to take forever for me to blink.

"How did you know I was on the bridge?"

He reached into his back pocket then held up his cell phone. A punch of a button and he showed me the display. "Sofie" it read, at ten past midnight.

I blinked back big, fat, hot tears. Obviously, my blind fumbling had netted me the right phone call.

"And the copter?" I asked, noticing how my drug-induced state made the sentence sound like one unintelligible word.

"Friends of mine."

"Ahhh." I tried to shake my finger at him but managed only to point. "Good to have friends like that."

He grinned. "That it is."

I stared at him. At the way his eyes held a shadow of concern along with amusement. At how his mouth cocked just a little bit to the side in a way that made me want to lick that spot. And his hair . . .

"Who are you?" I asked, sounding amazingly clear even to myself.

He broke eye contact and reached for a towel behind me. "Just a guy who got his girl out of a little trouble."

That's the second time that night someone had referred to me as his girl. I liked the thought of belonging to Porter loads more than the alternative.

I rubbed the heel of my hand against my nose, feeling a little too weepy for my liking.

He gently dried my ankles and applied some sort of gel stuff the doctor had given me. I was turned on by watching his fingers stroke my skin, but winced from the pain of that same touch.

Oh, that was so not the way it was supposed to go.

Touch me somewhere else, I wanted to say.

"Come on, let's get you into bed."

As he swept me up into his arms, I thought that was the best damn idea I'd heard all day . . .

Twenty-four

I BECAME AWARE OF THREE things at once.

First, my ankles hurt like hell.

Second, my tongue felt like it had swollen to twice its normal size and was threatening to choke me.

Third . . . I wasn't alone.

I jackknifed upright in bed, clutching the sheet to my chest and pushing my hair from my eyes.

"Morning."

The greeting came from the doorway to my bedroom and was said by Porter, who was leaning against the jamb looking like temptation revisited.

While I both felt and probably looked like shit warmed over.

"I notice you didn't preface that with 'good,'" I said.

I immediately detected an all too familiar odor.

"Oh, man." I pulled the sheet over my nose and mouth, staring at where Muffy sat wagging his tail apologetically from the end of my bed.

"Yeah. That's quite a little ripper you got there," Porter said. "Stunk up the place but good last night."

Little ripper. Was that Aussie speak for Muffy liked to let one rip? Only in the Jack Russell terrier's case, he liked to let *them* rip.

I blinked at Porter. "You stayed all night?"

And I wasn't naked and ravished? I peeked under the sheet. Nope. Purple thong and sports bra still fully in place. Under-the-skin-itch still there. And ankles red and raw.

I'd been hoping the whole bridge incident had been some kind of really bad dream. Instead, it turned out to be a really bad reality.

I tossed off the sheet, grabbed a few items of clothing from my dresser drawers, then headed for the bathroom and the shower beyond.

"Whoa. Where's the fire, luv?"

It felt like it was around my ankles. "Is that coffee?" I asked, salivating after Porter's mug. It was a porcelain one I'd lifted from my grandpa Kosmos' café, sky blue with a white Greek key design around the rim.

He held it out.

I took the mug and downed half the contents, making a face at the unsweetened, bitter brew. But it did manage to shrink my tongue somewhat.

"Did you make that?"

"Australian blend."

"Mmm."

"Mind telling me what you were doing on that bridge wearing

cement overshoes last night?" he asked, working a finger under the strap of my bra and righting it.

I followed the movement, aware of a completely different kind of burning.

I caught myself scratching my arm and stopped.

"I'll tell you if you tell me how you got there so quickly and with so many . . . friends."

His answer was a grin.

"Well, then," I said, drinking some more of his coffee when what I really wanted was him. Then again, right now I'd settle for a frappé.

"Did they get DiPiazza?" I asked.

A shadow flickered through his eyes. "The only person we found was you."

I stared at him. Not a single one of DiPiazza's crew or Tony himself had been captured? Not even the one who'd been shot with some kind of dart?

The knowledge sent a shudder skating over my very exposed skin.

Porter nodded toward my room. "That's some interesting décor you've got there."

I squinted at him then followed his gaze to the wedding gifts still stacked up against the opposite bedroom wall, along with the boxes holding the *boubounieras*.

Oh, boy.

"Souvenirs?" he asked with a raised brow.

"Revenge," I answered.

Then I passed him and disappeared behind the closed door of the bathroom.

I don't know if I was shocked or disappointed to find Porter gone when I came out. Then again, I hadn't expected him to be there so maybe I was just pleased that he'd stayed, in essence protecting me, while I healed from my ordeal.

And seeing as none of DiPiazza's crew had been arrested . . . well, I guess I needed the protection.

What came after a failed hit attempt? A point blank, bullet-between-the-eyes whack?

I picked up the phone and dialed the agency. Rosie picked up on the second ring.

Even though it was the weekend, she held down the fort until about one since we received a lot of customers on Saturday morning. I think it might have something to do with so many people working nine-to-five and Saturdays being the only free time they had to do things like, oh say hire a PI to get dirt on their spouse.

"Sofie! Omigawd, girl, did you hear what went down at Astoria Park last night? DiPiazza was doing something to someone and I heard there were helicopters and SWAT teams and frogmen and everything . . ."

"I heard," I said, looking down at where my beige capris left my ankles free from material. And since my K-Swiss were history, I wore a pair of tan leather sandals I'd picked up in Greece last year and had to dig out of the back of my closet.

I didn't think it was a good idea to tell Rosie that I'd been DiPiazza's target last night, seeing as she'd probably quit and I'd never see her again.

But I also didn't think it was a good idea to go to the agency either, just in case DiPiazza's next step involved gunfire.

"I've got some off-site stuff to see to this morning," I told her.

"I've got gossip this good and you're not coming in?"

"Call if you need anything."

I rang off and called information next. Moments later, I dialed the number for Plato's butcher shop.

Surprise of surprises, there was no answer.

I stalked toward the kitchen to make myself a frappé, Muffy following on my heels. I stopped just inside the doorway. There, sitting in the middle of my kitchen table, was a cell phone and my Glock, all shiny clean and—I picked it up and checked the clip—fully loaded. I checked the cell, surprised to find it was one of those with all the bells and whistles that did everything but supply toilet paper . . . and that it held my number.

Bless Jake Porter's romantic little heart.

I'M NOT SURE HOW I knew, but I was pretty sure that wherever I went, Porter was along for the ride. I didn't see his truck anywhere. But since I knew he wouldn't have left my place without handcuffing me to the radiator unless he'd arranged for protection, well, I felt semi-safe getting into my car—which was parked right in front of my apartment—and driving to the butcher shop. I pulled up behind Uncle Tolly's Mercedes, which still bore the FOR SALE sign. I wasn't all that surprised to see a CLOSED sign in Plato's shop window. But whether it was closed because Plato had never made it home last night—my throat tightened as I imagined what might have happened to him had DiPiazza's guys caught up to him—or if it was because he was in his upstairs apartment hiding, I didn't know.

I got out of the car and dialed the number for the butcher shop again. His home number was unlisted, but Rosie had ways of getting stuff like that, so I called her and within minutes she had a number for me. I dialed it. No answer.

Still, that didn't stop me from knocking on his door and ringing the doorbell. "*Kirie* Plato? It's Sofie," I called up, you know, just in case he was listening.

Of course, I'd identified myself hoping it would encourage him to open up to me, but I realized the information might have the opposite effect as well. After all, hadn't it been me who had brought unwanted company to our meeting last night, no matter how unintentional?

I looked at the busy dry cleaners and sighed. Now I had two missing persons on my hands. Leave it to me to go looking for one and send another one missing.

I got back into my car and sat for long moments staring at the back of the Mercedes. What had Plato said last night before we were so rudely interrupted? Not much. But maybe there was something there for me to work wi—

There was a tap on my trunk and I nearly hit my head on the ceiling of the car.

"Hanging out again where you shouldn't be, Metro?"

I stared at Pino. Was he referring to last night? "What do you mean?" I croaked.

He gestured toward the Mercedes and the cleaners. "I told you I've gotten complaints about your being here."

"And where else have I been lately that I shouldn't?"

He looked at me as if I was an ice cube short of a full frappé. "Move along, Metro. Go cause trouble somewhere else."

It dawned on me that, like Rosie, he didn't know about my connection to last night.

Which made the incident seem all that much more surreal.

It reminded me of the question "If a tree falls in a forest and no one's around to hear it, does it make a sound?"

If no one knew about what had happened last night, had it really happened?

And just where had Pino been last night? I mean, since it appeared he worked 24/7, didn't it stand to reason that he should have stopped what went down before Tony got my friggin' feet in that cement?

Actually, that was the sixty-four-thousand-dollar question, wasn't it? Where was Pino last night?

And why didn't he know anything about what happened?

Or did he . . .

I gave him my best casual smile. Which, had I been thinking, should have been enough to put him on alert. "Hey, Rosie tells me something happened down at the park last night. Do you know anything about that?"

It was strange talking in third person about things I had all too real first-hand knowledge about.

He hiked his pants up. I winced.

"The Feds had something going on. Kept us barred from our own territory."

"That's all you're going to give me?" I asked.

"What you got to barter with?"

I gestured toward the butcher shop. "Plato might know what happened to Uncle Tolly."

"Tell me something else I already know. Why do you think I've been hanging out here lately?"

The thought honestly hadn't crossed my mind. Probably because I believed Pino was naturally where I didn't want him to be.

"Yeah, but he was part of what happened at the park . . ." I led on.

I'm not sure, but I think Pino's ears actually swiveled so he could hear me better. "Go on," he said.

"And now he's missing too."

Pino's head snapped toward the butcher shop.

"So what else do you got?" I asked.

He shrugged and gave me a grin that revealed he'd eaten something doughy for breakfast. Blech. "I already gave you everything I got."

"Fine."

I started Lucille.

"Where you going?" he asked.

I eyed his hands where they gripped my door, warning him without words to step away from my vehicle, sir.

He stepped away.

"I've got some unfinished business to conduct with my father," I told him.

AND I DID. HAVE UNFINISHED business to finish with my father, that was. I mean, it sucked not being able to stop in at home anytime I wanted. And with my mother hounding me to give her information I didn't want to give . . . well, I couldn't do that. Which meant my refrigerator was bare. And my hunger for Greek gossip was growing.

Only when I parked near his restaurant, I wasn't all too sure I was up for this. As it stood, my role in the family used to be pretty pat. I was the oldest daughter from whom nothing much was expected but to work in the family restaurant, get married, and have cute little Greek children who would wear authentic Greek costumes and take part in the Greek Independence Day Parade on Fifth Avenue every March.

Okay, so I really didn't want to confront my dad. Mostly because he was my dad. But the only alternative was to tell my mom. And that was definitely not something I could do. Mostly because I wanted to keep dad around.

I climbed out of the car, not realizing I was scanning the street until I spotted a truck pull to the curb a ways up.

Porter.

I immediately relaxed and walked into my father's restaurant.

You never really appreciate all that goes into running a restaurant until you go into one when it's closed. The lights were on bright for cleaning purposes. The tables were bare. The booths empty. And in a few short hours there would be food and people everywhere, with countless staff making sure water glasses and bread baskets were kept full, the customers kept smiling, and the tips piling up.

I knew my father was there because I'd parked behind his old Caprice. Efi and I used to joke that dad got the car because that's what the NYPD and some federal agencies called their car of choice—but while everyone else had moved on, Dad stuck with a car they didn't even make anymore. "Uh-oh. We're in trouble now," we used to say when he'd be in charge of taking us all somewhere. He'd laugh it off but we could tell his shoulders used to inch back just a hair.

I guess one of the reasons I was indulging in the memory right now was because, first, last night I'd almost lost all rights to create any new memories.

And second, depending on how this meeting went, there

might be few opportunities for warm and fuzzy father and daughter memories.

Oh, sure, Greeks divorced. Just ask my uncle Spyros. But when it happened, it wasn't pretty. And I didn't want to be the cause of it happening in my own family.

Don't get me wrong, I don't think the effects of divorce are different in any other family. But with the Greeks, it's almost as if the husband, the father, ceases to exist. Oh, he's still there. Physically. But gone is any kind of solid connection. Because, let's face it, most men aren't good with intimacy. And without a sympathetic woman—like my mother—around to balance things out, well, the man's connection to his children is cut. Then either the children take the mother's viewpoint (as is the case with my uncle Spyros, whose estranged son is connected enough to keep popping up to lift money from his office, but never once asks if we've spoken to his father or indicates he wants to talk to him), or without the mother there to encourage the connection, it just kind of vanishes.

I didn't want that to happen to my father. To our family.

I heard laughter from the kitchen. I looked at my watch. It was just after nine-thirty. Most of the staff would be showing up in a half an hour to an hour to begin prepping for the midday rush. Which meant my father was in there with somebody.

And that somebody had better not be Magda.

I stalked toward the kitchen without calling out and opened the door.

There stood Magda making something at the counter; my father had one arm around her shoulder and was showing her something.

"Get away from her, you lech."

Twenty-five

I WASN'T SURE WHO WAS more surprised at my words: my father or me. We stood there in the kitchen of the Metropolitan Restaurant, the place he had owned for as long as I could remember, the place I had spent most of my teenage years working, staring at each other like strangers.

Okay, that's the way my father was looking at me. I . . . well, I was pretty sure I looked mad enough to chew glass.

"Magda?" my father said, clearing his throat. "Can you leave me and my daughter alone for a few minutes, please?"

"Actually, Magda, you're fired," I said, crossing my arms over my chest. "If you know what's good for you, you'll get your things and never come back again."

"Sofie!"

I stared at my father. He was looking at me as if I was the one in the wrong.

"Magda, go home. I'll call you after I've sorted things out with my daughter."

I opened my mouth to tell her she'd better change her number between then and now, but she was already gone, having run from the room like her apron was on fire.

And if I'd had a lighter on me, it would have been.

I tightened my arms across my chest and stared at my father. We both heard the outer door slam shut.

"That was uncalled for," my father said, looking sterner than I'd seen him in a long time. At least since I was seventeen and I'd invited ten of my closest friends to the restaurant kitchen on a Sunday night when the place was closed for an impromptu party and been caught by him. How was I supposed to know there were ordinances about that kind of stuff? And, of course, we'd gotten into the liquor and two of my so-called friends had ralphed all over the prep counters.

Still, I stood my ground. "I think it's exactly what was called for," I told him.

We stood locked in some sort of strange Greek standoff, neither of us saying anything.

Then my father scratched his right brow with his pinky finger and cracked a grin. "Did you really just call me a lech?"

"I wanted to call you worse. I still want to call you worse."

He chuckled and I got angrier.

"Come on," he said. "Let's go have a cup of coffee. It looks like you and me need to have a nice long talk."

"We can talk just fine here," I countered.

He stood for long moments without saying anything, but at least he wasn't grinning anymore.

"All right. If that's how you want it. Then talk."

I gestured toward the door. "I want you to stop . . . whatever it is you're doing with that woman. Now."

"Excuse me?"

"You heard me. Whatever shenanigans that have been happening in this restaurant, here's where they end."

That grin again. Then he looked me straight in the eye. "No."

Okay. I didn't know quite how to respond to that one. It had taken so much mental mustering for me to confront him that I guess I'd assumed the moment I called him on his activities he'd stop them.

I hadn't made a contingency plan for his refusal.

That was it. Right now I was staring at the beginning of the end of everything that was familiar to me. My family. My parents' marriage. The life that I knew and loved.

And I wasn't quite sure how to handle that on top of everything else that had happened to me in the past couple of days.

"Tell me, Sofie. Just what do you think is going on?"

I gave an eye roll, but it was only half strength because I was afraid I was going to cry.

"Come on," he said. "Let's go have that coffee."

Five minutes later I was sitting at the bar in the main dining room, clutching a frappé in my fingers although I had yet to drink any of it.

"So," my father said, taking the stool next to me and sipping his own regular coffee, which the Greeks called either boiled coffee, or French, but neither really mattered to me right now. "You think I'm having an affair."

I stared at him. "Are you trying to deny it?"

"Ah. Denial implies guilt. And I'm not guilty of the crime you've tried and convicted me of." He cleared his throat. "What put such a stupid idea into your head anyway?"

"Mom said . . ." How much did I reveal? I mean, as a detective, I knew that in cases of infidelity the injured party's having the information before the guilty party sometimes made all the difference in the world. I'd seen cheating spouses run away with all the marital assets because they'd known the ax was going to fall.

But we weren't talking about your run-of-the-mill cheating spouse. We were talking about my father. My dad. My papa.

"Your mother put you up to this?" he asked. "I should have known."

"Should have known she'd see right through your games," I said.

"Sofie, Sofie, Sofie," my father said in that head-shaking way that had always made me bristle and feel more than a little dumb. Because it usually prefaced the sharing of information that would shine an unflattering light in my direction, if not spotlight me dead on. "I'm not cheating on your mother with Magda—"

"What about Aunt Aliki?"

"I'm not cheating, period."

I wasn't following him. What was he doing if he wasn't cheating on her? Almost cheating on her?

"I'm arranging a surprise thirtieth wedding anniversary party for your mother."

I stared at him.

In my twenty-six years on earth, my parents had never celebrated their anniversary. I couldn't even tell you the day they'd gotten married, only that it was in summer sometime because my mother had talked about how much she'd sweated in her dress, and how it had been so much better that I was going to get married in the spring when it wasn't so hot.

"What?" I breathed, feeling that all too familiar dumbness beginning to settle in. Especially when I remembered my mother having mentioned thirty years of marriage. It hadn't even dawned on me that it was a milestone worth celebrating.

"Why didn't you tell me?"

I watched the man who had just changed back into my dad chuckle again. "Because you have the biggest mouth on earth."

I gaped at him.

"Admit it. You never would have been able to keep a secret like that under your hat. You would have blurted it out to your mother five minutes after I told you."

He put his arm around my shoulder and crowded me to his side.

"*Och, morie Calliope,* what am I to do with you?"

The words warmed as well as embarrassed me. That's what he used to say to me when I was a kid and I hadn't heard him use it for a good ten years. It made me feel . . . I don't know. Like maybe everything would be all right.

"So Magda and Aunt Aliki—"

"Are helping me plan the event."

I balled my fist and half-heartedly punched him in the ribs, causing him to take his arm from around me. "You could have told me. I could have kept a secret."

He lifted a brow.

"Okay, maybe I couldn't have. But, trust me, whatever would have happened as a result of my spilling the beans would have been a whole helluva lot better than what I've been going through for the past week—not to mention Mom."

He seemed to consider this.

"Admit it. The last thing you wanted to do was make your wife think you were being unfaithful to her."

"Maybe. Maybe not." He looked at me. But where I might have expected a smile or a grin, I got a sober expression. "It's not a bad idea to remind your spouse every now and again what they have."

"What? Why?"

"I don't know. I've been thinking that Thalia and I both take each other too much for granted. Our marriage. You kids. Our livelihood." He shrugged. "That's why I thought this surprise party would be a good idea. You know, show your mother how much I still love her."

I looked at him and saw one hundred percent truth.

This time it was me who put my arm around him. "That's sweet."

"I'm not doing it to be sweet. I'm doing it because your mom and I should be marking every anniversary like it's the first day of the rest of our lives." He fell silent for a moment. "Thirty years ago, your mom saved my life. I think it's important she knows that."

As I sat there absorbing what I'd learned, and correcting every wrong idea I'd had about my dad over the past seven days, I thought that that's exactly the type of love I wanted. Like the kind my parents had.

"So when is this party?" I asked.

"Tonight. Think you can keep a lid on until then?"

I nodded, determined to keep quiet about the information if only to prove that I could.

"So, what's happening with you?" he asked me.

I made a face, thinking of last night, of the cement boots I didn't want but I'd worn, and the red rings I still had around my ankles as a result.

My father got up and took my empty frappé glass. "How about a refill?"

I smiled at him. "I'd love one."

———

WHEN I CLIMBED INTO MY car a little while later I felt much better about life in general. I hardly even noticed how the leather seat scorched my behind because it had been sitting in the direct August sunlight. I did, however, notice the petition papers that I had fastened with a rubber band to the rearview mirror.

Call me fickle, but somehow the conversation I'd just had regarding my parents' marriage made what happened last night drift a little farther into the past. Oh, I was all too aware that Tony DiPiazza wanted me dead. And that he probably would until I pieced together what had happened to Uncle Tolly, but I figured I was pretty safe for now. Aside from the fact that Porter was watching out for me—I gave him a little wave when I came out of my father's restaurant—probably DiPiazza would be laying low for the next day or so after the entire Third Battalion had descended on the Hellgate Bridge last night.

"Say hello to my little friends," I thought, borrowing one of my favorite lines of all time, said by none other than one of my favorite actors, Al Pacino, in *Scarface*. Al's performance aside, the movie was so-so. But that line was great.

I knew that in the cop world, backup was called upon all the time. "Suspect at Ditmars and Twenty-ninth. Need backup." That kind of thing.

But what did a PI do when she needed backup? I mean if she didn't have a hunky Aussie named Jake Porter to look after her?

I added that to the long list of questions I had for my uncle Spyros when—if ever—I caught up with him.

I pulled the papers free and stared at them. Was it all right to deliver them on a Saturday? I knew Sundays were free zones for recipients. Eugene Waters could be dancing a jig in nothing but his pink robe, grilling chicken in his front lawn, and I couldn't legally approach him. But what about today?

I opened the papers. And as I did, I remembered my uncle's words to me when I'd delivered my first papers when I was seventeen and looking for some extra cash to buy my first car (a 1976 Pacer that ended up in the junkyard a month after I bought it).

"Rule number one when it comes to process delivery: never read the document."

I'd nodded my head several times like his rule made perfect sense.

I hadn't understood at all.

I'd since reasoned it had something to do with the law. But now I wondered if it wasn't to keep a professional distance between the server and the servee.

Well. I'd just thrown that right out the window.

Seemed Mr. Waters' ex-landlord was petitioning to sue for back rent. Not on the place he was in now, but a place from which he'd been evicted last month.

I refolded the petition. Great. Now I knew that not only was Waters having far worse money problems than I was (I considered the fact that I couldn't afford a complete Lucille makeover a problem with money), he had been kicked out of his home.

Probably he'd deserved it. Probably he'd had money and hadn't paid his rent. Spent it on things like pink robes and reefer instead.

Unfortunately, my attempt to return to professional distance wasn't working.

But it did give me an idea . . .

Twenty-six

I WAS WELL ON MY way to Waters' house when I spotted Porter's truck in my rearview mirror, some three car-lengths back. I blindly reached around for my new cell phone where I'd put it on the passenger's seat, then found the auto dial button for him.

"Yeah," he said.

"You know, while I appreciate the extra attention, you don't really have to follow me. I don't think DiPiazza is going to try anything again so soon. Not after the fear of God you and your friends put into him last night."

"No worries," he said, which I took to mean, "Don't worry about it."

"What I'm trying to say is that I'm going to be making some pretty routine stops. I don't want to bore you or anything."

"Luv, you do anything but bore me."

I was pretty sure my cheeks flushed at that. "Oh."

Silence, then, "Are you sure?"

So much for feeling special. "I'm sure. I've got my trusty new cell phone and my cleaned and shiny gun with me. If I need anything, I'll call. Or shoot. Or both."

He didn't say anything.

"Put it this way: if you're going to be following me all day, you might as well be riding with me."

"Not a good idea."

"Why?"

"Let me know what general area you plan to be in."

I noticed he didn't respond to my question. He did that a lot.

I said, "I'm heading over to Jackson Heights, then I'll be back in Astoria. I'll let you know if that changes."

"Gotcha."

I rang off then put the cell back on the seat, watching as Porter turned and disappeared down a side street. And for some reason I immediately regretted telling him he didn't have to follow me. Somewhat like a girl who'd accidentally gone out wearing a short skirt and no underwear only to find it unusually gusty that day. No, that wasn't right. How could someone accidentally forget to wear underpants?

Okay, so I felt naked. And vulnerable. And I didn't particularly like feeling either way.

I found myself checking my rearview mirror and side mirrors and eyeing other cars, not just for Porter but for Rokko or DiPiazza, or one of his tens of other goons who did his dirty work for him, and I contemplated calling Porter back.

At the next crossroads, the black truck pulled behind me again.

The profound sense of relief I felt made me shiver.

My cell phone rang.

"Yeah?"

"It's me. Just thought I'd let you know I was behind you again."

I didn't bother to ask him why. I was just grateful he was there.

I smiled at him in the rearview mirror on the off chance he could see me. "Thanks."

I rang off again.

Five minutes later, I pulled into the parking lot of Waters' apartment complex. Porter parked on the street outside in clear view. I plucked the papers from the visor then climbed out of the car. I considered the dark clouds that had been gathering in the sky since last night and walked to the door to apartment number sixty-nine.

"Who is it?" Waters asked.

"It's Sofie Metropolis."

He pulled open the door and stared at me. "You again?"

I nodded, trying not to notice that today he had on an ice blue nightie.

Interesting life he must lead.

"What happened to your ankles?" he asked.

"Bungee jumping. Now are you going to take this petition or not?"

"Not."

I crossed my arms. "Actually, I bet you ten dollars I can convince you to not only take this petition, but to sign that you got it yesterday."

"Oh?"

"Yeah. By offering you a job."

"A . . . job."

I nodded. "Since this is a petition to sue you for unpaid rent, and since you seem to be here all the time, you must be out of work. And I figure since you know so much about avoiding be-ing served, you'd make a helluva process server."

He stared at me.

I tried to look around him. "This your girlfriend's place?"

He made a face. "Something like that."

"So how about it."

He crossed his own arms, pulling up the hem of the nightie higher than I would have liked. "Let me get this straight. If I take this petition, you'll give me a job serving?"

"Uh-huh."

"Deal."

He swiped the papers from my hand then slammed the door.

I knocked again.

"What?" he said, opening it.

"Here's my card."

"I don't need your card. I already know you. You're the PI who shot that guy in the knee."

The door slammed again.

Okay. I suppose if I was to be remembered for something, the knee-shooting incident wasn't bad. It was miles better than being known as a pet detective.

Or the girl who'd bought and paid for a new pair of cement boots.

MY NEXT STOP WAS MY parents' house.

Since it had been some time since I'd visited (okay, it had only really been a couple of days, but hey, my supplies were running low and I was actually getting tired of eating souvlaki, no matter how blasphemous the proclamation sounded).

Besides, since I now believed what I'd been telling my

mother over the phone every time she called, I no longer had any reason to be afraid of her prying me for information that I didn't want to give.

Of course, there was the whole blabbermouth reputation I also had to live down. If only to prove it to myself, I had to go over there and not say anything about the surprise anniversary party my father was throwing that night.

"My God, tell me it's so," my mother said, smacking her hands to her chest when she saw me. "Is it really my long lost daughter?"

I looked at my grandmother who was stirring something or other at the stove. I wondered if she knew about the party. Probably. Probably everyone knew about the party but me. Because I couldn't keep a secret.

My mother grabbed my arm and pulled me into the roomy pantry filled with all sorts of yummy stuff. "So what's her name?" she asked.

"Whose name?"

"The woman your father is sleeping with, of course. Who else would I be talking about?"

"You really want it?" I tried my best deadpan look on for size.

"What happened to your ankles?"

"Allergic reaction. You didn't answer my question."

She busied herself with straightening cans on the top shelf. And I felt immediately guilty for torturing her the way I was. A few simple words and all the worry would disappear from her eyes, her forehead.

"Mom?"

She looked at me and in that one moment appeared ten years older than she actually was.

"I don't want to know."

"Well, tough. After all this I'm going to tell you anyway. The name of the woman Dad is sleeping with is—"

Yiayia had gotten closer to the pantry, wooden spoon in hand. My mother closed the door.

"The name of the woman Dad is sleeping with is . . . Thalia Kalamaras Metropolis."

She looked like I'd just put a pin to her balloon. "Again with this nonsense." She opened the door and stalked out.

"I'm telling you the truth, Ma. Why won't you believe me?"

"Because I know differently." She picked up another wooden spoon and waved it at me. "He's late coming home. He gets strange phone calls from a strange woman. He smells like another woman's perfume . . ."

My grandmother snorted as if to say "What do you expect, my son deserves a better woman," and this time I was the one who pulled my mother aside.

"I want you ready for a girls' day out in twenty minutes."

"Girls' day out? Sofia, I haven't been a girl for over thirty years."

I marveled at the fact that my mother kept throwing the number "thirty" around and hadn't a clue my father was planning an anniversary party. Of course, I hadn't caught on either, but I wasn't married to my father.

"Well, maybe we should turn back the hands of time a little."

"But your father's dinner—"

"He can eat by himself."

She stared at me.

Had my mother really never left my father to fend for himself?

I crossed my arms over my chest. "If you won't believe me about Dad, then why don't you do something to make him wonder what *you're* up to?"

She shook her head. "Two wrongs don't make a right."

"How is getting your hair done and buying a new dress wrong?"

She put a hand to her hair. Hair I was used to seeing shot through with gray but that could use some definite updating. She really was a pretty woman. But with a little help from my stylist, Mano, she could be drop-dead gorgeous. Make her feel that not only was she capable of keeping her man, but that he would be a fool to even think of leaving a woman like her.

I opened my cell phone and searched my directory for my hairstylist's number. "Yes, Mano. I know this is last minute, but can you fit me in. Oh, and I'll be bringing in . . . a friend, as well. She needs the whole nine. Thanks, M, you're a doll."

Of course, it was also going to cost me double, but hey, I figured this could be my anniversary gift to my mother.

It wasn't until an hour or so later that I realized that not only hadn't I told my mother about the party, but that I hadn't even come near accidentally breathing a word about it.

I smiled to myself even as I caught sight of Porter outside the salon window leaning against his truck smoking a cigarette.

Yes, this was definitely better than being left out in the cold.

I WAS JUST DROPPING MY mother off at home looking like she could be Exhibit A in one of those makeover shows when my cell rang and I picked up to talk to Porter.

"How's it hanging?" I asked.

He sounded like he was choking on something. I looked

back to find him drinking probably coffee from one of those blue and white Greek deli cups. "Pardon me?"

"Never mind. I'm heading to the agency."

"You think that's a good idea?"

"You mean so long as I keep busy at the hairdresser and do some shopping I'm safe?"

"Something like that."

"Yeah, well, I think solving the Uncle Tolly case is the only thing that will keep me safe."

He didn't say anything.

"Is there something you know about Uncle Tolly's case that you're not telling me, Porter?"

"You know, it's looking a bit like rain. Do you have an umbrella with you?"

I hung up, deciding that if he wanted to play games, I might just take him for a cruise by DiPiazza's.

Then again, no.

A few minutes later, I parked around the block from the agency. Hey, I didn't want to advertise that I was there.

I watched Porter pick a spot a little closer and turn off his engine. I walked over to his truck and knocked on the window. He rolled it down and I leaned my arms on the door.

"You want to come in for some coffee?"

He lifted his cup. "Taken care of, thanks."

I squinted at him. "I have the feeling you're avoiding me."

"I've been following you all day."

"That's not what I mean. I mean you're avoiding spending time within ten yards of me."

"I'm having a bit of a prob getting the image of all those unopened wedding gifts you got piled up in your bedroom out of my head."

I smiled. "Want to help me open them?"

"No, I'd prefer you got rid of them."

"That's what helping me open them would do."

"No thanks. I'll pass."

I reached out and stuck my finger inside the neck of his T-shirt. God, but he smelled good. Like some kind of fresh soap, or that Shower-to-Shower stuff or something. Whatever it was, it made my mouth water with the desire to lick him.

"What's the matter, Porter? Afraid of the word 'wedding' coming anywhere in the vicinity of your name?"

He met my gaze, his expression serious. "No, I would prefer it if your own wedding was more a part of your past than your present."

Oh.

"My wedding is a part of my past." I waggled my left hand at him. "See. No ring."

"That's because I had to fish the mangled thing out of your garbage disposal a couple of months back."

I dropped my hand to my side, not sure if I was willing to concede the point.

"As far as I'm concerned, that damn fake rock might as well still be on your finger."

Ouch.

I gripped the car door tightly, then released it. "Well, okay then." I backed toward the door to the agency. "I shouldn't be long. You might want to keep the engine running."

"Where to next?" he asked, his eyes narrowing.

"To prove no man is above accepting a free television."

I turned my back. Let him make what he wanted out of that one.

At any rate, he would find out what I meant soon enough.

Twenty-seven

IT WAS AMAZING WHAT A little green placed in the right hands could accomplish.

I sat in my Mustang in my usual spot, up the street from comp case Charles McCutcheon's house, watching him lounge in his usual spot in his lawn chair on his porch knocking back a cold one. Truth was, I was getting tired of this same old routine and while I was getting my nails done at Mano's, a thought occurred to me. Rather the UPS guy inspired an idea when he'd delivered a box to the salon. A box that had obviously held a television that Mano had had delivered to the salon rather than his house, even though it was obviously a personal purchase. (Probably he was going to write it off on his taxes.)

At any rate, I hoped the ruse I'd come up with would take care of the McCutcheon case once and for all.

I glanced into the rearview mirror, spotting Porter in his truck a block back. He was talking on his cell phone. And not to me.

I wasn't sure what bothered me more. That he was behind

me doing something other than keeping completely focused on me. Or that I needed him to be behind me for reasons other than activities we could do in my king-sized bed.

A familiar brown truck rolled by, momentarily blocking my view of McCutcheon's porch and, by extension, McCutcheon himself. I craned my neck to see around it, but as luck would have it, the truck stopped in a spot that didn't allow me clear sight.

Damn.

I grabbed my camera and climbed out of the car, waiting for an old Chevy to drive by before hurrying across the street and to the sidewalk a few houses up from where the UPS truck was parked. Thankfully, McCutcheon's attention was on the delivery guy who retrieved the box he'd given to Mano only a short time ago.

"Mr. McCutcheon?" he asked as he made his way up the walk toward the house in question.

I tried my best to look inconspicuous as I flicked the cap from my camera lens.

"I ain't expecting no deliveries," McCutcheon said, not budging from his chair or releasing his beer can.

I had to slow my stride or else I'd end up passing the house altogether. Then where would I be?

"Expecting or not, you've got one," the guy in brown said. "Sign here."

He thrust one of those digital signature boards at McCutcheon.

"What is it?"

"I don't know. But from what's on the box and the weight of it, I'd judge it to be a television."

Come on, come on. Go for the bait.

"Speaking of which, could you hurry it up?" the delivery man said. "This thing weighs a ton."

Finally, McCutcheon put his beer can down and got to his feet, a smarmy grin visible as he eyed what he apparently thought was a gift from the gods. He walked down the steps and met UPS John on the sidewalk, then signed his name with a flourish.

"Here," the delivery man shoved the box at McCutcheon and he took it.

Giving up all pretense of appearing to be merely out for a stroll, I lifted my camera and squeezed off shots of McCutcheon hefting an eighty-pound box with little or no effort and walking up his five cracked cement steps with it before bending over to easily put it down on his porch. He spotted me just as I was finishing up. I dropped the camera to my side.

"Sorry, Charlie, but your ex-employer thought it might be a good idea for you to learn that there really is no such thing as something for nothing."

The UPS truck pulled away, well worth the fifty I'd invested in the ruse.

McCutcheon cursed at me as he turned to open the box. He then kicked it over, the two cinder blocks inside hitting his porch with a thunk, the white Styrofoam peanuts drifting around them like snow in August.

I thought it might be a good idea if I made my escape just then. After all, I didn't want firsthand proof of Charlie's physical capabilities. I hurried for my car and squealed off in the opposite direction, watching as he ran into the middle of the street after me, shaking his fists. I aimed the camera over my shoulder and took a couple of additional shots.

Ah, yes. You had to love it when a plan came together . . .

AS MUCH AS I WOULD have liked to have skated into my parents' party that night on the wings of victory, the truth was exposing McCutcheon for the lazy would-be thief that he was turned out to be little more than a brief blip on my professional radar screen. A couple of months ago, it probably would have been enough to see me through an entire week of cheating spouse cases. Now, five minutes after driving away from the scene of the crime, the rush of triumph was gone, leaving me alone to stare at the other items of unfinished business that littered my path.

Then, of course, there was the other bit of unfinished business following me in his truck.

Porter had shaken his head and grinned at me when I passed him at McCutcheon's. I took that to mean that while he didn't approve of my methods, he might be a little impressed with the outcome. Or at least that's how I was determined to interpret his reaction.

In any event, a little while later found me knocking on the door of Widow Vardis' house. I glanced at my watch. Just after five. My parents' anniversary party started at nine. Plenty of time. And since I really didn't have anything to do between now and then—you know, besides driving Jake nuts following me all over town—I figured I wouldn't truly relax until I squelched the hunch that had been bothering me much like that itch I couldn't seem to scratch.

The door opened and I stood considering the flustered widow who never looked anything but cool, calm, and collected. "Hi, *Kiria* Vardis. I was hoping I could talk to you for a minute?"

"Whatever for?"

Not exactly Miss Manners material. Not exactly typical Greek behavior either. In my experience, women of Mrs. Vardis' age, especially women who lived alone with kids well out of the house, welcomed visitors, rather than trying to scare them away.

"I was wondering if you might know where *Kirios* Plato is."

She stared at me so hard I thought her eyeballs might fall out and roll down the porch. "Plato? Well, why would I know where Plato is?"

I gave her my best from under-the-eyelashes look. "*Kiria* Vardis, I already know the two of you have been seeing each other on the sly for some time now."

"Who told you that?" A liver-spotted hand went to the white lace collar of her black dress. It was already buttoned up to her nose, but I guess she wanted to make sure she hadn't forgotten to do one up. "Did Plato say something?"

"*Kiria* Vardis, where is he?"

She looked like she was about to stonewall me some more but sighed instead. "He's at the airport."

Damn. "The airport? Which one?"

She appeared confused.

"Did he say which one? LaGuardia or Kennedy?"

"LaGuardia, I think. But I can't be sure."

"Thanks."

I turned and booked for my car. If Plato was skipping town, I needed to catch him before he flew away.

I SPED DOWN ASTORIA BOULEVARD toward LaGuardia, aware that Porter's truck was trying to keep up with me.

My cell phone chirped.

"Where's the fire, luv?" Porter asked.

"I've got to get to the airport."

Silence, then, "Going somewhere?"

"No, but Plato the butcher is. And I've got to catch him before he goes."

"Which airline?"

Which airline? What kind of stupid question was that?

A completely legitimate question. But one I didn't have the answer to because Widow Vardis hadn't seemed to know for sure which airport Plato was flying out of.

"I don't know."

"What was that?"

"I said I don't know." Trust Porter to make me repeat myself.

Thankfully, LaGuardia wasn't as big as Kennedy was. If Widow Vardis had said Kennedy, I wouldn't be in my car right now racing for the airport. Too many terminals, too little manpower.

Still, even at LaG, trying to find one Greek butcher in a crowd of hundreds was going to prove a challenge. Especially if said Greek butcher had already gone through security.

"How are you with airport security?" I asked Porter, hoping he hadn't hung up yet.

"How do you mean?"

"Can you get us through without boarding passes?"

"Hold on a second."

I heard a click and guessed I'd been put on hold.

I took the left-hand turn onto ninety-fourth a little too fast, and with the cell phone pressed to the side of my face, I had to do some quick thinking to stop my fishtail from sliding me right into a telephone post.

A moment later, I picked up the cell where I'd let it drop to my lap.

"Not pretty, that move," Porter said into my ear.

"So? Can you?"

"That's being looked into now."

Looked into? By whom?

I gunned the engine to make the yellow light then watched in my rearview mirror as Porter cruised through the red light at normal speed as if he had a right to do so.

LaGuardia lay ahead to my right. A few winding entrance roads later I was parallel to the main terminal.

"Anything yet?" I asked Porter.

Then I spotted the last thing I would have expected to see at LaGuardia. Uncle Tolly's Mercedes, with the taped up passenger's side window and FOR SALE sign, parked outside the arrivals terminal, hazard lights flashing.

Interesting . . .

"Never mind," I said to Porter then disconnected the line.

I pulled up behind the empty Mercedes that was even now being written up for a ticket while another security guard was most likely radioing for a tow truck. How had Plato gotten access to the Mercedes? Had Aglaia given him the key? But if Aglaia had had the key, why had she broken the window? Oh, excuse me, a very large pigeon/hawklike bird had flown into the window.

I scratched my head, watching as Porter passed me.

It didn't make any sense . . .

Then, suddenly, everything came into clear focus, much like a freshly taken Polaroid picture. Because walking from the terminal doors was Plato, looking like his ole butcher self minus his apron . . . and right next to him was none other than a very much alive Uncle Tolly aka Apostolis Pappas.

I scrambled out of my car, gaping at the remarkably healthy-looking man in a tropical print shirt and Bermuda shorts, his legs looking skinny but tanned. He wasn't trying to disguise himself, wore no extra-large overcoat or hat as if he were trying to hide from anyone. In fact, he looked a little too much like he'd just returned from a vacation somewhere warm and fun.

Holy shit. Uncle Tolly had never truly been missing; he *had* run away.

Something my grandfather said early on echoed in my brain: "If you ask me, he finally wised up and left that old battle-ax he's married to."

I drew even with the men at the same time they reached the Mercedes, and Plato began arguing with the officers in charge even as a third officer chased me down.

"Ma'am, you can't park there," she told me. "The temporary lots are right over there."

I stared at the young woman who looked like she graduated high school yesterday. "Do I look like a 'ma'am' to you?"

She drew her head back and I half expected her to say, "Oh no, you didn't."

I ignored her. "Uncle Tolly," I exclaimed, kissing both of his cheeks then drawing back to look at him. "You have no idea how good it is to see you. Alive."

I pinched his cheek a little too hard and he winced.

"Come on, why don't you let me give you a ride home," I said.

I tugged on his arm, but Uncle Tolly resisted me. "I have my car here."

I blinked as if just now seeing it. "Oh, you're right." I patted his hand where I had it gripped tightly in my other lest he try to disappear on me again before I got some answers. "But since Plato apparently has the keys and drove it here," I stared at the man in question, "Plato can drive it back." I pointed at Uncle Tolly then myself. "You and me, we need to have a talk."

"Fine, fine," he said. "I'll go with you. What happened to your ankles?"

"Compliments of a pair of cement boots I received as a gift from DiPiazza and his boys because I wouldn't give up trying to find you. Come on."

I all but shoved him into the passenger's side of my car and slammed the door, then ran to the driver's side before he could get out again.

"Don't you have air-conditioning?" he asked.

"Suffer," I said.

Twenty-eight

UNCLE TOLLY HAD WANTED TO retire to the Bahamas and open up a tiki bar . . . alone.

So there we sat inside the closed butcher shop, myself, Uncle Tolly, and Plato, with Porter standing off to the side in the shadows, un-introduced, his presence unexplained. Next door, Aglaia had already closed up shop, none the wiser that her long lost husband was alive and well and sporting a new suntan.

I listened as the two men tried to explain everything to me.

"Wait, wait, wait," I said, lifting a hand to stop them from talking over each other and occasionally shouting at each other. "Let me see if I'm getting this right. You wanted out of every-thing," I said to Tolly. "You didn't want to run the dry cleaners anymore, you didn't want to be married, you wanted . . . well, out."

He nodded his head, his hands folded between his knees

where he leaned toward me on his plain wood chair. "Right."

"No. Wrong." I shook my head. "If it was as simple as that, why not just get a divorce and divide up your assets?"

Plato snorted, a typical sign of disgust in Greek speak. "Because he wanted to go to the Bahamas and open one of those stupid tiki bars."

I sat back in my chair. My ankles hurt like crazy. Probably I should put some of that gel on them or something, because with all my movement so far today, I'd stretched the healing skin to its limits. "He still could have done that."

"You don't understand. Greeks my age don't get divorced."

I stared at him.

Uncle Tolly continued. "Forget me. I would have been all right. But my Aglaia would have been destroyed."

His Aglaia . . .

"Why not just take her with you?"

The two men shared a knowing look.

"What? It's a reasonable question."

"Because I thought forty years with the woman was enough."

He looked like maybe he didn't feel that way anymore. Which was good, wasn't it? I mean, he had come back when he'd discovered his wife had been arrested for murder. Maybe all wasn't lost.

Still, my mind was ticking off the details. "So you made it look like the mob knocked you off because you were laundering money for them."

He nodded. "Better to make Aglaia appear a widow then a divorcee. A divorcee . . ."

Again, that shared look, but this time Plato looked away.

"A widow stands a chance of marrying again. Yes, she grieves but she moves on. A divorcee . . ."

A Greek divorcee was forever branded a loser and lived the rest of her days on the fringes of the Greek community, with married women afraid to let them near their husbands and men afraid of what she'd done to scare off her first husband.

I rubbed my fingertips against my temples.

"And your connection to DiPiazza?"

Uncle Tolly sat up and shrugged. "I did his laundry."

I squinted at him.

"I washed his clothes. Is that clear enough for you?"

"So you weren't involved in any kind of illegal activity with him?"

"No. Never."

I thought of the double set of books. The Mercedes parked outside. Rokko following me for days, then DiPiazza deciding I was getting too close to something and trying to off me with a shove off the Hellgate Bridge.

"You are stupid," Plato told him. "Everything happened just the way I said it would."

"How could you know what would happen?"

Plato waggled his finger at Tolly. "Didn't I say that Aglaia would probably be arrested? Didn't I tell you that buying that damn Mercedes wouldn't be the gift you wanted it to be, but the item that put her behind bars, implicated her in a murder that never happened?" He threw up his hands. "All this so you could stick your pudgy white toes in the sand and sip those damn drinks with umbrellas in them."

"What? It should have worked just the way I planned. The police find no body. The books prove a blurry connection between me and the mob. My being missing is written off as a suspected homicide. I live happily-ever-after with my tiki bar, free as a bird, and Aglaia gets to sell the Mercedes and live happily-ever-after as a widow."

There was a fuzzy kind of logic to the plan. And it could very well have gone down as planned.

Except that I'd gotten involved.

No one had to say it. We all knew it as we sat there staring at each other.

So essentially I was to blame for the mementos I'd gotten from my brief affair with cement boots.

My head suddenly hurt.

I got up.

"Where you going?" Uncle Tolly asked.

"It's not where am *I* going. It's where *we* are going."

Plato rose. "This is where I take my leave."

"Oh, no. I need you as a character witness. Probably the police will think I brought in a double for Uncle Tolly just to clear my client." I gave him a once over. He'd lost a good ten pounds and the tan and weight loss looked good on him. "Let's just hope Pino is around somewhere so he can play second witness."

But, of course, Pino was never around when I wanted him around. Only when I didn't want him around.

UNFORTUNATELY, CLEARING AGLAIA WASN'T AS simple as all that. No, Pino hadn't been there, but a desk sergeant had called him in and he'd grudgingly verified that the man in the tropical print shirt and Bermudas was indeed one previously missing Apostolis Pappas. But, I was told, there were procedures to follow. Number one, the case was no longer in their hands, it was in the prosecutor's. They'd need signed affidavits and had to go before a judge before Aglaia could get off for murdering a man that was still obviously very much alive.

One aspect I was having a hard time accepting was that I had nearly died for a man who was never truly missing.

The thought gave me chills.

I left the 114th, alone, Aglaia's destiny safely in the hands of her estranged husband and attorney. And I didn't want to be anywhere in the immediate vicinity when Aglaia found her "dead" husband letting himself into their apartment saying something along the lines of "Honey, I'm home." Probably she would kill him. Probably she'd get away with it because of extenuating circumstances.

Either way, the case of Uncle Tolly was officially closed for me.

But as I drove toward home, watching big fat raindrops plop against my front and rear windows, preventing me from getting a good look at where Porter was behind me, I knew that wasn't it. That wasn't all that was required for this entire fiasco to end.

I turned my car toward Queens Boulevard even as a rumble of thunder rattled the ground under me.

"Where you going, Sofie, girl?" Porter asked over the cell he'd called me on a few minutes into the journey.

"You have to ask?"

"I'd advise against it."

"Advise all you want. It wasn't your feet stuck in those cement containers last night."

He didn't appear to know how to respond to that, so I closed the cell and wiped my sweaty palms one by one on my pants legs.

As I rounded the corner to Tony's club, I immediately spotted Rokko's sedan . . . along with him just getting into it. Since my car kind of stuck out like a sore thumb because of all the bondo, he stopped and stared at me. That's when I noticed the gauze taped to his right ear.

Yikes. Had I done that?

I couldn't help a satisfied smile. Yes, I had. And if he didn't watch it, I might take it into my head to shoot him again. And this time he wouldn't get off so easy.

I parked and got out of the car, looking over my shoulder across the street to where Porter was doing the same with his truck. I tucked my Glock into the back waist of my capris. He leaned against the front of his truck and lit a cigarette, tipping his hat to me.

I was glad for his presence.

"If it isn't little Sofie Metro," Rokko said, slamming his car door and stepping toward me.

"Fuck off, Rokko. It's your boss I'm interested in talking to."

He looked an inch away from reaching for the firearm that was probably hiding under a jacket it was way too warm to be wearing. The guy with him hurried inside the club. Moments later, Tony DiPiazza stepped out, his attention on the cell phone he held to his ear and the sidewalk ahead of him. He stopped walking and ended the phone conversation at the same time, then looked up at me.

I stared back at him.

"I just heard the news," he said. "Uncle Tolly's still alive."

"Mmm," I agreed.

I felt the weight of my Glock in the back waist of my capris, a monster of a gun that was undoubtedly clearly visible under my shirt and pants. My palms itched with the desire to take it out and shoot Tony right there. Oh, not in the head or anything. But maybe in the shoulder. Serious enough to be a constant

reminder of what he'd done to me and my revenge for that vio-
lation. But nothing that would endanger his life.

Then again, maybe I didn't think I could trust myself not to
shoot him in the head.

He grinned in that way that made me blink, and shrugged.
"Hey, no hard feelings, huh? Truth is, the bosses were out of
town when everything went down and, well, I didn't know
what the family's connection was to the old man. But what I
was hearing didn't look good. And those ledgers . . ."

The ledgers Uncle Tolly had forged to both skim money to
finance his secret retirement fund and make it look like there
was a connection between him and the man in front of me.
The ledgers I'd gotten from Aglaia and that Tony had stolen
from me after duct taping my dog to the commode.

"You mean a simple phone call to your boss could have kept
any of this from happening?"

Probably he'd wanted to prove himself capable of holding
down the fort while the bosses were away. Probably he'd been
in way over his head. I eyed a tall, dark, sinister-looking guy in
a suit standing off to the side and noticed the way Tony's gaze
kept going to him. Obviously, Tony's plan hadn't quite turned
out the way he'd wanted.

"Hey, what's wrong with your ankles?" he asked.

I stared at him, deciding to shoot him.

"Oh." He apparently realized what had caused the red burn
marks. "Like I said, no hard feelings. When all is said and
done, nobody got hurt, did they?" He scratched his chin. "Well,
not bad anyway."

Depended on your definition, really. My ankles burned like
hell. But that was a far sight better than swimming with the
fishes at the bottom of the East River.

"Hey, I'm not going to be around for a while," Tony said, looking more than a little awkward. "I'm going to visit the old country. When I get back, maybe we can go for that pasta we talked about."

I took out my gun and shot in the general direction of his face, hitting the door to the club behind him. Rokko was just coming out and screamed as he put a hand to his other ear.

At least now he had a matching pair.

The only problem is, within a blink of an eye I found myself surrounded by at least a half dozen men pointing guns of their own. Namely at me.

"Whoa, whoa, whoa," Tony said, holding up his hands. "No harm, no foul."

No one moved, including me. I still held my Glock mere inches away from Tony's head.

He glared at his men. "Put the friggin' guns away already, will you?"

They all hesitated then did as he asked.

"Now it's your turn, sweetcakes," he said to me.

"Give me a minute," I said. "I'm not going to shoot you. I just want to enjoy the sensation of knowing I could for a few more seconds."

He chuckled at that. "That's quite a pair you've got on you, Metro. And back at school, I thought you were going to turn into one of those girly girls. You know, the type that gets married and has a houseful of screaming brats before she's thirty? Nothing more pressing on her agenda than soccer practice and lingerie sales."

Hearing his take on what essentially would have been my life had things worked out differently . . . well, made me drop my Glock to my side.

I took a deep breath.

"Bygones?" Tony extended his hand toward me.

I ignored his hand, stuffed my gun back into the waist of my pants, then walked toward my waiting car.

Porter didn't appear to have moved from where I'd last seen him. He grinned at me then climbed into his truck at the same time I got into my car.

Twenty-nine

PORTER'S SIMMERING LOOK MADE THAT itch I'd been feeling for the past week kick up a notch. It was all I could do not to scratch as I walked down the front steps of my apartment building in my strappy black stiletto heels and red halter dress. Mrs. Nebitz had opened her door as I was leaving my apartment and readjusted her glasses as if unsure I was, indeed, me. She'd said I'd looked *shaineh,* which I think is Yiddish for "lovely," and asked if I would be seeing my nice Mr. Porter.

Of course, I would be seeing my nice Mr. Porter, but it wouldn't be in the way she apparently expected. Rather, I would be seeing him as a reflection in my rearview mirror.

I stopped on the sidewalk and shifted my weight to one foot, sliding the chain handle of my purse over my bare shoulder. Then again, maybe not.

I stepped to the truck and opened the passenger's side door. It took a little inventive maneuvering to climb inside without flashing my undies to anyone who was watching, but it was worth the trouble if just to see the shocked look on Jake's handsome face.

And witness his apparent struggle to find something to say. You know, along the lines of, "Have I forgotten something, luv?"

"I hope you don't mind giving me a lift to my father's restaurant," I said, popping open my purse and taking out a tube of lip gloss. I flipped down the sun visor and used the mirror to slowly move the roller over my lips.

I was pretty sure I heard Jake gulp. But that couldn't be possible. If only because everything I'd seen up to this point indicated that Jake Porter wasn't a gulping kind of guy.

"Your father's restaurant?"

"Hmm-mmm." I put the gloss away and smiled at him. I knew I looked good. Well, aside from the redness around my ankles that I'd used the straps of the shoes to disguise. There was also something about knowing I was getting better at my new job that was a major turn-on.

And that I was turning on Jake as a result was a reward all its own.

"I figure I'm entitled to do a little celebratory drinking tonight and probably shouldn't be driving." I shifted on the seat, taking special care to allow him a more than decent flash of bare thigh. "I'll catch a ride home from a cousin or something later."

He put the truck into gear, heading in the direction of Broadway and my father's place.

Unsurprisingly, we arrived all too soon. Mostly because Jake was speeding as if on his way to a fire.

Silence settled as he pulled to the curb a couple of doors up from the restaurant.

"Would you like to come in?" I found myself asking.

I wasn't sure who was more surprised by the question, him or me. But I was relatively sure we both wore the same wide-eyed expressions.

Was I really inviting him in to meet my parents, so to speak?

There weren't many hard-and-fast rules in the dating game. But when you added "Greek" to the mixture, you did run into all sorts of logistical problems. At the top of the list was that you absolutely, positively, did not introduce someone who was not Greek to your parents unless you were so besotted you forgot yourself for a moment, or as in Yanni Protopsaltis' case, you'd already married them.

Jake cleared his throat. "Sorry, luv, but I'm going to have to pass. I'm not exactly dressed for the event."

I almost sighed my relief.

"By the way, I've come across some info you might like."

"Oh?"

"You won't be bothered by DiPiazza or his goons anymore."

I liked that I already knew this particular information. "I know. His bosses aren't very pleased, so he's taking a vacation to the homeland."

Saying "homeland" made me think of some sort of summer camp for mafia members in training.

Jake stared at me. "If you'd call a year a vacation."

A year wasn't a vacation; a year was exile.

I shivered, almost feeling sorry for Tony. Almost.

"Shame," I said. "He and I were supposed to go out for pasta."

I took some joy in the glower he gave me.

I opened the car door and made the same awkward maneuvers required to get out, pretending the instant I had my feet on the sidewalk that I'd been in complete control all along.

"So . . ." I said. "Does that mean I'm no longer going to have the pleasure of your company?"

I fought the urge to bite my lower lip.

"Have a good time tonight, Sofie Metropolis."

I closed the door and he drove away from the curb, leaving me to make what I would with another of his nonanswers.

"Sofie! Sofie, is that you?"

I turned around to find my aunt Aliki motioning to me wildly from the door to the restaurant. "Get in here. Your mother's due here any second! And she'll know for sure something's up if she's see you out here wearing a dress."

I glanced back in the direction Jake had gone even as I walked toward the corner . . .

NOBODY, BUT NOBODY, KNOWS HOW to put on a party like the Greeks.

It seemed like a long time since I'd been to one, I'd forgotten that. And as I watched my mother, looking like a million bucks in her new dress and hairstyle, beam under the attention my father and the family showered on her, I thought it also had been a long, long time since I'd seen her this happy.

A half hour into the festivities, Thalia had gripped my arm in that way that only mothers know how to do.

"You . . . you," she said, shaking her finger at me. "You knew all along that your father wasn't having an affair? That all along he'd been arranging this, didn't you?"

I took her hands in mine and gave her a lingering kiss to the cheek. Of course, she couldn't know that I hadn't been in on anything going on tonight. Next to her, I had been the last to know. "Would tonight be as sweet had I told you?"

She hugged me so hard I thought I heard my ribs crack.

"Mind if I cut in?" my father said, smiling at me, then my mother.

"Not at all." I handed Thalia off to her husband of thirty years, watching as a Greek *bouzouki* band my father had hired for the night struck up the first number . . . and my father and my mother led in the dancing.

My sister Efi and my brother Kosmos came to stand on either side of me. And in that minute, it didn't matter that all of them had kept me in the dark about tonight. That the past week had been a living hell for me because I'd thought my father was cheating on my mother.

What did matter was that our parents appeared to be just as in love as the first day they met.

Efi elbowed me. "Good show on the visit to the salon. Mom looks great. I wish I'd thought of it."

"If you had suggested it, she would have figured out something was going on for sure."

Koz chuckled. "You mean unlike you, who had no idea something was going on that didn't have anything to do with Dad's fidelity?"

I gave him a faux glower then we leaned into each other and laughed.

The band launched into another number, this one a traditional song from my father's family's area near ancient Olympia, Greece, a *tsamiko*. First Kosmos was pulled in to dance in the line, then Efi. I stopped a passing waiter, emptied a plate of bread, then tossed it to the floor at their feet.

"Opa!" the cry went up from the guests.

I caught the eye of someone familiar on the opposite side of the dance floor. He was smiling at me and, for reasons I couldn't immediately identify, I smiled back. It took me a minute to place him. Constantinos. Or, rather, Dino. The pastry shop owner and would be suitor to Efi.

My father moved the white napkin he was holding from his left to his right hand and held it out to me, indicating he wanted me to lead.

I hesitated. Truth was, while I enjoyed watching the traditional dance, I'd really never been very good at doing it. It involved some tricky steps and some originality by the lead dancer. Neither of which I'd ever been particularly good at.

But rather than duck the invite as I usually did, something made me reach out and grasp that napkin. My gaze met my father's. In his eyes, I saw love and pride.

And in my heart, in that one moment, I felt joy about everything I was. Greek. A cherished daughter. A loved sister.

And one helluva good PI.

And I danced like I'd never danced before.

Thirty

the anniversary party for my parents had ended and the skies had opened up, unleashing a harsh summer storm, I sat at my kitchen table putting the finishing notes on the Uncle Tolly file and dipping a pickle into my morning frappé. I figured the meager price I'd quoted in the beginning, you know, in order to allow Aglaia to keep her pride, had at least quadrupled—which would bring the fee up to the normal charge—and I would be taking my bill over to the couple in person sometime next week, well after Aglaia readjusted to having her estranged husband back.

I couldn't actually bring myself to call Tolly (whom I'd decided I wasn't going to refer to as "Uncle" anymore because, well, his seemingly innocent little stunt, no matter how funny, had nearly gotten me killed), so I'd called Plato instead. He'd told me that after everything was set to right, Tolly would be returning to his old routine as the dry cleaner and husband of Aglaia. As it turned out, Plato had said, the time Tolly had spent away from his wife had given the couple a fresh new perspective. There was word of a second honeymoon and there was more laughter than harsh words coming from the direction of the shop now.

Go figure.

Muffy's toenails clicked against the kitchen tile as he came in from his spot on the Barcalounger. He barked at me. I leaned down and absently began patting him until I touched a bald patch and he leaned against my right ankle. I winced and plucked him up from the floor, holding him in front of my face.

There was a time not too long ago when I wouldn't have dared such a move for fear of losing my nose to . . . what had Porter called him? Oh, yeah. The little ripper.

But now . . .

We openly considered each other, trying to figure out how we felt about this new closeness. Then he licked my chin.

I smiled and cuddled him close, bald spots and all.

"Quite a pair, you and I, aren't we?" I said.

After a few moments, he gave me a low growl and we parted company as he jumped from my lap. It was a start. Seeing as he was used to Mrs. K, and I wasn't used to pets, I thought it was a pretty good start indeed.

It was just after eight A.M. and all was quiet on this Sunday morning, if not entirely well. It would probably be some time before I felt completely safe again. Call me nuts, but I reasoned being the target of the mob—even for a short, dangerous time—had that effect on a girl.

I caught myself scratching my arm although the storm had finally broken the heat wave.

"The heat makes people do strange things," my father had said that day when I'd learned Tolly was missing.

I'd agreed then. But now I wondered if heat was just an excuse for bad behavior. Tolly's . . . Tony's . . . my own.

Only I hadn't really been bad, had I? Not in the way I wanted to. I crunched on the last of my pickle when Muffy decided to grace me with one of his room-clearing clouds.

"Jesus." Holding my breath, I rushed into the living room then to the open window.

It had long since stopped raining and the air was fresh and even a little cool. Leaves had been ripped from branches by the fierce wind and dotted the damp, shiny pavement with spots of green. The sun was more yellow than hazy orange. And the world at large seemed brighter.

Of course, my new outlook could have as much to do with my having gotten a whiff of death as it did the weather.

At any rate, I welcomed the change. Swapping my old Mets T-shirt for a pair of shorts and a tank, I got a towel from the bathroom and draped the thick terry cloth over the fire escape landing outside my window. Then I scooted out to sit.

The neighborhood looked cleaner somehow and a light breeze brought the smell of all things green to my nose. Much better than Muffy's personal smell as of late.

Probably I should give the vet another call. Maybe take Muffy in for another visit.

Speaking of the mutt in question, he jumped out onto the fire escape alongside me. I made a face, hoping he didn't plan on dirtying the air out here. But he made a dash for the roof instead, his little paws climbing the wrought-iron steps as if they'd been put there specifically for him to see to his business.

I leaned my head back and closed my eyes. Everyone seemed to have their windows open, happy to welcome in the air after long weeks of being closed inside. I heard music probably coming from the business students' place. The sound of a cartoon from Etta Munson's. Then I made out the click click of Muffy's toenails on the fire escape. Only I quickly discovered he wasn't on the one leading to my apartment.

I opened my eyes and looked to my right.

"Here, doggie, doggie, doggie."

I lifted my brows as Mrs. Nebitz called for Muffy through her open window.

"There you are," she said, patting Muffy while he wiggled his furry little butt like his tail was on fire. "Here. I made your favorite this morning. Especially for you."

Seemed I wasn't the only one she was feeding.

"Mrs. Nebitz?" I said.

She jumped and put a hand to her chest. "Sofie! Are you trying to scare an old woman to an early grave?"

I smiled. "Sorry. I didn't mean to startle you." I shifted to face her better, a good ten feet separating us. "What's that you're feeding Muffy?"

She continued to pet the mangy-looking Jack Russell terrier as he tore into a plate of something. "Just some fried chicken liver I had left over."

Liver . . .

All this time I'd been feeding Muffy bland dog food to try to clear up his little gas problem, and all this time Mrs. Nebitz had been feeding him liver, causing his little gas problem.

I laughed.

"What is it?"

"Nothing. Nothing at all, Mrs. Nebitz."

She gave the dog another pat then disappeared back inside her apartment. I sat back, deciding I could take another day of noxious clouds. I'd ask Mrs. Nebitz not to feed him any more liver later on tonight. Maybe give her a bag of his dog food, or better yet biscuits, so she could continue to get visits from him. For now, let her have her fun. Obviously, she enjoyed cooking for someone, even if that someone was an ornery dog. And me.

There you had it. Another mystery solved.

I thought back on all that had happened to me over the past week. Being awakened by Muffy growling and yanking on my sheet. The events of two nights ago on the bridge. My struggle to serve papers and ending up with a new server. Michaela Lopez's smile when we recovered Fred. My parents dancing together last night as if it had been hours since they'd exchanged vows instead of thirty years. Porter necking with me, appropriately enough, at Little Neck Bay . . .

I drew in a deep breath.

No, I didn't think only the heat could be blamed for people doing strange things. I theorized that it was pretty much our nature to be strange, period.

I heard a car pull up on the street below and glanced down to find Porter getting out of his truck. My gaze locked with his and for a moment it didn't matter that he was one big mystery to me. Or that I didn't know what would have happened had he not been there Friday night. Or what might have happened had I sent Debbie to get that money shot. All that mattered was that he was there.

And he was holding a bag from my favorite donut shop.

He grinned, and I smiled.

"Just a minute," I said. "I'll buzz you up."

And off I went to see what other strange, natural things I could do to make my life more interesting, and what excuse I could come up with to blame it all on . . .

Telos

Recipes

Dear Reader,

If we made you hungry during Sofie's food-laden adventures, we're sorry. Okay, maybe we're not. The truth is, food, and lots of it, plays a huge role in Greek culture. And like Sofie's family, we keep a very Greek kitchen. Some recipes are unchanged from when they were created millennia ago. More of them are modern variations, both for the sake of convenience and taste. We've provided three recipes from our own personal archives here. You can find more on our Web site at www.sofiemetro.com.

Kali Orexi!
Lori & Tony

ZESTO NESCAFÉ
(Hot Nescafé Coffee or Nes)

1 cup boiling water
1 heaping teaspoon Nescafé Classic instant coffee
2 teaspoons sugar (or to taste—Tony goes for three—but sugar is required)
1 teaspoon water
milk or cream (optional)

Put water on to boil. Add next three ingredients to a sturdy mug. With a spoon, "hit" the mixture (stir vigorously, making sure to "hit" the mix against the sides of the cup) until creamy and smooth—about three minutes or until water boils. Add boiling water (and milk or cream, optional) and violà! You have a frothy cup of Nes. *Sten eyeia sas!*

SPANAKOPITA (Greek Spinach Pie)

$^1/_2$ cup extra-virgin olive oil, plus additional for greasing the baking pan
10 scallions chopped—including green stems until about an inch from the end
$^1/_4$ cup fresh dill, finely chopped
2 packages pre-washed baby spinach (10 ounces each)
1 teaspoon salt
$^1/_2$ teaspoon freshly ground pepper
2 cups crumbled feta cheese ($^3/_4$ pound)
1 package frozen Pepperidge Farm Puff Pastry Sheets (2 sheets, thawed)
1 egg beaten with 1 teaspoon water, for egg wash

NOTE: defrost pastry sheets overnight in refrigerator before starting recipe.

Preheat oven to 350 degrees. Heat olive oil in a large pan over medium-high heat. Add the scallions, stirring, until lightly cooked. Add the dill, then the spinach, little by little (adding more as the previous batch shrinks), and stir until completely cooked. Season with salt and pepper. Switch off heat and stir in feta.

Brush olive oil lightly over a 9- by 13-inch baking pan. Pastry sheets are just an inch or two shorter than the pan, so you'll need to roll each out slightly lengthwise on a lightly floured surface. Spread one puff pastry sheet over the bottom and press into sides and corners. Add spinach mixture, and then top with other pastry sheet, cutting away excess with a sharp knife. Make a couple of one-inch steam slits in the middle of the top sheet, then brush the surface with egg wash. Bake until golden brown, about 35 to 45 minutes.

Let cool, cut into squares, and serve with a fine *boutari*—Greek red wine. *Kali Orexi!*

TONY'S FAMOUS BAKLAVA

1 box thawed Greek phyllo sheets (in your grocer's freezer section)
2 sticks real, unsalted butter (melted)
4 cups chopped walnuts
1/2 cup sugar
2 teaspoons cinnamon

Syrup
4 cups sugar
2 cups water
honey (from ¼ cup to ½, depending on taste)
a pinch of vanilla (½ teaspoon if liquid extract)
a one-inch piece of lemon rind

In a regular 13- by 9-inch Pyrex baking pan, layer 8 to 10 sheets of phyllo (cut to fit the pan, about half the phyllo sheet), brushing melted butter on each sheet before adding the next sheet. Sprinkle 2 cups of the walnuts, ¼ cup of the sugar, and 1 teaspoon cinnamon on the prepared phyllo (use more or less of each depending on taste). Layer five more sheets of phyllo, again buttering each as you go. Sprinkle the remaining walnuts, sugar, and cinnamon on top of this. Then layer about 15 to 18 more sheets of phyllo on top of this, buttering each sheet as you go. Then you want to cut the pieces before baking in the pan, going diagonally to get that diamond shape. This takes some finesse. Make sure your knife is sharp and you get all the way down to the bottom of the pan. Then bake in a 350-degree oven for approximately half an hour or until top and bottom of phyllo is golden brown. Let it cool, then make the syrup.

Syrup: Combine ingredients in a medium saucepan and bring to a boil. Then turn down the heat and simmer for five minutes. Pour hot syrup over the baklava, then let cool until the syrup is absorbed. You're done! *Opa!*